Caught in the Act

*Other Five Star Titles
by Joyce Lamb:*

Relative Strangers

Caught in the Act

Joyce Lamb

Five Star • Waterville, Maine

This novel is a work of fiction. Names, characters, places and incidents are either the product of the author's imagination, or, if real, used fictitiously.

First Edition, Second Printing.

Set in 11 pt. Plantin by Minnie B. Raven.

Printed in the United States on permanent paper.

Library of Congress Cataloging-in-Publication Data

Lamb, Joyce, 1965–
    Caught in the act / Joyce Lamb.—1st. ed.
        p. cm.
    ISBN 0-7862-5335-5 (hc : alk. paper)
    1. Newspaper publishing—Fiction.   2. Women editors—Fiction.   3. Journalists—Fiction.
    4. Florida—Fiction.
    I. Title.
    PS3612.A546C38 2003
    813'.6—dc21   2003049010

For my dad, Joe Lamb.
My mentor, my friend and
an extraordinary newspaperman.
I miss him.

Acknowledgements

Thanks to everyone who had a hand in helping me get this book written. In addition to my amazing family and friends who have always been there for me, I want to thank Belinda Stewart for sharing her perspective as a newspaper editor; Karen Feldman, Ruth Chamberlain, Chantelle Mansfield, Nancy Christiansen, Mary Hotlen and Lucy Fischer-Pap for offering encouragement and always-constructive criticism; Lisa Kiplinger, Lisa Hitt and Chris & Mary Clay for saving me from some embarrassing errors; Amy Kinsella and Ed Clements for passing on their photo expertise; Jennifer Pollock and the *Rockford Register Star* staff for their unflagging support; Cheryl Turnbull for sharing her connections so enthusiastically; Russell Davis for being a truly wonderful editor; and my agent, Kay Kidde, for never giving up on me. A special thanks goes to Linda Grist Cunningham, for her input, inspiration and never once saying, "Comments? Observations?"

Chapter 1

Jessie Rhoades squinted through the rain, flinching as lightning skittered across the black sky. The rain raced down the windshield so swiftly the wipers couldn't keep up. She knew she should pull over and wait out the storm, but there wasn't much of a shoulder flanking the island's narrow main drag. The storm was probably just a usual southwest Florida thunderstorm. Rain would fall in a torrent for several minutes, then clear skies would claim the rest of the evening.

Besides, it had been another stressful, eighteen-hour Monday at the newspaper, and she was eager to kick off her shoes and relax. Her destination was only a few minutes away. All she had to do was slow down and be careful. In fact, the familiar curve before her best friend Mel's driveway was just ahead.

She put her foot on the brake to slow for the small hill that preceded the curve.

The brakes didn't respond.

Oh great, she thought. Black ice.

It usually caught visitors by surprise, especially Northerners. They didn't realize that when rain on the road mixed with the oil left by heavy traffic, the resulting surface could be as slippery as ice. Jessie wasn't a visitor, but she had relocated here from Illinois, so she knew how to handle ice.

She pumped the brakes.

Still, the car didn't slow. She pumped more frantically. And then she saw the tree.

Clay Christopher watched lightning spider-crack like splintering glass through the dark clouds. The thunder was almost continuous, deep and rumbling, rattling the foundation of the house. It was a reflection of his mood as he watched the storm over the Gulf of Mexico. It had been three years ago today that Ellen had died. No, was killed.

They had been covering the never-ending unrest in Bosnia for *The New York Times.* Clay remembered it so clearly, how they had dashed across Sniper Alley in Sarajevo. They hadn't been thinking, high on adrenaline, feeling invulnerable. He had been in front, head down, flak jacket flapping, when he'd stumbled and gone down on one knee. Ellen had paused to help him, and he'd shouted at her to go. *Go, go, go!*

He heard the shot again. Like a firecracker.

He again tasted the dirt their scrambling feet had kicked up, felt Ellen's slim body twitch against his. Her Nikon flew out of her hands, and he caught her in his arms as she sank to the ground, her round, pale face a mask of bewildered pain.

"El?" At first, he was as puzzled as she looked. Until he realized his hands were already slippery with blood. Ellen's blood.

"Oh Jesus, oh Jesus. You're hit." He stared down into her brown eyes in shock, his mind blank about what to do. Her fingers gripped his arm hard, then went lax as her eyes threatened to roll back.

The ping of a sniper's bullet off a nearby car fender snapped him out of it. He clutched his wife's limp body to his chest and carried her to safety, where he lowered her to the dusty ground. She tried to speak, her lips barely moving, but he shushed her. "Save your strength, honey, please." Raising his head, he began to yell for help.

Now, Clay gulped down the last of his drink, crushing the remaining ice cube between his back teeth. The cheap gin had stopped burning his throat hours ago. Yet, he still felt the pain in his chest, the ache that never went away. It receded most of the time, subsided into a dull throb that flared only when something, or someone, reminded him of her. Or every March.

He got up to pour another drink. A roar filled his ears, the only place he felt the alcohol.

Damn it, he should have been over it by now. Why didn't the pain go away? Why couldn't he forget?

He glanced around the house, with its tall windows, arched ceiling and ceramic tile floors. He and Ellen had searched for months for the lot and had found it on Captiva, a tiny barrier island off the southwest shore of Florida. They'd bought it with money he'd inherited from his grandfather, and construction had begun only three months before they'd headed to Bosnia for a voluntary, six-week tour of newspaper duty. They had decided it would be their final war-zone assignment, and then they would settle down to start a family.

Now, plastic hung from the ceiling, cutting off the unfinished third of the house, marking the place where a baby's room would have been. Clay had canceled the contractor's work the week after she'd died, unable to bear to have the house finished without her and unable to sell it.

He drained the liquor. He wanted his head to spin. He wanted to be falling-down drunk.

He didn't feel a thing.

Except for that annoying sound in his ears. He focused

on it, strained his ears as he realized it was not the buzzing that went with the drunkenness that eluded him. It was a car horn.

Damned car alarms. People, tourists especially, didn't have a clue when it came to car alarms. Florida thunderstorms were violent enough, with the beating rain and shaking thunder, to set them off by the dozens.

He ambled to a front window and stared out at the water that fell in relentless sheets. Wind ruthlessly bent trees to its will, let them snap back, only to bow them back the other way. It beat at the trees the way life beats on some people, Clay thought. The ability to bend was all that kept most from snapping.

He needed more gin.

Determined, and resigned, he didn't bother with a raincoat or umbrella. Neither would be any match for the rain. His destination was a block up—a small grocery with a liquor department.

Opening the front door, struck by a wall of moisture, he almost changed his mind, put off by the violence of the storm. But the prospect of slowly going insane if he stayed sober on this particular day urged him on.

As he stepped outside, he ducked his head, telling himself he was an idiot, a pathetic, crazy idiot, to be so desperate. But he didn't turn back.

The rain, colder than he expected, soaked him in seconds.

He had his head down until the blaring car horn brought his chin up. Water streamed into his eyes as he saw the car. Its front end was flush against the trunk of a banyan tree, steam, or smoke, billowing from under the crumpled hood.

Clay narrowed his eyes against the stinging rain, his heart jackhammering as he realized someone was in the car.

He wrenched open the driver's side door. A woman was slumped back in the seat, unconscious, her face turned away from him. He put a wet hand on her shoulder, hesitant to move her, aware of the damage he could cause if she had a neck injury.

Then he saw the flames licking around the edges of the hood where it had been wrenched back to expose the engine. The gushing rain didn't seem to be having any effect on them.

Clay made a decision. Better alive and paralyzed than dead.

Trying to be gentle even as the flames grew, he unbuckled the woman's seat belt and began to ease her out of the car, alarmed when her head lolled toward him and he saw blood.

He lifted her free, grateful she wasn't pinned. She hung limp in his arms, her head back over his forearm, one hand dangling, as he carried her to the house. The cold rain drenching her face, washing away blood in rivulets, did nothing to revive her.

Inside, Clay placed her on the sofa, drawing the throw balled up in the corner over her saturated khaki slacks and white sleeveless blouse. A small amount of blood trickled down her temple.

Retrieving a towel from the bathroom, he dabbed at the blood as he took his first look at her. She was young, probably in her late twenties, with shoulder-length blond hair. Her nose was narrow, her lips full. A striking woman, he thought. Whose breathing seemed too shallow.

Fumbling with the cordless phone with one hand, he pressed his fingers to the inside of her wrist, where her pulse was thready and irregular.

His alarm grew as it became apparent that the storm had killed the phone.

13

Cursing under his breath, Clay dropped the towel and phone and scooped her up. He got her into his SUV in the garage and buckled her in, blanket and all. He would have preferred to take her to a better-equipped hospital on the mainland in nearby Fort Myers, but he worried that would take too much time. As he drove through the deluge toward the island's immediate-care clinic, he watched her for signs that she was coming to. She didn't stir.

When he carried her into the clinic's waiting room, a woman in blue scrubs met him halfway, calling over her shoulder for assistance.

"What happened?" the woman asked.

"Car hit a tree," Clay said.

A woman wearing a white doctor's coat and a man wearing blue scrubs slammed through swinging doors with a gurney. As Clay deposited the patient on it, the woman checked for her pulse. A gold name tag pinned to the lapel of her jacket read "Dr. Marta Lewis."

"How long has she been unconscious?" Dr. Lewis asked.

"Uh, I don't know for sure. Half-hour, forty-five minutes."

"She's awake," the man in scrubs said.

Clay looked down. Her eyes were the color of swirling smoke, the outer rims of her irises ringed in dark blue.

"David?"

He had to lean down to hear the whispered name. At first, he thought she had mistaken him for someone else, but then he saw fear in her eyes, and another, terrifying thought occurred to him. "Was someone else in the car with you?" he asked.

Blinking slowly, she seemed to force herself back from the edge of unconsciousness. She pressed her hand against the front of his shirt, as if to push him away.

14

"Was someone in the car with you?" he repeated.

Her hand dropped away, and her head rolled to the side.

Turning, Clay stumbled toward the door. He imagined the car, a burned-out shell by now. No one had been in the front seat with her. He was sure he would have noticed. He tried to remember the back seat. Had there been a car seat back there, a child strapped in? Helpless.

"Sir? We need you to fill out forms."

"Not now."

Outside, the driving rain struck him, and he broke into a run.

Chapter 2

Jessie opened her eyes to an unfamiliar ceiling. She knew the smells, though. Hospital smells. Panic had her bolting up. Pain shot through her temples, sent the curtained cubicle revolving as hands grasped her arms. "Whoa. Take it easy."

She blinked to try to clear the haziness. Finally, the face of a friend swam into view. "Mel." Relief had her sagging back against the pillow.

Melanie Holbrooke, a redhead with green eyes and soft features, was wet and bedraggled in black slacks and a green silk blouse. Stress lined the lightly freckled skin of her forehead. "Welcome back."

Jessie smiled. She felt weird—floaty, disconnected. "Think I had an accident."

"No kidding. How do you feel?"

"Like I had an accident."

"You're your usual smartass self, so that's a good sign. How's your head feel? You knocked it a good one."

"What are you, a doctor?" A pause, then, "Oh, yeah, you are. It's okay, I think."

"The ER doctor gave you something for pain. You've got a broken wrist, some bruises and a knot on the head, but nothing major. In other words, you're going to hurt like a son of a bitch tomorrow. But it could have been a lot worse. Want to sit up?"

Nodding, Jessie let Mel help her into a sitting position

that sent her head whirling again. "God."

"Just give it a minute."

Closing her eyes, Jessie tried to focus on something other than the urge to be sick. "How'd you get here?"

"Firefighter salvaged your purse from your burning car and found my card in it."

"Good thing I threw out that circus clown's card."

Mel laughed, her growing relief evident. "How're you doing? Head spinning?"

"Like a top."

"Just breathe."

"Did you say my 'burning car'?"

"Yep. It's a goner."

"I loved that car."

"You needed a new one anyway. In fact, if you'd gotten a new one last year like you should have, an air bag might have spared you that headache and busted wrist."

Jessie didn't respond as she examined the splint on her hand. A dull ache throbbed inside it. Her blouse was gone, replaced by a hospital-issue gown that gaped open in the back. The last thing she remembered was straining to see through driving rain.

"One of my neighbors brought you in," Mel said, rubbing a soothing hand over Jessie's back. "Firefighter said he saved your life."

Jessie didn't know what to say. It amazed her that she had been in danger so grave that a stranger had had to save her.

Mel's hand moved to the back of her neck, lightly massaged. Jessie let her head fall forward, closing her eyes as her friend's expert fingers worked the tension out of her neck.

"The neighbor who brought you in said you asked for

someone in the ER," Mel said, her tone light, conversational. "He thought it was a child or someone in the car with you."

Jessie kept her eyes closed. She recalled sheets of rain, slick streets, lightning jagging out in dozens of directions. Nothing more. "I don't remember."

"Jess, you said 'David.' "

Raising her head, she met Mel's worried gaze. She hadn't seen or spoken to her ex-husband in two years, had made sure of it. She couldn't imagine why she would have said his name. "I must have been pretty out of it."

"So you haven't heard from him?"

"Of course not."

"You'd tell me, wouldn't you? If you had heard from him."

Jessie saw the uncertainty in her friend's eyes, the apprehension, and wished that she'd never told Mel what had happened between her and David. She grasped her friend's hand. "I'm not going to hear from him, Mel. There would be no point."

"I don't believe you, but seeing as how you're under the weather, I'll let you off the hook for now."

"I'm probably going to be under the weather for a long time then."

Mel arched a reddish brown brow. "I doubt that." She patted Jessie's knee like a fussing mother. "Your hero wants to see you. His name's Clay Christopher."

Jessie smiled at Mel's choice of words. "The name of my 'hero' sounds familiar."

"It should. He's the investigative reporter jerk whose little exposé on sick buildings closed down my former employer."

"That *little* exposé was a Pulitzer contender. And you got

a much better job at the hospital because of it. In fact, if it hadn't been for that new job, you wouldn't have moved into that fancy house on Captiva last year."

Mel waved an impatient hand. "Whatever. He wants to see you. I think you scared him with the dramatic way you drove your car into his tree." She became serious. "You didn't fall asleep at the wheel, did you?"

Jessie didn't need a mother. She had Mel. "You're not going to lecture me, are you? 'Cause I have a really big headache."

"You're lucky you're not dead. No job is worth that, no matter how exciting it's been the past two days."

"Hello?"

The man who poked his head around the edge of the privacy curtain that surrounded the cubicle had dark blond hair that was sun-streaked and shaggy. Even though his beard needed a trim, it didn't distract from very blue eyes made even bluer by a deep tan.

Mel turned. "Clay, come in."

As he entered, Jessie took in the holey jeans that fit muscled legs and lean hips like only well-worn denim could. His white, untucked T-shirt was damp and spattered with blood.

Suddenly, she understood why she had said David's name when she had been semiconscious. Her former husband had also had a beard and blue eyes, though they had not been nearly as blue nor his eyelashes as long. Even though she had assured Mel that there was nothing to worry about, there had been a niggling doubt that perhaps David really had tracked her down. She couldn't help feeling relieved now.

Clay approached the bed with an easy grace, and her ex was forgotten.

19

He extended a hand. "We met earlier."

His hand, warm and dry, clasped hers. She sensed the strength in it, yet his grip was gentle. "Sorry about the shirt," she said.

His gaze stayed fixed on hers. "It's old. You look like you're feeling better."

Her face went hot, and she felt ridiculous for blushing because the man had looked, really looked, into her eyes. "Thanks for . . . you know."

If he noticed her discomfort, he didn't acknowledge it. Releasing her hand, he pocketed his. "The car's a wash, I'm afraid. You hit a banyan tree—sturdy old one. The engine caught fire. You must have been in a hurry, from the looks of the car."

"I don't remember."

"You must have been," Mel said. "You were an hour late to dinner with your best pal."

Jessie shot Mel a sheepish glance. "Sorry about that."

"She's devoted to that damn newspaper," Mel told Clay. "Sometimes it jeopardizes her health."

"Mel, please," Jessie said.

Clay smiled, and the tanned skin around his eyes crinkled. "So you are the Jessie Rhoades I know."

Jessie gave him a blank look. "Excuse me?"

"You were a reporter at *The Star-News* in Fort Myers, weren't you? I stopped seeing your byline last year. I thought maybe you'd moved on."

"I'm the city editor now."

"An exhausted one," Mel said.

"I'm not surprised," Clay said. "That was a huge story the newspaper broke today."

"Don't get her started on corrupt cops and exotic dancers," Mel said.

"I'll take that as my cue," Clay said. "I just wanted to see for myself that you're okay. It was nice to meet you."

Jessie laughed softly. "Funny."

"No, it really was."

When they were alone, Mel said, "A gorgeous, gorgeous man."

"Down, girl."

"He's not my type. You know I'm much more into dark-haired nerdy guys. But he's totally *your* type, Jess."

"Please."

"If that man does not get your pulse tripping, I'm going to check you into the nearest clinic for treatment for this self-imposed abstinence, stat. Did you see the way he looked at you? And talk about a romantic way to meet. He pulled you out of a burning car. He's your hero."

Jessie let her head fall back to the pillow, too tired, and wary, to consider the possibilities. When she'd left David, she had sworn that she was done with romantic relationships. She wasn't good at them. And trusting a man . . . well, that wasn't likely to happen again anytime soon. "How long before I'm sprung?"

"Your wrist needs to be set," Mel said. "The doctor wanted to keep you overnight for observation, but I persuaded her to let me take you home with me and poke you awake every few hours to make sure you don't go comatose on us."

Jessie smiled, her eyelids drooping. "Thanks for taking care of me. You're a good friend."

"Didn't you think his eyes were amazing?"

Jessie already was drifting off. "All of him was pretty amazing."

Chapter 3

Clay settled back in the wooden deck chair and stared out at the waves that rolled lazily onto the shore, retreated and rolled again. The sun had risen at least an hour before, but he hadn't noticed. He couldn't stop thinking about Jessie Rhoades.

He supposed it was normal after such a dramatic accident. She could have been killed in his front yard. If he hadn't been so determined to spend the night drunk . . .

But it was more than that. The fear in her gray eyes when she had thought he was a man named David haunted him. And made him intensely curious.

Shaking his head, he picked up the glass that had held gin and tonic and was now in need of a refill. As he rose, the phone rang.

He answered it on his way inside to the fridge. "Yeah."

"Didn't know whether you'd be up, pal."

Clay, hearing the voice of Steve Cronk, an old friend and his former editor, chuckled. "I'm surprised myself, Steve. What's up?"

"Got a story idea you might be interested in."

"No kidding?"

"Yes, it's true. I call only when I've got a pitch that I think could suck you back into the journalistic grind."

"That's what makes you a good editor."

"Yeah, well, I've been a lousy friend. How are you?"

Clay dropped ice into the glass, followed by a splash of

tonic and more than a splash of gin. "I'm doing great."

"I know it's a rough time of year for you."

"This year, it's been a breeze."

"You're a terrible liar."

"I'm working on it. What's the story?"

"I heard there's a bit of a scandal going on down there."

The day before, *The Star-News* had run a major story about police officers engaging in illicit behavior—while on the job—at a local strip club that defied a city ordinance. The headline: "Copulating cops: Your tax dollars at work." The story had been accompanied by what would have been very explicit photos had they not been censored for public consumption. Everyone from the officers themselves to the police chief had vehemently denied the allegations, even when presented with the photographic proof. One police officer, though, had broken the silence of his colleagues and corroborated the evidence.

It was the kind of story that Clay would have jumped on in a heartbeat three years ago. He'd have doggedly pursued the truth, driven by adrenaline and righteous determination to expose the villains who abused power and used those less fortunate. Once the story broke, he'd feel powerful and useful, because he would have made a difference. Somewhere along the way, though, that drive had taken a wrong turn and vanished around a curve.

He attributed the loss to getting older, to becoming more cynical. Stories about the evil that people did, the misery that innocent people suffered, no longer fired him up. Disgust and frustration had replaced the desire to expose the bad guys. No matter how many were exposed, there was always someone out there to pick up the slack, who would exploit or take an innocent life just because they could.

"You there?" Steve asked.

"Uh, yeah. So you heard about our little scandal all the way up there in New York?"

"It's hardly a little scandal from where I'm sitting. We're talking corruption in law enforcement, always a hot-button issue." Steve paused a moment, then sighed. "Come on, Clay, we both know I'm preaching to the choir here. This is right up your alley."

My former alley, Clay thought. "The paper here is reporting the hell out of it," Clay said. "I don't know what I could turn up that it hasn't."

"Well, here's something the newspaper there hasn't reported: there's a rumor that the story's a hoax."

Clay paused with his drink halfway to his lips. "A hoax?" He thought about Jessie Rhoades. A bogus story on such a scale would be devastating, to the newspaper and the careers involved, hers included.

Steve chuckled. "I knew that'd hook you."

Clay didn't respond right away as he recalled that he'd been skeptical when he'd first seen the story. But then he remembered what had put his doubts to rest. "A respected cop ratted out his buddies," he said.

"Which makes this story all the more intriguing, don't you think?"

"I don't know. The pictures they ran were pretty graphic."

"They could have been doctored. Hell, the newspaper itself doctored them by putting all those unsightly black bars over the naughty parts."

"Where'd the rumor come from?"

"The Fort Myers mayor is a friend of a friend," Steve said. "Swears by all that's holy the cops were set up."

"You're asking me to possibly make fools of the reporters and editors at this paper."

"If the story's bogus, then perhaps those journalists should have done a better job of reporting. Think about the cops whose careers, hell, whose *lives* have been ruined. I'm not asking you to make fools of anyone. I'm asking you to find the truth. That's what we do."

"Jesus, Steve. I'm not a rookie who needs a damn pep talk."

"No, you're a damn good investigative reporter who's let yourself go soft. It's time to get back to work, Clay."

"I don't have to work, remember?" He had a few million in the bank between his inheritance, Ellen's life insurance and what the *Times* had paid out because she'd been killed on the job. Technically, he wouldn't have to lift a finger to support himself for many years, if ever. Except that the payouts resulting from Ellen's death sat untouched, collecting interest, because the thought of spending one penny made him feel sick. Blood money. That's what it was to him.

"What else are you going to do?" Steve asked. "Sit in that half-finished house on your little island and drink yourself to death? Is that what Ellen would have wanted you to do?"

Clay clenched his jaw against the urge to hurl the phone against the wall. "Look, you want this story so bad, get someone else to dig for it."

"I want the best. I want you."

"I'm done, Steve. You can't reel me back in."

"Just ask some questions. That's it. See what you can turn up and let me know. If you sense there's something going on, I'll send someone else in. Come on, you owe me."

"For what?" Clay asked.

"Hell, I don't know. We've known each other a long time. You must owe me for something."

Clay laughed in spite of himself. "Oh, for God's sake—"

"Thanks, buddy," Steve cut in. "Knew I could count on you. Call me when you've got something."

Jessie rubbed absently at the ache in her temple, struggling to concentrate on the words that seemed to float in a jumble on the computer screen. The painkiller she'd taken in the morning had already worn off, leaving dull, gnawing aches in her wrist and head.

Barely eleven hours had passed since her car had slammed into a tree in Clay Christopher's front yard. A full day had passed since the newspaper had broken the biggest story in its history, a story that still had issues that bothered her. The file on her screen was the start of yet another follow-up.

"Well? What do you think?"

Pulling off the glasses she used for reading, she squinted up at the reporter pacing beside her desk. Greg Roberts had his hands in his pockets, worry lines creasing his forehead. His long, dark hair was in a ponytail, drawing attention to the diamond stud in his earlobe. With the silver, wire-rimmed glasses with tiny oval lenses, he looked both hip and intelligent. Of all her reporters, he was her youngest—twenty-three—and most promising: eager as hell to do a good job and hungry for the guidance she happily lavished on him.

Now, though, he was as stressed as he'd been two days ago when he'd been writing the lead story that went with photos showing local cops doing the nasty with exotic dancers. The story she was reading now was about the cops involved being put on unpaid leave until a full investigation had been completed.

Jessie wished she could ease his anxiety, but she wasn't

doing so well with it herself, so instead, she said, "Why don't you take a break outside in the sunshine while I read this?"

He gave her a chagrined smile. "I'd rather pace right here and make you crazy. If that's all right."

She focused on the computer, slipping her glasses back in place. "Just keep in mind that driving me crazy today would be a short trip."

"Since you mention it, several of the reporters have expressed concern about your, uh . . . condition."

"They'll get over it."

Greg sighed. "I suppose we'll have to."

She didn't glance up as she recalled the shock that had greeted her when she had walked into the newsroom several hours before. The news of her accident had been well circulated by that time, the reporter on the police beat having heard the scanner traffic about it the night before. Most of her morning had been spent assuring co-workers that she was perfectly capable of performing her duties even if she felt a little queasy and stiff and even if the cast made typing a challenge. For the first time in the months since she had become city editor, she wished she had insisted on having a PC in her office. Then she could have closed the door on the concerned looks and motherly advice. But she had wanted a work station among the reporters—to promote better communication. And it had. Now, however, she wanted less communication about her accident.

After another minute of reading, she glanced up at Greg. "This looks like a good start. You assigned photos, talked to the graphics department?"

"Yep." He pocketed his hands again, nervously glanced around.

Leaning back in her chair, she crossed her arms. "Okay,

out with it. What's going on?"

"One of the women from the strip club wants to meet with me," he said.

Jessie pulled off her glasses. "Again? Why?"

"She wouldn't say," Greg said. "Wouldn't even hint."

"Whatever she says, it has to be on the record."

"I know."

"When are you meeting her?"

"Tomorrow morning."

"Excellent," she said. "We'll have all day to pull something together for Wednesday's paper. What—"

"Hey, Jess."

She winced a little as she turned her head toward the news assistant who had called her name. "Yes?"

"Someone here to see you," the young woman said, gesturing over her shoulder.

Greg was saying, "I'll catch up with you later," when Jessie spotted her visitor.

She gave Greg an absent wave as she rose. "Mr. Christopher."

Clay smiled. "Hope you don't mind me dropping by unexpectedly."

Jessie tucked stray hair behind her ear. "It's no problem."

He had shaved his beard, revealing an angular chin tempered by a dimple. The lack of tan lines on his face told her his skin had been exposed to the sun before the beard. His clean, white T-shirt was tucked into jeans that looked new. Even when he'd worn shabby clothes and a shaggy beard, she had thought him attractive. Now, she noticed his sun-bleached hair, blue, blue eyes and arms that were well-muscled and tanned, as if he spent much of his day in the sun.

Realizing that the silence had grown while she'd checked him out, she cleared her throat. "What brings you to *The Star-News*, Mr. Christopher?"

"I called Mel's, and she said you insisted on coming to work today. I suppose she chastised you on the absurdity of that," he said.

"Is that why you came by? To continue the chastising?"

"Have you eaten?" he asked.

"No time." The phone rang, and she reached for it.

"I've got it," Greg called from his desk.

Clay shifted, regaining her attention. "You need to eat."

"You sound like Mel."

"She admitted to buckling under your glare."

She frowned, faintly annoyed. What else had Mel told him? "I hardly glared."

"You're glaring now. There's a crease between your eyes."

She massaged the spot that wrinkled whenever she had a nasty headache. "Look, I'm really—"

"In pain," Clay cut in, concern replacing his smile. "Did you take something for it?"

She shook her head, irritated with herself for letting it show.

"A break would help," he said.

"It would just put me further behind."

"You don't have assistants?"

"People are on vacation and out sick. And if you've been reading the newspaper lately, you know we're up to our eyeballs in follow-ups."

"Working yourself into a coma won't help. In fact, it would just create more work for your staff because not only would they have to cover for you, but it would probably be the first work-related coma, warranting even more work for your staff."

"Nice." Her lips quirked into a small smile. So he was a flirt. An incredible-looking flirt. For an instant, she allowed herself to regret that she wasn't the kind of woman who could fall in love, or at least into bed, easily. "Is there something else you wanted?"

"To take you to lunch." He arched a brow, undaunted.

"That's very nice of you, Mr. Christopher, but—"

"You bled on me and ruined my favorite T-shirt. You can call me Clay."

She decided humoring him would encourage him. "I'm afraid I'm still pretty—"

"Hey, Jess."

Grateful for the interruption, she turned. "Yes?"

A co-worker was leading an unfamiliar man toward her. "Another visitor. You're popular today."

This visitor was about forty-five, with thinning salt-and-pepper hair, a dark mustache and equally dark eyes. Wearing black slacks, a white short-sleeved shirt and plain black tie, he didn't smile or offer his hand as he flashed a badge. "Detective Mubarek, Fort Myers police. Ms. Rhoades?"

"Yes." She squared her shoulders. She'd gotten plenty of irate calls from law-enforcement types since the newspaper had broken the copulating cops story, but no one had shown up at the office. "What can I do for you, detective?" she asked.

"Is there somewhere that we can talk privately?"

She cast a glance at Clay, thinking this was where he would exit, but he waved her on. "Go ahead. I'll wait." Helping himself to her chair and the copy of the day's newspaper on her desk, he leaned back, opened it to an inside page and gave her a look that indicated he had all day.

His confidence that she would want him to wait

amused—and baffled—her as she led the detective into her office. Shutting the door, she braced for a verbal attack.

Detective Mubarek flipped out a notebook as he sat in the chair across from her desk. "I'm investigating your accident. Can you tell me what happened?"

Relieved that she wasn't going to be put on the defensive, Jessie leaned a hip against the desk and folded her arms across her chest. The front walls of the office were glass, and she could see Clay studying the newspaper with interest. Focusing on the detective, she said, "I'm afraid it's a blur. It was raining, hard to see. I don't remember much."

"That's not unusual with head injuries." He stared down at his notebook for a beat. "Can you think of any reason someone might try to kill you, Ms. Rhoades?"

She stared at him, thrown. "Why?"

He raised his head, dark eyes narrowed. "Your brake line was cut. That's why you hit that tree."

Feeling lightheaded, Jessie sank onto the chair behind the desk. "Could it have been normal wear and tear on the car? It was old."

"The brake line was sliced clean. Nothing normal about that. Have you received any threats, Ms. Rhoades?"

She was vaguely aware of Clay turning to a new page outside the office. "Other than readers threatening to cancel their subscriptions, no."

"Anything at all? No matter how minor it seemed at the time?"

"No. Nothing. I'm not exactly in the public eye."

"Any disgruntled employees? Someone you've recently disciplined or fired?"

"You'll find plenty of disgruntled employees in this newsroom, detective, but I don't think—"

"Any of them disgruntled with you specifically?"

She glanced past him at the bustle of the newsroom. Everyone she saw she considered a friend. "Maybe one," she said.

"Name?"

"I don't think—"

"I'm trying to do my job here, Ms. Rhoades, which amounts to finding out who tried to kill you. Name?"

Her stomach started to churn. "Stuart Davis."

He jotted a note. "His problem?"

Pulling in a breath, she released it, slow and easy. "Stuart's beat was recently changed, and he's not happy about it."

"He threatened you?"

"He expressed his extreme displeasure."

"How so?"

"He threw something. Look, detective, I'd hate for you to waste your time considering Stuart as a suspect. He's really not—"

"What did he throw?"

She told herself she was being honest. That didn't equate betrayal. "A chair."

"He threw it at you?"

"No."

"What happened after he threw the chair?" he asked.

"I had no choice but to suspend him for three days without pay."

"When was this?"

"His suspension started Thursday. He's due back today."

"When you suspended him, did he make any threats, say he was going to get you or make you pay?"

"No."

"Has he ever said anything like that before last week?"

"No. I don't consider Stuart a threat, detective. He's an angry person. That's all."

As if she hadn't spoken, he asked, "Does Mr. Davis know what kind of car you drive?"

"Drove. It's totaled."

"Whatever. Does he?"

"I don't know," she said. "Maybe."

"Where was your car parked yesterday?"

"In the lot here."

He scribbled more notes. "Have you received any odd phone calls here or at home? Hang-ups or otherwise?"

"No."

"Is your home number listed?"

"No."

"How long have you been in Fort Myers?" he asked.

"Two years."

"And before that?"

"I relocated from Chicago."

"Married?"

"Divorced."

"How many?"

"How many what?" she asked.

"Ex-husbands."

Her temper started to heat. "One. You thought there'd be more?"

He shrugged. "A looker like you? Sure."

The spark in her temper turned to flame, and she latched onto it to counter the trepidation that was spreading with each question. "Are you making an effort to insult me, detective? Or is this happening naturally?"

"No effort, Ms. Rhoades. Where is your ex?"

"Chicago. We don't keep in touch."

"Why not?"

"We just don't."

"He ever threaten you?"

"No." She didn't hesitate, reminding herself again that she was being honest. *David* had never threatened her.

"His name?"

"Why?"

"I'd like to ask him a few questions," he said.

"I told you he never threatened me." She hoped the sudden thudding in her chest wasn't obvious.

"I'd like to cover all the bases, if that's all right with you."

"I'd prefer you didn't contact him."

"I can find out his name without your help." He was poised to write, as if he thought she would give in.

"Fine," she said.

Impatience darkened his gaze. "You're not going to tell me?"

"I don't see the point. He has nothing to do with this."

"You're not being very cooperative, Ms. Rhoades."

"Do you have other questions, detective?"

He glared at her a long moment, then, when she didn't buckle, he pursed his lips as if considering his next question. "Any boyfriends?"

"None."

"Recent ex-boyfriends?"

"No."

"You have no current or former boyfriends?"

"That's correct."

He arched a dubious brow. "What about the surfer dude you were talking to when I walked in?"

She laughed in spite of her annoyance. Surfer dude, indeed. "Mr. Christopher is an award-winning journalist."

"Award-winning journalists aren't allowed to surf?"

"Look, detective—"

"Lovers, male or female?"

"No one. I don't understand how this is productive—"

"I'm trying to find out who tried to kill you, Ms. Rhoades. Surely that's productive in your eyes."

His words, as much as his tone, were a slap of reality. Someone tried to kill me, she thought. Jesus. Swallowing hard, she said, "No lovers, male or female."

"If you were having more fun, Ms. Rhoades, perhaps your newspaper would have been able to avoid embarrassing this city and its fine police department."

Another slap, this one more like what she'd expected when he'd arrived. Irritation chased away the fear that had been encroaching, and she straightened. "Perhaps you should take up your frustration with the person who took pictures of your co-workers in compromising positions and gave them to a reporter."

"If you give me that person's name, I will."

"I don't have that person's name, detective. Like the newspaper reported, it was an anonymous informant." And the dead-last choice on her list as a reliable source, but it hadn't been her decision.

Snapping his notebook closed, the detective stood. "When are you expecting Mr. Davis?"

"He should be here any minute. He's working a later shift today."

"If you point out his desk for me, I'll wait for him."

After she indicated which desk was Stuart's, Mubarek said, "I recommend you get yourself a bodyguard and lie low until we figure this out." He flicked a business card onto her desk. "If you think of anything to add, give me a call. Home number's on the back."

He left her alone, and Jessie stared at his card. *Someone*

tried to kill me. The pain in her head began to pound in time with her heart.

"Jessie?"

Clay stood in the door, blond and gorgeous, a question mark in his eyes. She didn't know what to say to him. Someone wanted her dead.

"My brakes were tampered with." As soon as the words were out, she wished she could take them back. It was personal, and she didn't know this man.

But it was too late as he stepped into her office and shut the door. "What did the detective say?" he asked.

Yanking open a drawer, she rummaged for some Tylenol or Advil, anything that would stop the throbbing. "That someone tried to kill me." A bottle of Tylenol tried to roll away from her questing fingers, but she snagged it up and fumbled with the child-proof cap.

The cast on her hand stymied her, but before she could swear in frustration, Clay eased the plastic container away from her and popped it open. As she dumped the last two pills into her palm, she was chagrined to see that her fingers were visibly trembling.

"What are you going to do?" Clay asked.

She chased the pills with water from a bottle she kept on her desk before meeting his gaze. The concern in his startling blue eyes rattled her. Why should he care? They'd just met. Then it registered what he'd asked. *"What are you going to do?"* Running was definitely an option. Except she'd already done that once in her life . . .

Closing her eyes, she told herself to get a grip. It was too soon to panic. When she opened them, he was still there, watching her with those clear blue eyes. A woman could drown—she cut the thought off. "I'm going to get back to work."

He stayed where he was, between her and the door. "Someone tampering with your brakes isn't something to take lightly," he said.

"I'm well aware of that, and I'll take care of it. I appreciate your—"

"How?"

She faltered. "Excuse me?"

"How are you going to take care of it?"

His persistence surprised, and irritated, her. It wasn't often that two men managed to annoy her in the course of one hour. "It's none of your business."

"I'm making it my business."

"Well, I'm not. You don't even know me."

He almost smiled, as if enjoying her growing agitation. She suspected he would have had a full-blown grin on his face if a detective had not just delivered such disturbing news. "I planned to change that over lunch," he said.

"Which I already said no to."

"You're allowed to change your mind, you know."

"Thanks for your consideration, but the answer is no."

He sighed. "I have a confession to make."

"There's a church down the street. Thanks for stopping in." She started by him, but he shifted to block her way. A whiff of his aftershave—clean and crisp—forced her back a step. He looked good, and he smelled good. And that couldn't be good for her ability to resist him.

"I cut a bit of a deal with our mutual friend," he said.

"Great." Dropping into her chair, she folded her arms across her chest, already knowing she'd been outmaneuvered. Mel had always been the craftier one. "What is it?"

"She said that if I couldn't get you out of the office for a leisurely lunch, she would send orderlies with a strait jacket to haul you out of here."

Jessie couldn't suppress a smile at the thought of how her co-workers would react to that. "She wouldn't dare."

"I don't know her as well as you do, but do you want to risk it?"

As she shook her head, she saw Stuart Davis walk—no, stalk—into the newsroom. He was heading straight for her office, his red face set in determined angles. Describing him as a difficult personality was not adequate. He was the stereotypical reporter: cynical, hard-bitten, crass, hard-drinking. Mix in paranoia and a complete lack of diplomacy, and that was the man who possibly wanted her dead.

As Detective Mubarek intercepted Stuart, Jessie glanced at Clay. She couldn't deny that as the lesser of two evils, he could have been much worse. "All right." Fishing her purse out of her bottom desk drawer, she shouldered the strap. "We'll make it a quickie—" She broke off, horrified that her mouth had said what some part of her brain thought every time she looked at him. "I mean—"

Clay's grin grew. "I like the way you think."

Chapter 4

"You used me to avoid unpleasantness, didn't you?" Clay asked, enjoying the way Jessie dug into her lunch without the delicate pretense of many women eating in the presence of a man for the first time. He'd been pleased when she had ordered a cheeseburger and fries rather than a salad as he had expected, and he hadn't bothered to argue when she paid for her lunch without a glance at him.

Jessie swallowed a bite of burger. "As if you didn't use Mel to get me out here."

They had chosen a tiny burger joint with vinyl, red-and-white-checked tablecloths and booths carved from dark wood. The lights were dim, the air thick with the scents of fried food, and an old Pac Man machine blipped and gurgled near the door. Customers—young and not-so-young, professional and blue collar—occupied every booth, and a steady throng of patrons kept the women at the counter busy.

Savoring his deliciously greasy cheeseburger, Clay tried not to be too obvious watching his lunch partner. She seemed unaware of his scrutiny, hadn't noticed the appreciative glances she'd gotten when they'd arrived. Clay had noticed, but he couldn't blame anyone for looking. She was striking, even dressed simply in a white, short-sleeved, mock turtleneck that displayed nicely toned upper arms and black slacks that seemed tailored especially for her slim curves. Her blond hair fell straight with only the hint of curl at the ends that brushed her shoulders. She wore little, if any, makeup, which drew his attention to the deep blue ring around her gray irises. A low-maintenance woman, he decided, who had no idea that high-maintenance fantasies kicked in when she walked into a room.

He swallowed some Diet Coke, surprised at himself. He had not looked so closely at a woman who wasn't Ellen in years. The thought of his dead wife changed the direction of his thoughts, and he sought a neutral topic for conversation.

"I noticed the detective was talking to Stuart Davis when we left," he said. "Did that have something to do with your brake problem?"

"I don't think so." She seemed so unflustered by the attempt on her life that he searched her eyes for undercurrents of fear. He saw none before her gaze darted away, foiling further assessment. "How do you know Stuart?" she asked, munching on a french fry.

"We worked together about ten years ago at a daily outside D.C. We called him Bulldog because he was such a hard-news man."

"Still is. Were you friends?"

"Acquaintances really. He had quite a reputation."

"He smells conspiracy in every story," she said. "Sometimes he's right."

"He hasn't changed then."

"He's a decent reporter with some impressive behind-the-scenes sources. Unfortunately, his attitude doesn't help. He doesn't care for me."

"You're a woman in a power position. Triple whammy."

"Triple?"

"You're a whippersnapper."

She laughed, some of her stiffness dropping away. "A

whippersnapper. Haven't heard that in a long time."

He liked her laugh. Soft, without pretension or self-consciousness. "I would think you'd hear it all the time in your position. You're not even thirty, are you?"

"Thirty-two."

Her tone wasn't the least bit defensive. Finally, he thought, a woman who wasn't hung up about sharing her age. "City editor for a midsize paper and so young. That's impressive. But then, you were a damn good reporter."

"Smooth." Grinning, she tipped back her can of Diet Coke.

"I'm not blowing smoke."

"Please," she said. "You're so transparent."

So she thought he was trying to charm her. He began to tick off points, starting with his thumb. "The series about the state of local mental health care? So well done that it got state lawmakers going on new legislation. It helped that it was an election year, of course, but still." He held up his index finger. "The developer who left town after your very thoroughly researched report exposed him for the con artist he was? Excellent reading, and let me just say, what a jerk." His next finger popped up. "Exposé of abuse at the dog tracks? Enraging and wrenching at the same time."

Wariness began to replace the amusement in her eyes. "You're not stalking me, are you?"

He chuckled. "I'm just supporting my statement that I think you're a good reporter. When your byline disappeared, I thought you'd moved on to a bigger and better newspaper. While I'm pleased that you're still here, I'm wondering why you haven't."

She shifted, obviously uncomfortable with such praise. "I've been here only two years."

"So? Someone with your talent should be writing for

USA Today, The Washington Post, The New York Times. Hell, if you worked for a corporate-owned publication, you'd be on the fast track."

"Maybe I don't want to be on the fast track."

"Everybody wants to be on the fast track. And a story like those copulating cops of yours could put someone like you in the national spotlight."

"They're not *my* copulating cops."

"No, but that's your story, isn't it? As editor, I mean."

"I'd rather not talk about it, if you don't mind."

That stopped him. Journalists as a breed loved to talk about their big stories and how they landed them. "Come on," he said, unable to blunt his disbelief.

When she bristled, he realized he'd made a major misstep in assuming that she'd be eager to share her war stories. As he fumbled for a way to regain his footing, she glanced at her watch. "I should—"

"Don't," he cut in. "Please."

She met his eyes, and hers narrowed.

He gave her a conciliatory smile. "Don't cut lunch short because I'm an idiot."

She returned his smile, her shoulders relaxing some. "At last, a man who can admit when he's an idiot."

"Ouch," he said, and laughed. Biting into his burger, he wondered at his relief that she wasn't walking out on him right now. He wasn't normally driven to earn anyone's approval. He'd lived his life the way he'd wanted, even when his senator father and stockbroker mother had expressed disappointment in their son's choice of career. Certainly, as a teenager and a young adult, he'd fallen all over himself to impress a beautiful woman or two. But never as the man he was now. In fact, the women were usually the ones trying to impress him. None, with the exception of his wife, had intrigued him as much as the woman sitting across from him now. And very few had proved to be as immune to his charm.

Swallowing, he said, "I can't help getting carried away sometimes. I love the news business."

"If you love it so much, why aren't you in New York or D.C., where all the action is?"

He shrugged. Now she was treading into territory he wanted to avoid. Turnabout, he thought. "I'm semiretired."

"You're not nearly old enough."

"And you're wondering how I can afford to live on a very pricey barrier island and not work."

"That's none of my business."

"How unreporter-like of you," he said.

"I prefer refreshing."

He grinned. "If you must know, my grandfather left me some money, which I invested well." He paused to devour a french fry. "The occasional freelance project helps out."

"Like the one that pissed off Mel."

"Right," he said. "Sick buildings. I hear there's still no cure."

She smiled. "I'll let Mel know."

He focused on her cast as she finished off her burger. The plaster was still pristine white, and he thought it sad that no one had scrawled goofy messages across it. Then he noticed the tremor in her fingers, and his stomach clenched. "Is it bothering you?" he asked.

"This?" She made a negligent gesture with her injured hand. "I'm getting used to it."

"I was referring to what the detective told you."

"Oh, that." She focused on something over his shoulder. "Who wouldn't be bothered by it?"

"It's okay to be scared." Wanting to touch her, to offer

comfort, he brushed his fingers over the back of her hand.

She jerked back as if he'd just dropped a tarantula on her. Then, blushing, she turned her attention to crumpling into a ball the white paper bag that had held her lunch. "It's time for me to get back to work, Mr. Christopher."

"Your barriers are daunting, Jessie."

"Barriers?"

" 'Mr. Christopher.' You just reminded me of where we stand. Strangers."

"Which we are." Sliding out of the booth, she discarded the bag before walking outside.

He caught up with her beside his Jeep Liberty. By then, sunglasses shielded her eyes from the sun while a light breeze toyed with the ends of her hair.

"What are you going to do?" he asked.

"About what?"

He struggled to keep her cool nonchalance from frustrating him. "Whoever tried to kill you failed. That person might try again."

"My income can't handle a bodyguard, if that's what you're suggesting."

"It would be money well spent."

"Probably."

"I'd be happy to—"

"You're kidding, right?"

The hitch in her voice—panic? fear?—surprised him. So she wasn't coping with what had happened as well as he'd thought. Some people were artists when it came to hiding their feelings. Unfortunately, he had no idea how to handle people like that. He tried for a light touch. "Let me help. I'd hate for my efforts last night to be for nothing."

She frowned. "This is an unsettling conversation."

"I know some people. A couple of phone calls and—"

She shook her head. "That would be panicking. I don't panic."

"You can't be overly cautious."

"I know that. I just don't think this is a situation that—"

"Someone *messed* with your brakes. To me, that's a situation that calls for some panic. You need protection."

"If I need some, I'll get some. I don't need handouts."

"It's hardly a—"

"Are you going to give me a ride back to the newspaper, or am I looking at a long walk?"

He tried to stare her down, but her sunglasses thwarted him. For all he knew, she wasn't even looking at him. And, he thought, who was he to force what he wanted on her? She was an intelligent, strong woman who had been taking care of herself long before he came along. Unlocking the door of the SUV, he opened it for her.

Jessie had settled down at her work station and signed on to the computer system but couldn't focus. She kept telling herself that Clay had invaded her personal space and that's what had unnerved her so. But when he had touched her hand, she had felt the shock to her system. She wasn't the kind of woman who was comfortable being touched, even casually, by people she didn't know. But she also wasn't the kind of woman whose body responded independently of her head. And it had responded as if his fingers had held an electrical charge.

She reminded herself that he had caught her at a bad time. She'd just learned that someone had tried to kill her. Who wouldn't be shaky?

Sitting back, she stared at the phone. Maybe Clay was right. Maybe she did need protection. Would "bodyguards" be a heading in the Yellow Pages?

She closed her eyes. Even the memory of the last time her life had been threatened couldn't change the fact that protection had a price. And she simply didn't have the cash.

Her anxiety was forgotten when a news assistant raced across the newsroom to the police scanner that sat atop some metal filing cabinets. As he cranked the volume, Jessie joined him.

"What's up, Jon?" she asked.

"Someone just called us with a bomb threat."

"Here?"

"The water park."

"Jesus, that place is packed on days like this. Did you call 911?"

"Yeah."

"Where's Greg?" she asked.

"Lunch. No scanner traffic yet."

"Stuart?"

"Don't know," Jon said. "He left shortly after he got here. Everyone else is at lunch."

Yanking open a drawer, she snatched up one of the newsroom cell phones. "I'm going out there."

He gaped at her. "You're going to cover it?"

"We don't have anyone else at the moment. Photog?"

"Tracy just got back from an assignment."

"Have her meet me in the parking lot. She's driving." She headed for the door.

"Are you sure you're up to it, Jess?"

She waved over her shoulder, annoyed that her accident the day before had her colleagues treating her as if she would disintegrate if she had to work too hard. They didn't get that work helped.

Twelve hours later, Jessie dragged herself through Mel's

front door. Her friend, clad in a Winnie the Pooh T-shirt that hung to her knees, kinky red curls piled on top of her head, met her there with anger snapping in her green eyes.

"It's two. Did we not make a deal this morning?" Mel demanded.

"I fumbled my end of it," Jessie said, smiling wearily. "Cute jammies."

Mel glared. "Don't change the subject."

Jessie managed a contrite face. "Sorry. We had news."

"Where did you get into mud?"

Jessie glanced down at her caked shoes. "Did I track it in?" she asked, scanning the plush, gray carpet.

"No, it's dry. Don't tell me you were in the middle of that bomb threat."

Jessie nodded as she slipped out of the wrecked footwear. "No one else was available." Settling onto Mel's black leather sofa, she dropped her head back with a sigh. "How'd you hear about it?"

"Saw something on the news. They didn't have much, though."

"God, what a day."

Jessie hadn't realized how much she had missed her reporting days, living on adrenaline, firing off a breaking story within seconds of deadline, heart thudding with the excitement of everything happening at once. Chaos. It made her feel gloriously alive.

Being an editor was a different sort of chaos, the stress more intense because of the pressure from higher-ups to squeeze more sales out of a saturated market, the pressure to wring award-worthy enterprise out of overworked, underpaid reporters who struggled some days just to get one decent story out of their beats. Some days, like today, she wondered what she had been thinking when she had agreed to leave behind the job she truly loved to climb a management ladder that often frustrated the hell out of her.

Mel plopped down next to her. "You look like hell, champ."

Jessie rolled her head toward her friend, relieved to see that her anger had faded. "Thanks."

"I'm not kidding. You pushed it today. Too far."

"I'm fine—"

"It isn't about the fact that you allowed yourself no recovery time before jumping back into the fray, Jess. It's about how much you work every day, how much you push yourself every day. It's not healthy, and exhausting yourself is not going to make it go away."

Pushing herself up, Jessie padded into the kitchen, her stockinged feet sliding a little across the white tile floor. They'd had the conversation before and never verbally identified "it," though they both knew what "it" was. "Got anything to eat? I'm starving."

Mel followed her with a groan. "Leftover spaghetti in the fridge. Family recipe."

"It's my lucky day." Jessie retrieved the bowl with a grin. "Want some?" she asked. She had gotten used to the cast, and it didn't get in her way as she whipped open a drawer in search of utensils.

"I ate it eight hours ago when I came home at a reasonable hour," Mel said.

"And you're not hungry again?" Jessie asked as she heaped a generous portion on a plate.

Mel's longing gaze fastened on the pasta. "Maybe I will have a little."

"Have this one," Jessie said, scooting the plate over. She began filling another without missing a beat.

Minutes later, Jessie twirled pasta around her fork.

"Your Uncle Don, may he rest in peace, was the greatest sauce-making man on Earth. This recipe should be set in gold."

"It probably is, somewhere."

Jessie popped open the refrigerator to fetch some bottled water. "Want anything?"

"What you're having. So what's the story on the bomb scare?"

Uncapping her water, Jessie said, "Someone called it in to the paper this afternoon. Police cleared the water park and hunted about three hours before they found it. It was real."

"Wow."

"The part the TV news didn't have was the cops detonated the thing in a field around midnight. They said it was powerful enough to level three city blocks."

"My God, all those people could have been killed."

"But they weren't, so it's okay to love the hell out of this story," Jessie said. "Plus, the police got to redeem themselves some. They handled the whole thing perfectly, kept people calm and cleared the park in record time."

"So what's the headline?"

" 'Police thwart water park bomber.' A screamer."

"Ah, much less troublesome than 'copulating cops.' "

Jessie winced. "You know how much I hated that headline."

"I know," Mel said with a grin. "The water park story makes two screamer headlines just a day apart. What more could an editor want?"

"A hot shower and about ten hours of sleep."

"The night you allow yourself ten hours of sleep, I want it documented by a notary public." Mel sipped her water. "Clay Christopher stopped by the hospital this afternoon."

Jessie paused with her fork in midair. "Why?" She tried to be nonchalant as her stomach knotted with tension. She remembered how he'd looked at lunch—the angles of his face clean-shaven and tan, his blue eyes looking into hers so intensely she'd had to concentrate to avoid squirming. It wasn't often that she met a man she had trouble looking at without being distracted by such silly things as the dimple in the center of his chin.

"He told me about your visit from the police," Mel said.

Jessie's tension shifted to aggravation. "He had no right."

Mel's lips tightened. "You weren't going to tell me."

"I guess I hadn't thought about it."

"That's insulting. Do you know how insulting that is? I'm your closest friend. If someone is trying to kill you, I deserve to know."

"So you can worry even more? You don't need an ulcer because of me."

"You're staying in my home for a few days—the only part of the bargain we made that you're sticking to. Do you think you're safer here than you were in your car?"

Jessie pushed her plate away, the pasta only half-eaten. It hadn't occurred to her that she could have brought danger to her friend. Feeling nauseated, she braced a hand on the counter. "I didn't think."

"Did you tell the police about David?" Mel asked.

Her ex-husband's name brought her head up. "I told the police the truth, that we don't keep in touch. It didn't seem necessary to elaborate."

"Someone tried to kill you yesterday. I think it was damn necessary to elaborate."

No, she thought. Not David. He wouldn't. "I'm tired." She started to turn away, but Mel caught her wrist from across the counter.

"Look, Jess, I didn't know you when you were with him. All I know is what you told me, and I know you well enough now to suspect that you left out big chunks. I think you're being foolish for not telling the police."

Jessie gently reclaimed her arm, leveling a steady look at her friend. "David was not behind the attempt on my life, Mel. End of discussion."

"Look, I'm sorry. I care about you. Whatever happens to you affects me."

"Nothing's going to happen to me."

"How are you going to prevent that? Are you going to run away again? Am I going to get up tomorrow and find you're gone? Because I think you owe me more than that, Jess."

Jessie gazed at Mel, her chest tightening. She'd never had a closer friend. When she'd walked out on her life two years ago, there hadn't been one friend like Mel. She'd thought then that she would never trust again, would never even speak of what had happened to make her leave behind her entire life. But then she'd met Mel, and her perspective had shifted as Mel became someone she could trust, someone who demanded nothing, expected nothing, yet freely gave support, space and friendship.

After a year of weekly dinners, morning jogs, many shared bottles of wine and shakers of martinis, Jessie had told Mel about David and why she had left him. It had been the cheating, yes, without a doubt. Betrayal like that sliced deep, had left ribbons of scar tissue that sometimes seemed to be healed only on the surface. The deepest wounds still ached. But that particular betrayal hadn't been all. It had been enough, certainly, to force her out of her marriage. But it hadn't been enough to force her out of her life.

That particular event happened the day after she'd discovered David's indiscretion. She'd gone to work at the suburban newspaper where she was a reporter and tried to escape, to stop thinking. She didn't know what she was going to do. Leave him, of course. But to go where? Both her parents were dead, her father when she'd been a teenager and her mother recently. She had no siblings, no family, no close friends.

She'd buried herself in work that day, which wasn't all that different from most days. She'd been focused on reporting a story about a city councilman who'd slugged a colleague in the hall after a council meeting when her boss had invited her into his office and closed the door. He had told her that the newspaper had been quietly working on a story about law firms filing fraudulent insurance claims. David's firm was among those that would be exposed when the story went to press that Sunday.

Her boss had been kind, sympathetic, saying he understood that the story would put her in an awkward position with her husband's law firm and perhaps even with her co-workers reporting the story. He suggested she and David take a few weeks of vacation until the scandal died down. She had protested. She needed to work. It grounded her. But he insisted. It would be best for everyone involved, he said.

She'd left his office, numb and shell-shocked. As she had walked through the newsroom to gather her things, no one had met her gaze, no one had offered comfort. It had been a telling and painful moment.

She'd gone home and packed. Still, she hadn't known where she would go. When the doorbell rang, she hadn't thought much of it. As she'd gone to open it, she'd expected a solicitor or a Census taker. But one of David's law partners stood on the porch.

He'd shoved the door open, forcing her back several paces, and had walked right in. He hadn't wasted time with formalities. After accusing her of tipping the paper to the firm's unlawful activities, he'd told her what would happen if she failed to prevent the publication of the story. It hadn't mattered to him that she'd had no idea what the firm was doing or even that the newspaper had been tipped off. It hadn't mattered that she had no control over the top editors or that it wasn't the newspaper's practice to respond to threats. He'd told her, very simply, that if the story ran, he would quietly make her disappear.

The minute the guy left, shaking so hard she had to dial twice, she had called David at work. He was incredulous. She tried to tell him that his life might be in danger, that hers had been threatened. It had taken all her effort not to dissolve into a quivering mass on the floor.

He told her in a tight voice that they'd discuss it when he got home that night. His disbelief hurt, almost as much as the cheating, and it had knocked the shock out of her. Grimly resigned, she advised him to be careful, called her editor to let him know others might be threatened, then quietly walked away from that life.

Two years later, she felt safe, having decided long ago that the threat had been empty, a scare tactic by a desperate man who was now serving time in federal prison. Technically, that man had done her a favor. His intimidation had flung open the door for her, had given her an excuse to flee a life that didn't make her happy and seek one that did.

Her life now was more full than the past one had ever been. And much of that she owed to the best friend she'd ever had.

Jessie looked into Mel's eyes. "I'm not going anywhere. I promise."

Chapter 5

The next morning, Greg was waiting for Jessie as she walked into *The Star-News* newsroom.

"We need to talk," he said.

"Good morning to you, too," she said with a smile that faded when he took her arm and steered her toward her office. Ordinarily, she would have been annoyed by his aggressiveness, but it was unusual for him, as was his grave expression.

"I'm onto something," he said as he shut the door.

She settled behind her desk. "What is it?"

He seemed to brace himself before he spoke. "The woman I met with this morning—Sandi from the strip club—said she lied about the cops, uh . . . partaking of the services of her and her co-workers at the club. They were there, she said, but nothing improper happened. They were completely cop-like and threatened to shut the place down if it didn't adhere to the law."

Anxiety knotted Jessie's stomach. "She told you this on the record?"

"Yes."

"Did you ask her about the pictures?"

He gave her an insulted look. "Of course. What kind of reporter do you think I am?"

Jessie waved him on. "You're very thorough, blah blah blah. Go on."

He gnawed at his bottom lip. "She says the pictures are fake."

Jessie sat back as if the words had been fists hammered against her chest. She pictured lawsuits, ruined careers and public scorn. The newspaper's credibility would be shot. Without credibility, it wouldn't be much more than a recyclable, something to wrap around the day's catch or pad the breakables during a move. Recovery could take years, and even then it would never be complete because residents would gleefully tell newcomers about the time the local paper had been hoodwinked. Advertisers and thousands of subscribers might even abandon the newspaper, forcing it to slash costs to make up for the lost revenue, which would no doubt lead to layoffs and shattered lives. She searched for something, anything, to make what Greg had just said implausible.

"Shawn insisted the pictures hadn't been tampered with," she said.

Graphics editor Shawn Witherspoon was a Macintosh wizard. He knew all things computer. Moments after Greg had handed her the computer disk that a man on the street had slipped him, she had taken it to Shawn. They had discovered together the very explicit, very damning photos. She'd thought that if anyone could determine whether they'd been altered, Shawn could.

"Sandi says it's her and her co-workers in the pictures," Greg said. "But not the cops. She was paid to lie for the story."

Jessie thought of Taylor Drake, the respected police officer who had backed up the dancers' stories and corroborated the photos. Her initial anxiety about retractions and unemployment began to ebb. Cops like Taylor Drake didn't lie. And he definitely wouldn't rat out fellow cops without a damn good reason. If he hadn't come forward, the newspaper never would have run with the story. Even then,

Jessie would have preferred not to run with it as quickly as they had, but she wasn't the boss. "Who paid her?" she asked.

"She doesn't know," Greg said. "The deal was arranged over the phone, but the voice was distorted. She doesn't even know if it was a man or a woman. The day we ran the story, an envelope of money arrived in her mailbox."

"You believe her?"

"Credibility is an issue, of course," he said.

"When you talked to her, how was she? Nervous?"

"Yeah. Real nervous."

"She could be lying about lying."

"It didn't seem like that kind of nervous," he said.

"Does she still have it?"

"What?"

"The envelope."

"Why?"

"There might be fingerprints," she said. "And see if you can get her phone records. It's unlikely whoever allegedly set up the cops called from a traceable number, but you never know."

Whipping out his narrow reporter's notebook, he jotted notes. "Okay."

Jessie thought a moment. "She sought you out?"

"Yeah. And she insisted we go for a walk because she was afraid her place might be bugged."

"If she's so freaked out, why did she fess up? Why not take the money and run?"

"She said she feels guilty and wants to set the record straight."

"She didn't ask you for money?" she asked.

He shook his head.

Jessie tapped a nail on her desk. She knew Taylor Drake,

56

and he was the most honest cop she'd met when she'd worked the police beat. The dancer *had* to be lying. But the only ethical thing to do was check out her story. If they didn't, the newspaper could be accused of trying to cover its own butt instead of striving for accuracy in its reporting. "Have any of the other women contacted you?" she asked.

"No. I'm trying to track them down, though. I've only managed to hook up with two so far."

"Did you tell them why you want to talk to them again?"

"A follow-up story."

"Good. What about the guy who gave you the photo disk? Any leads?"

Greg shifted, tugged at his tie. "No. Like I said, he handed it to me as I was leaving the ATM and walked away. Looked like a homeless guy."

"Taylor Drake?"

"I haven't tried him. I thought maybe you'd want to call him since you're the only one he would talk to before."

She nodded. When the police officer had confessed the transgressions of his co-workers, as well as his own, she'd been stunned that he was involved at all. She'd even hesitated—before her journalistic duty kicked in—to report his involvement, knowing the price he'd pay when the story broke. It was exorbitant: not only did he lose his friends in the police department, but his wife walked out on him, taking their children with her. How many others had paid a similar price? If the allegations were untrue . . .

"You need to keep this to yourself for now," she told Greg. "There are too many unanswered questions, and if anyone gets wind of this—"

"I know. Hell to pay." He started to rise, but paused. "If it turns out the dancer's telling the truth, where do we stand? I mean, professionally."

She liked him too much to give him platitudes. "It's not good."

"Are we talking a strongly worded reprimand or long-term unemployment?"

"It's too soon to worry about that."

"Something like this can break a career, can't it?"

"Greg—"

"Or a newspaper," he said.

"We did our jobs thoroughly."

"You mean as thoroughly as we were allowed."

She caught a glimpse of red across the newsroom. "Here comes Gillian."

Greg glanced over his shoulder. "Looks like she's ready to rip someone's head off." Before opening the door to leave, he flashed her a strained grin. "Glad I'm not you, Jess."

"Bite me." She said it with a smile as he slipped out.

A moment later, Gillian Westin stepped in and shut the door. "Got a minute, Jessie?"

As if Jessie had the option to say no. "Sure. Have a seat."

Gillian was a willowy woman with rich auburn hair and eyes so brown they were almost black. Her dress today was silk and clingy, showing off the curves of a woman who relentlessly worked her body to keep it firm and conditioned. Sitting in the chair facing Jessie's desk, she crossed shapely legs, at ease in her power position.

It was a position that had been handed to her rather than earned when her father, the much-respected and beloved Richard Westin, had retired last year. He'd given her the reins to *The Star-News* with undisguised difficulty, his decision dictated by a heart ailment that would worsen if he didn't give up the long, stressful hours of being a newspaper editor.

The day before he'd retired, he'd told Jessie he was making her the new city editor, replacing a man who had quit as soon as he'd learned Gillian would be his new boss. Richard said he needed someone like Jessie to keep the newspaper on the right track. If he'd had his druthers, he'd said, he would have hired someone outside the newspaper as his own replacement. But his father and grandfather had both been *The Star-News'* top editor before him, and Gillian had her heart set on inheriting the role in the family tradition. If he chose someone other than his only child, he feared the humiliation would devastate her. So he was giving Gillian two years to prove she could handle it, and he wanted Jessie there as a sort of incognito safety net.

Incognito punching bag was more like it, Jessie thought as Gillian smoothed her already-smooth skirt. "Let's talk about the water park bomb story," Gillian said.

Jessie hated the way her stomach muscles tensed. "Is there something wrong with it?"

"No, no. It was fabulous. Circulation said our numbers were way up this morning."

"Good." Jessie relaxed some. When circulation was up, Gillian was happier. She had reason to be. Six months into her tenure, her father had informed her that circulation had slipped since she had stepped into his shoes. Jessie could have told them both why: Gillian had promoted a softer edge for *The Star-News* rather than the hard-hitting investigative journalism that made mediocre newspapers great. Page One exposés had given way to fluff—kids frolicking in the surf, residents raising money to pay the medical bills of the child with the "disease of the week." Jessie didn't have anything against such "feel-good" stories. But she didn't think they belonged on the front page in place of hard news.

Apparently, readers had agreed, and when circulation

started dropping, Richard had issued an ultimatum to Gillian: bring the numbers back up, thereby increasing ad revenue, or he would sell *The Star-News* to the highest bidder. Gillian had been a bitch on heels ever since, so any good news about circulation could mean a more tolerable working environment was on the horizon.

Clearing her throat, Gillian said, "I noticed the water park story had your byline."

"No one was available when it broke," Jessie said.

"You see, that's the problem."

"Problem?"

"No one else was available, so you covered it yourself," Gillian said.

"I have a reporter on vacation, two out sick and three others working on projects. The rest are picking up the slack and still trying to cover their own beats."

"That's not the point, Jessie. The point is, what's the best use of your time? I'm paying you to be a department head, not a reporter."

"I understand that, but there was an immediate need, and no one else was available," Jessie said, careful to keep her tone level. Any sign of defensiveness would earn a lecture.

"Then there's a management issue here," Gillian said. "Your role is to delegate, not pick up the slack."

"I responded to breaking news," Jessie said, then winced inwardly. So much for not sounding defensive.

Gillian gave her a patient, somewhat triumphant smile. "I'm not reprimanding you. I'm simply pointing out that perhaps you need to re-evaluate your role as a department head. It's irresponsible to drop everything to cover breaking news. What happened to the rest of your department while you were out there traipsing through the mud? Your reporters were left with no guidance. Yes, the water park bomb was the best damn story in the paper today, but there were a half-dozen others that needed more editing. Do you see what I'm saying?"

Not that it ever would have occurred to Gillian to pitch in with the editing herself. But Jessie didn't dare point that out. "I understand," she said, opting to seek safety in submissiveness.

Gillian's smile turned maternal, as if she had just put an errant child back on course. "You're new at this. You're young, perhaps too young for such responsibility. But you're good at your job. I wouldn't have chosen you as city editor if I hadn't been absolutely convinced of your ability to do it and do it well."

"I appreciate that," Jessie said, not bothering to remind her boss that her father had been the one who'd made Jessie city editor.

"Good," Gillian said. "So how are you this morning? You look tired."

"I'm fine."

"No, you're not. What's bothering you?"

Jessie forced herself not to bristle. "Nothing."

Gillian leaned forward in her chair, her dark eyes as sympathetic and quizzical as a therapist's. "Come on. Spill it."

Worrying her bottom lip, Jessie figured she'd have to tell Gillian eventually. She might as well get it over with. "Greg says one of the dancers is claiming she was paid to lie."

Gillian sat back, eyes going to slits. "Really."

"He's going back to the other women to see how wedded they are to their stories."

"What about Officer Drake?"

"We haven't contacted him yet," Jessie said. "I'd like to see what Greg turns up before talking to him again."

Gillian nodded, her lipstick red lips pursed. "So you're not sure this woman's legit."

"I don't know."

"What's your gut say?"

"Someone's putting pressure on her."

"Want to know what my gut says?" Gillian asked.

"Of course."

"The woman had her fifteen minutes of fame, and now she wants more."

"That thought also crossed my mind," Jessie said.

"I suppose the thought also crossed your mind that this newspaper would be severely damaged if the story turns out not to be what we reported."

"We were thorough."

"Not as thorough as you would have preferred, however."

Jessie picked up a pen to give her antsy fingers something to do. "You know my concerns about the photos."

"Yes, you made them known. Loudly."

It was rare for Jessie to argue so heatedly with her boss, especially in front of their colleagues. But she had wanted to hold the story a day so outside experts could examine the photos for tampering—especially considering the mysterious circumstances under which Greg had received the disk. But Gillian had been eager to get the story out there before radio and TV got a whiff of it. Jessie understood the fierce desire to beat the competition—she had it, too. But Gillian often took it too far, probably because of an intense desire to please her father. Unfortunately, that led to the newspaper running stories that hadn't been fully developed. It happened so often that they had a saying in the newsroom: don't let the facts get in the way of a good story. This definitely had seemed like one of those times.

"I felt strongly," Jessie said. Diplomacy was always the way with Gillian.

"We might have come to blows if your buddy Taylor hadn't come forward," Gillian said with a small smile, as if she savored the idea.

An exaggeration, Jessie thought. "I think it's even more imperative now that we have some outside experts look at the disk."

"Where is it?" Gillian asked.

"Shawn's office."

Gillian smiled. "Doesn't it feel clandestine?"

Jessie didn't share her enthusiasm for being furtive, but she nodded. "Thoroughly."

Rising, Gillian went to the door. "Let's sit tight on the disk for now. As soon as Greg gets a handle on this woman's story, I want to be informed immediately. If we have to backpedal on this thing, we need to do it before the TV people get hold of it and make us look like idiots."

"Okay."

"Comments? Observations?" Gillian didn't wait for a response.

Alone, Jessie let herself sag back in her chair, exhaling the breath she'd been holding. She always felt as if she had dodged a bullet after she and Gillian chatted.

She'd turned on her Palm handheld computer to retrieve Taylor Drake's phone number when Greg appeared at her door. "Hey, I'm on my way out. Clay Christopher called while you were with the dragon lady."

All thoughts of lying dancers and ruined reputations fled. "What did he want?"

"A hot date."

She didn't know what to say.

Greg laughed at her look of shock. "Hell if I know. We

didn't have a heart-to-heart."

"Jerk." She looked around for something to throw at him.

"I e-mailed you his number."

After he was gone, Jessie resisted the urge to check her e-mail and call Clay back right away. There was something else she needed to do first. After finding his number in her Palm handheld, she called Taylor Drake. His answering machine picked up.

"Taylor, it's Jessie at the paper. I need to talk to you ASAP. Please give me a call." She rattled off her work, home and cell phone numbers. Then, after getting his number from Greg's e-mail, she dialed Clay, blaming her sweaty palms on leftover stress from her talk with Gillian. Lord, the woman intimidated her.

Clay answered on the second ring. "Yeah?"

"Hi. It's Jessie Rhoades."

"That was quick. I called about two minutes ago."

"I was in a meeting."

"A good one, I hope."

"Not really," she said. "What can I do for you?"

"How's your day going?"

"If you're asking whether there have been any attempts on my life, the answer is no."

"That's excellent news. Planning to eat dinner tonight?"

She almost smiled. He didn't ask if she had dinner plans, just if she planned to eat. "I will probably eat dinner, yes."

"Will you eat it with me?"

She hesitated, tempted but wary. Her life was complicated. Getting involved with him, or any man, would make it more so. "I'll be here late." At least it wasn't a lie.

"You work too much," he said. "Mel said so."

"Mel should talk. She's a doctor."

"What kind?"

"Pardon?"

"What kind of doctor?" he asked. "I've always wondered."

"Oh. She's in internal medicine."

"Huh. I would have guessed plastic surgery."

"Why?" she asked.

"Don't know. She did say that you work more than she did as an intern. That's too much."

"Whatever," she said, trying to keep up with his shifts. "I'm having a busy day—"

"I'll cook."

She laughed, caught off guard yet again. "Well, that changes everything."

"Does it?" He sounded pleased.

"I was kidding."

"And here I thought my culinary skills had somehow gotten back to you."

"Guess your culinary skills aren't as widely known as you'd hoped."

He chuckled. "Do you like Thai food?"

Either he already knew which bait to dangle or it was a lucky guess. Regardless, she was hooked. "I love it."

"I make it."

"Get out."

"How do you feel about chicken galangal soup?"

"My favorite," she said.

"I thought so."

"Mel could be in big trouble."

"Don't be too hard on her," he said. "I had to call on some rusty torture skills to get it out of her."

"Sure you did." But she was smiling.

"I also make a mean Popeye chicken."

"Like the fast-food joint?"

"Not even close. Mine is chicken and spinach in a peanut sauce."

Her stomach rumbled. "You're killing me here. I really do have to work late."

"If you won't take the whole night off, just give me a couple of hours. *The Star-News* can function without you for a couple of hours, can't it?"

She knew she was giving in far too easily and couldn't imagine why it mattered. "What time?"

"Eight."

"I'll bring wine."

"Excellent."

After hanging up, she sat for a moment. It had been a long time since she had had dinner with a man, other than the occasional platonic co-worker. She no longer knew the rules.

Before she could second-guess her decision to accept his invitation, she glanced up. Stuart Davis stood in her office door, looking more disheveled than usual, his silver hair unwashed and messy, his jaw unshaved. Despite the Florida heat, he always wore a long-sleeved shirt and a simple tie, which was loose at his throat today. His flinty gray eyes were unfriendly as he waited for her to ask him in.

"Hi, Stuart," she said. "What can I do for you?"

"That detective talked to me yesterday," he replied, his voice gruff from years of cigarettes.

"Why don't you come in and close the door?"

Standing just inside the door, he said, "He asked me questions that made me uncomfortable."

"I'm sure Detective Mubarek felt they needed to be asked. Do you want to sit down?"

He ignored the invitation. "You told him I threatened you."

She rose, feeling the need to meet his accusing gaze on the same level. "That's not quite how the conversation went."

"Then why would he ask me those questions?" Stepping forward, he braced his hands on her desk so he could lean close enough to invade her personal space. "You're trying to get rid of me."

The desk was between them, but she still had to fight the urge to step back. "Stuart—"

"I didn't cut your damn brake line, lady. If I were going to try something, it would be far more subtle than fiddling with your brakes."

The veiled threat startled her, and she didn't know how to respond. Maybe she had underestimated him after all.

"And I was available to cover that water park story yesterday," he said.

The swift change in subject threw her for an instant. "You were out of the office."

"My cell phone was on."

"I didn't think to try it."

He straightened. "Of course you didn't."

"Look, Stuart, I don't know what you think is going on here—"

"I don't think," he cut in. "I *know*. I won't go down without a fight."

"There is no conspiracy here to—"

"Bullshit." Growing fury reddened his face. "You think I don't see your little closed-door meetings with Gillian Westin? I know how this business treats aging journalists. There isn't an ounce of respect. There's just the concern that we're grossly overpaid and too old to keep up with the youngsters. We get shuffled off to cover the festivals and the balloon rallies until we give up and quietly go away. I won't go away quietly."

Realizing that there was only one way to deal with this man, Jessie skirted the barrier of the desk. She was a foot shorter, so she had to tilt her head back to meet his gaze, but she did it with her jaw set and her eyes narrowed.

"Don't you think I had a reason last week to fire you, Stuart? You threw a chair. And while it wasn't *at* me, it came damn close. I don't need to trump up attempted murder charges to get rid of you. The only reason I didn't can your ass is because you're a good reporter with solid sources, and it wouldn't have served me as city editor to have to replace you. So take your woe-is-me attitude back to your desk and get to work. And if I see you harassing anyone or even giving any of your co-workers a dirty look, I'll haul your butt back in here and we'll have another heart-to-heart that very well could lead to termination of your employment here. How does that sound to you?"

He gaped at her, his gray eyes wide.

Jessie glared back, knowing that if she wavered even slightly, she would lose him.

Squaring his shoulders, he cleared his throat. "I suppose that sounds fine."

Jessie gave a perfunctory nod. "Good. Anything else?"

"No."

"You're working with Greg on the water park follow-up?"

"Yes."

"That will probably be the biggest story in tomorrow's paper."

He nodded, apparently getting her point. "It's good to be thrown a bone every now and then."

She ignored that. "Have the police turned anything up on a suspect?"

"They found some footprints in the mud, but they're not releasing details."

"I look forward to seeing the story by five."

"I don't think we can get it done by—"

"Five," she repeated. "We have deadlines for a reason."

Though he scowled, he didn't grumble as he left her office.

Her heart tripping on adrenaline, Jessie sank back onto her desk chair. As workdays went, this one was shaping up to be stellar.

Chapter 6

In front of Clay's front door, Jessie took a breath and held it. It was foolish to be nervous. He was just a man. Make that: a gorgeous man with sun-streaked hair, a sexy dimple in his chin and piercing blue eyes that could make her heart skip a beat.

Closing her eyes, she told herself to get a grip. It was unlike her to be so rattled by the way a guy looked. But it was more than that—

The door opened, and Clay stood there, wearing denim shorts and a T-shirt that revealed the impressive muscles of his suntanned upper arms. With a dishtowel thrown over one shoulder, he grinned at her look of surprise. "I saw you drive up." Peering past her at the rental car in his driveway, a red Mustang convertible, he whistled. "Nice replacement wheels."

She held out the chilled pinot grigio she'd picked up on the way over. "Will this do?"

He looked her up and down, his gaze not straying to the wine's label. She still wore her work clothes—khaki slacks, an olive T-shirt and a black, tailored jacket—but the glint in his eyes told her he didn't mind. "Perfect," he murmured. "Come in."

As she entered his home, her mouth began to water at the heavenly scents coming from the kitchen. Ginger, peanuts, garlic.

Then the décor commanded her attention: slate-gray tile

floors, simple and sparse furnishings in shades of gray and black, wrought-iron tables and lamps, and floor-to-ceiling windows that looked out on darkness now but no doubt by day framed the sparkling blue-green of the gulf. Delicate piano music wafted from hidden speakers.

As she followed him toward the kitchen, she noticed that plastic cut off an unfinished part of the house. She wondered what he was adding on, but then, seeing the kitchen, she stopped in mid-step to gawk. One word described it: sleek. From the black marble countertops to the black-and-white tile floor to the pot rack suspended above the island to the stainless steel appliances, it made her wish she were a gourmet cook and could play.

"You have a beautiful home," she said.

"Thanks." He went to work on the cork in the wine bottle. "Can you have wine, or do you have to go back to work later?"

"One glass won't hurt."

He poured them each a glass, then handed her one as she perched on a bar stool beside the kitchen's island. She took a sip, hoping the alcohol would calm her nerves. It didn't help that as he sampled his wine, his gaze wandered to her mouth and lingered.

She started to tuck hair behind her ear when she remembered that she had tried to tame the wreckage by trapping as much of it as possible in a loose ponytail. Hair-tucking was her nervous gesture, and she realized she did it a lot when she was around him.

"So how was your day?" she asked when the silence stretched on.

"Not as stressful as yours."

Surprise raised her eyebrows. How could he know what her day had been like?

"You have shadows under your eyes," he replied, as if he'd heard her inner question.

A soft, uncomfortable laugh escaped her. He noticed too much. "What's behind the plastic?" she asked.

"Baby's room."

Startled, she glanced at his left hand, saw the wedding band that she hadn't even thought to check for before now. Her stomach twisted with disappointment. He certainly didn't *act* married. In fact, she was certain he'd been courting her. Why else would he be cooking her dinner? And that made him a jerk. A *married* jerk.

Before she could do much more than set down her glass, Clay gave her a strained smile. "Can't believe I actually said that." He gulped some wine.

Sensing he had more to say, and that he wasn't a jerk, she kept quiet.

"The plastic's been hanging for several years," he said. "The stock answer when I have guests, which is hardly ever, is that it's going to be my new office." Turning his back, he opened the oven door and pulled out a covered dish. "Spring rolls?"

Jessie realized as he placed the dish on a trivet before her that this man was too alone to be married. So he was either divorced or widowed. When he looked at her, she saw his sadness and knew which it was. Her heart clenched in sympathy. "I'm sorry," she said.

"It's been three years." He offered no details.

Jessie touched the hand he had braced on the counter, and he stiffened. Drawing away, he nudged the spring rolls toward her. "Better try these while they're still hot."

She helped herself, as eager as he was to change the subject. Even so, as she sank her teeth into one, she wasn't prepared for the burst of flavor. "You made these?" she asked, incredulous that anyone but a professional could produce something so tasty.

"I did."

"They're fantastic."

His grin chased the sadness from his eyes, and he got busy preparing the rest of the meal. "So what's the news of the day?"

While he worked, she nabbed another spring roll, suddenly ravenous. Ignoring his amused smile, she said, "Follow-up on the water park bomb."

"Any leads?"

"Footprints in the mud. Cops aren't talking beyond that. But then, they don't have much to say to the newspaper these days."

"I don't imagine they do," he said. "Anything new on the scandal?"

Shaking her head, she licked stray spring roll juice from a finger. "School board made some stupid decision about busing."

"That's news?"

She laughed. "With this school board? Not really." She met his blue eyes over the rim of her glass as she sipped, then glanced away. Just looking at him unnerved her. He filled out his T-shirt so nicely, and as he moved around the kitchen, she got frequent glances at his very fine butt. Forcing her gaze away from that area, she focused instead on the way his hair curled slightly where it brushed his collar. Lust, she realized, had signed a lease with her belly and was moving in, whether she liked it or not.

Clay caught her staring and paused, a plate in one hand, serving spoon in the other.

Downing more wine, she tried to remember what they'd been talking about. Ah, yes. News. "Stuart thinks county accountants might be misappropriating festival funds," she said.

He didn't reply as he leaned a hip against the counter and studied her.

Lowering her glass, she cocked her head. "What?"

"You're wearing perfume."

She'd dug it out of a bottom desk drawer before rushing out of the office. It seemed silly now, but the fact he'd noticed still pleased her. "Why do you find that odd?"

"I don't," he said. "I was just noticing that it's subtle. Like you."

"That's so corny." She hated, yet was thrilled at, how much he unsettled her. It had been far too long since any man had been able to do that.

"You're a beautiful woman," he said. "Don't you know when you're being wooed?"

"I haven't been wooed in a long time," she said.

"I find that hard to believe."

"My life is complicated."

"Isn't everyone's?"

"My schedule—"

"Needs some adjusting." When he reached over and brushed a thumb under her left eye, she braced. For her, lust was strictly a hands-off experience. It was safer that way. So her instinct was to jerk back, to put distance between them. But for some reason, she didn't. She let herself appreciate the glide of his skin against hers, the subtle caress.

"These shadows bother me," he said. "You're burning yourself out."

Her laugh was nervous.

"You laugh, but I know the routine," he said. "I've been through it. Sometimes it sneaks up on you, and before you know it, you're flat on your back." His hand, warm and dry, slid over hers.

The heat of the gesture, and the explicit image that popped into her head, knocked the fluster out of her. *Too fast.* That's all she could think. It was happening too fast. Swiveling off the bar stool, she fumbled for words. "I'm sorry . . . I . . . I'm not ready for this."

Clay stared at her in confusion. "For what? We're having dinner."

"And what else?"

He arched an inquiring brow. "Dessert?"

"That's what I thought."

"We don't have to have dessert. It's just a suggestion."

"Like the 'flat on your back' suggestion?"

"Oh." He started to grin. "You thought I was—" He broke off with a laugh. "Oh, this is good."

He wisely stopped laughing, though, when she folded her arms across her chest and glared.

"I wasn't suggesting anything," he said quickly. "Though I admit the idea is quite appealing."

As it sank in that she'd misread him, that her well-honed defenses had kicked into overdrive, her face began to burn with embarrassment, and she dropped her arms to her sides. "I'm sorry. I'm . . . I'm . . ." She cast about for the right words, but they eluded her.

"It's okay to be scared, Jessie," he said. "I am. But I'm also glad you came."

"I'm not like this usually."

"Like how? Completely charming?"

She smiled. Talk about charming.

He gestured toward the dining room. "Why don't you have a seat while I serve the soup? I promise to keep the conversation innuendo-free for a while."

She took a steadying breath. That sounded safe enough. "All right."

As he set a bowl before her, he said, "I've wanted to ask you about something."

"Okay." While he lit candles then took a seat across from her, she sampled the soup, tasted chicken, lime and a hint of coconut. "This is wonderful," she said.

"That's chili oil floating on top. Gives it kick."

"You were saying?"

"How did the cops scandal unfold? It must have been pretty exciting."

Jessie sipped wine, his choice of topic stunting the growing mellowness that had been seeping into her muscles. Stress about the unanswered questions returned with a vengeance. "It certainly had its moments of excitement. It still does."

"I find it shocking that a police officer turned on his buddies," he said. "How'd your reporter get him to do that?"

"Taylor Drake approached us, well, me, actually."

"He's a friend?"

"Just slightly more than an acquaintance. He took me under his wing while I was learning the police beat when I first arrived in Fort Myers." Taylor had yet to return her afternoon phone call, but she imagined his schedule was as busy as hers. "What's this?" she asked. She held up her spoon, which had captured a thin-sliced, disk-shaped root. "Ginger?"

"That's the galangal. Very similar to ginger."

After they finished the soup, he gathered their bowls and carried them away. "Police corruption is a hot-button issue these days," he said from the kitchen. "We had that business with the Chicago police running drug deals with heroin they impounded after a drug bust. There were those Texas cops busted for being in cahoots with organized crime, that cop in Virginia who'd let women out of tickets if they slept with him. And those are just the tip of the iceberg. It would appear that police corruption is rampant."

"Sounds like a budget line to me."

He returned with plates heaped with chicken on a bed of spinach, smothered in peanut sauce. As he sat down, she noticed how the shadows danced over the angles of his face, making him look dangerous and sexy at the same time. Realizing she was staring, and that he had noticed, she tried the chicken.

A moment later, all she could do was say, "Oh my God."

"You like?"

"Oh my God."

"I'm glad." He sipped wine, watching her, his expression serious. "There's something I need to tell you."

Instantly, she tensed. She'd known he was too good to be true. "Okay."

He hesitated, as if thinking first about what he was about to say. "My former editor asked me to look into a rumor that your copulating cops scandal is a hoax."

Jessie fought to keep her face neutral as her stomach began to churn. It was one thing for the newspaper that reported it initially to uncover a hoax. At least some credibility might be salvaged. But if another publication exposed a bogus story, *The Star-News* didn't stand a chance. Everyone who worked there would look like fools.

Focusing on Clay, she noticed how he watched her, his gaze measuring. Suddenly, his invitations to lunch the day before and dinner tonight had a different context. He hadn't been interested in her. He'd been pursuing a story.

Clamping down on the disappointment, she forced her

brain to stay on track. None of that mattered now. The story mattered. "Where did your editor hear this rumor?" she asked evenly.

Clay angled his head, his eyes narrowed. "Why aren't you more surprised to hear about it?"

She closed her eyes. It would be easy to lie. Certainly, it'd be safer on a personal level. No humiliation there. But, ultimately, what would be the point? The truth would come out, and then she'd still be humiliated, not to mention devastated professionally.

She couldn't help but think of how handy it would be to have someone like Clay, a top-notch investigative journalist, on her side. He could do things that she couldn't, such as defy Gillian Westin, to get at the truth. He could expose it at the national level—perhaps in *The New York Times*—in a way that she would never be able to. Use and be used, she thought. That worked for her.

Jessie lifted her chin a notch. "It's not the first time I've heard the suggestion the story might be inaccurate."

His unwavering gaze never left her face, as if deciphering her every blink. "I see."

She shifted. In a matter of minutes, his scrutiny had gone from obvious interest to suspicion. "Would you stop looking at me like that? I feel like I just got caught doing something wrong."

"Did you?"

"Are you kidding me? Do you think the newspaper fabricated the story?"

"It's happened before. While police corruption is a hot button these days, so is the credibility of newspapers. The reporter who faked sources at the Baltimore newspaper comes to mind. As does the New Orleans journalist who made up a Pulitzer-winning story. That list could get as long as the one about corrupt law enforcement."

She dropped her napkin on the table and rose. "Thanks for dinner. I'll show myself out."

He followed her to the door. "So that's it? You're just going to walk away?"

She ignored him, made it to the door and started to open it.

His hand slapped against it, shutting it before she could slip out.

Jessie stared at his fingers braced against the wood in front of her face. They were long and tanned, with well-manicured nails. She noticed, too, that he was wearing cologne. It was very faint—clean, like freshly washed sheets. Still, having him so close behind her, his hand blocking her escape outside, his arm blocking her way back into the living room, made the air start to hitch in her chest. Trapped. "You can't keep me here," she said in a low voice.

"Running away isn't the answer, Jessie."

He had her pegged, she thought. She was a runner. At the first sign of adversity, she bolted. Her ex-husband could attest to that.

Clay's breath stirred the hair behind her right ear. "I wasn't suggesting that *you* fabricated the story," he said. "Or even anyone at *The Star-News*. But it's been suggested that *somebody* did, and it's our job to find out the truth. So we can work together on this, or we can go our separate ways right now. You decide."

She didn't like ultimatums, but she wasn't stupid either. They were the good guys, and two good guys on this story were better than one, especially when one of them had been in Pulitzer contention and had big-time connections. Turning, she pressed back against the door to put as much distance between them as possible. Even though she was about to agree to work with him, she was still irked that he'd been cozying up to her to find out all he could about the story. It would be imperative from here on in to remain on guard.

She took a breath, held it a moment, then took the plunge. "One of the sources, a dancer, has changed her story."

Backing off, Clay slid a hand to the back of his neck and massaged. "What did she say?"

"That she was paid."

"You have a reporter on that, I presume."

Her temper flared. "It's on my budget for next week, after we finish the investigative piece on the firefighter who pulled the kitten out of the tree without the kitten's permission. We have our priorities, you know."

A faint smile turned up the corners of his mouth. "You won't stay mad at me for long, will you?"

"I'm not mad." She moved away from the door into the living room and sat on the sofa, dragging a pillow onto her lap.

He joined her but kept his distance. "Sure, you are. And it's okay. You seem to think that showing emotion is a weakness."

She glanced sideways at him. "You've never been a woman in a power position. Emotion *is* a weakness."

"You're right. I wouldn't know the first thing about that. But, just for the record, I don't consider it a weakness. It takes a strong person to let emotions show, and follow them."

"There's no place for emotion in this story."

"Not the scandal, no. But we're another story, aren't we?" He stroked a hand down her arm.

The gentle caress suggested he would be a tender lover,

and she swallowed against the sudden tension in her throat. *Don't go there, Jess.* "Are we?" she asked. "I thought the scandal was what you were after."

"Maybe I was at first."

She shoved the pillow aside and stood, moving away from him and his clever fingers. At one of the floor-to-ceiling windows, she stared out at the dark. "I'd prefer to keep it about work, if you don't mind," she said.

"I've hurt your feelings."

"You tried to get close to me for a story. I don't respect that."

"I'm sorry."

She faced him. "No, you're not. You're getting what you wanted, aren't you? The inside scoop on the biggest scandal this town has ever seen. So why don't we just get to work and move on?"

He rose, his expression grim as he crossed to her. She resisted the impulse to back up. Pausing before her, he looked into her eyes, and she felt as if he'd pinned her to the glass behind her without touching her. "I wouldn't say I've gotten what I want," he said. "Not yet."

A heartbeat later, he smiled. "How about some coffee to clear our heads?"

Chapter 7

As Clay headed for the kitchen, Jessie let out her held breath. The man could disarm her with a look. The danger that presented would have, under normal circumstances, sent her running for the door. But that wasn't an option. She had to get over it and do her job.

Clay, grinding coffee beans, glanced over his shoulder when she resumed her seat at the island.

"How about you give me the rundown on how the cops story unfolded?" he said.

She studied the ridges in the cast on her wrist. Where to begin? "A reporter, Greg Roberts, was handed a disk at an ATM by a guy who was probably paid to be a courier. As you know, the disk held some very damning photos of several local police officers at a strip club. We didn't have much turnaround time. It was already late afternoon, and it was Sunday, when most people are off work. We immediately started calling people at home. The mayor, the police chief, the owner of the club. We started trying to ID the cops in the photos and sent someone to the strip club to talk to the women who work there. While reporters were doing that, I was trying to find outside experts to authenticate the photos."

He nodded as he filled the coffeemaker with water. "No luck?"

"Like I said, it was Sunday, so it wasn't easy. I had a line on a woman in Naples when our graphics editor decided the pictures were for real, and Gillian—the top editor—said that was good enough for her."

"What about you? Were you satisfied?"

"No, and I told her so. I wanted to hold the story a day so we could be sure."

The scent of fresh coffee began to fill the kitchen. "What bothered you?" he asked.

"Lots of stuff, but mostly the way we got the pictures: from an anonymous source. We don't know what that person's motives are or what their connection is to the story. Going with the story without knowing who gave us the material or knowing for sure that it was legitimate . . . well, it seemed irresponsible."

"So the graphics editor signed off on the photos, and you objected. What happened next?"

"Officer Drake confessed."

"And that changed your mind about it all?"

"It still felt out of whack. I don't know why. It was just a gut feeling."

"But you trust Drake. You said he's a friend."

"I do trust him," she said, accepting the coffee cup he handed her. "Or I did before he cheated on his wife. I was shocked that he could be involved at all, let alone in the middle of it. I thought he was a stand-up guy."

"So you still wanted to sit on the story," he said.

"Just for a day. It was huge, and I didn't feel comfortable dashing it off without time to think it through very carefully. By then we had IDs on all the cops in the pictures. This story was going to ruin a lot of people."

"But holding it wasn't your decision."

"Right," she said. "What it came down to, for me professionally, was going with the story or walking away from the newsroom and never looking back."

"And that wasn't an option?"

His phone rang, and they both started.

Clay answered it, then held it out to her. "It's for you. Greg Roberts."

"Oh. I left your number at work in case they needed me. Lost my cell phone in the accident," she said, taking the phone from him. "Greg, what's up?"

"She's dead, Jess. And the others are taking off."

She slid off the stool, every muscle tensed. "Who's dead?"

"Sandi White. The dancer I met with this morning. Coroner said she shot herself."

"Where are you?"

"I'm in my car. Damn it, Jess, someone got to her. I know they did. They got to all of them."

"Listen, don't say anything else. Meet me at the paper, okay? We'll talk there."

"She bought it because she told me the truth."

"Greg, you're on a cell phone. Others could be hearing this. Meet me at the office. Can you do that?"

He sniffed, gulped in a breath. "Okay, okay."

"It'll take me thirty, forty minutes to get there," she said. "Are you okay to drive?"

"Yes."

"Are you sure? I can pick you up."

"I can make it."

"All right. See you soon." Hanging up, she faced Clay. "I have to go."

"What's going on?" he asked.

"The dancer who recanted is dead. Greg's meeting me at the paper."

"Is anyone covering the scene?"

"He's too upset. I'll have to call someone in."

"I'll go."

"That doesn't do *The Star-News* any good," she said. "I have to send one of my own."

"I won't require a byline."

"It doesn't matter. I'd still have to tell my boss who covered it, and she'd freak." She gave him a grim look. "Your hoax rumor is looking less like a rumor."

After she was gone, Clay got into his SUV and headed for the Fort Myers police station. As he drove, he noticed the wedding band he had not removed since he and Ellen had married. There'd never been a reason to take it off.

But tonight, something inside him had shifted. Watching Jessie struggle with the weight of her responsibility, the way dread darkened her smoky eyes as she'd considered the implications of a bogus story, he'd wanted to protect her. The strength of the feeling both startled and fascinated him.

And he was compelled to help her.

It was the first time in three years that he'd been compelled to do anything other than mourn the loss of his wife.

Four hours later, Jessie had persuaded Greg to go to a friend's house and try to relax until they had a better handle on what was going on. He'd wanted to track down as many sources from the cops story as possible and question them again, but Jessie had told him no. They didn't know what they were dealing with. The circumstances of the dancer's death were suspicious. And if it was something other than suicide, that meant someone was willing to kill to keep the truth from being discovered. Putting a reporter in jeopardy wasn't an option.

Jessie sent Stuart Davis to cover the scene of the exotic dancer's death, where neighbors told him they heard a gunshot and called police. No one professed to know anything else, the police weren't talking, and the coroner had clammed up. Jessie assigned the six-inch story Stuart filed to an inside page.

Now, alone and in her office, she tried Taylor Drake again.

She was surprised when he answered. "Taylor, it's Jess. Did you get my messages?"

"Jessie?" He sounded disoriented, as if she'd awakened him.

"I need to see you. Tonight. Now."

"I can't," he said. "I'm on my way into work. I've been pulling double shifts as a security guard since I got put on unpaid leave."

"On a break then."

"What's going on?"

"I can't say over the phone."

"This sounds serious."

"It is. Sandi White is dead."

He was silent a long moment. "How?"

"She was shot."

"Shit. All right. As soon as my second shift is over. Noon."

"It can't be sooner?"

"I wish I could swing it, but I can't get away. This job is all I've got."

"Fine. Same place as last time?"

"I'll be there."

She hung up and stared at her watch. Eleven hours before she could talk to Taylor. There wasn't anything more she could do until morning.

Forty minutes later, she was home and had a shower. Wet hair combed back and her still-damp body wrapped in a robe, she opened the refrigerator for no other reason than to distract herself from the turmoil inside her head. She wasn't hungry, not after Clay's fabulous meal.

Thinking about him, she felt a flutter deep in her stomach, then admonished herself. He might have pretended interest in her, but she wasn't an idiot. The story was his ultimate goal, and if he managed to score a fling with her in the process, he would think that was nothing more than a bonus. Still, she almost wished she were a fling kind of woman.

The phone rang, and dread followed. Now what? she thought as she went into the bedroom to pick it up. "Hello?"

"You're home already? What, you're only working fifteen-hour days now? You slacker."

Jessie smiled, relieved. "Hey, Mel. What are you doing up? I thought you had early appointments."

"I do, but I wanted to check on you. I tried you at work earlier, and they told me you'd left for a few hours."

"I had dinner with Clay."

"Excellent. How'd it go?"

"You can check your romantic imagination at the door. He's wooing me for a story."

"No way." She sounded crestfallen.

"Sorry to disappoint you," Jessie said.

"That son of a bitch."

"Yeah, well, he's a reporter. Aren't we at the bottom of the ethical heap with lawyers these days?"

As Mel laughed, a thump behind Jessie had her turning toward the door that led to the other room. She imagined her purse falling off the table by the front door.

"So what story is he so hot for?" Mel asked.

"I can't get into it on the phone."

"I figured but thought I'd ask anyway. You sound wiped. You're passing on the trash TV and going straight to bed, I presume?"

The laugh caught in Jessie's throat as she switched on the light. "Damn."

"What's the matter?"

Jessie just stared at the mess—books tossed off shelves, plants spilling dirt on the carpet, cushions off the sofa. She had walked through this very room not half an hour before, and nothing had been out of place.

"Jess? Are you there? What's wrong?"

A movement in Jessie's peripheral vision snapped her head around. Something large and black leapt at her.

Chapter 8

Clay jerked open his front door to see Mel gasping for air. "Phone . . . need your . . . phone . . . to call . . . 911."

Half asleep, he stared at her in confusion. "What's the matter?"

She gulped in several breaths, wrapping an arm around her middle, and cursed. "Get me . . . the damn . . . phone."

He pulled her inside, seized the cordless off the table by the door and punched the numbers himself. "Tell me what's going on."

"Jess." She bent over, her chest heaving. "Damn it."

The bottom of his stomach dropped out. "What about Jess?"

Mel reached for the phone.

He handed it to her and listened as she haltingly gave the 911 operator Jessie's address and said something about an intruder. He didn't need to hear anymore. Snatching car keys off the table, he bolted for the garage. He heard Mel calling to him and had to force himself to wait for her to get into the SUV with him.

As he tore out of the driveway, he looked at her. She was still panting. "What happened?" he asked, deftly steering the Jeep through a sharp curve.

She braced a hand on the dashboard. "Jesus. Don't kill us before we get there."

"Damn it, Mel."

"We were on the phone," she said. "The son of a bitch

must have been there while we were talking."

"Who? Who was there?" It exploded out of him.

"I don't know. She just dropped the phone, and I heard—" She broke off when he took another curve, tires squealing. "You're going to total us."

"What did you hear?"

"She screamed. Or tried to."

His grip tightened on the steering wheel as Mel rushed on. "I tried to break the connection to call for help, but I couldn't get a dial tone. All I could hear was . . . and then my freaking cell phone was dead, so I ran like hell to your place to call the cops. Damn it, it would have been faster to drive, but I wasn't thinking. Damn it, damn it, damn it." A red light loomed ahead. "Run it, Clay. Just run it."

He didn't have to be told.

Dazed, on her back on the floor, Jessie blinked up at the intruder standing over her. He wore the typical cat burglar uniform: black pants, black long-sleeved shirt, gloves, ski mask. He seemed huge, menacing. And hesitant.

He didn't know what to do.

She stayed where she was, fear a raging fever behind her eyes. Maybe he'd run away. All he'd done so far was tear up the place and knock her down. She could live with that. Perhaps that would be enough for him, too.

But she realized that was wishful thinking when he leaned down and jerked her up by the lapels of her robe. "We're going to have us a chat," he growled. His breath was minty fresh.

Swinging her around, he shoved her toward the cushionless sofa. She stumbled, and he grasped her arm in a cruel grip. She tried to yank away, succeeded only in dragging her robe off one bare shoulder. The belt at her waist loosened, and she panicked at the thought of it falling open.

She drew in a breath to scream, but he cut it off with a punch that sent her reeling back against the wall. Stunned, bright lights bursting in her vision, Jessie slid down the wall.

The intruder leaned over her, and she imagined he smirked behind the mask. "You're making this harder than it has to be," he said.

She nailed him in the temple with her cast. As he lurched back, she pushed to her feet and followed, striking him again, this time under the chin, hard enough to snap his head back. The impact sent pain singing up her arm, but she ignored it, focused instead on getting to the front door. It was the only way out, at least ten feet away. Her glass coffee table stood between it and her.

She'd taken two steps when the intruder grabbed her from behind and jerked her back against him, locking his arm under her chin and shutting off her air.

She clamped her good hand around his forearm, dug in with her fingers, tried to knock him in the head with her cast. But he was too strong and easily dodged her flailing hand.

Black spots started to make her vision splotchy at the same time that she heard sirens.

Clay and Mel saw the red flashing lights before they pulled into the parking lot of Jessie's complex. At least six police cars were there, parked haphazardly, doors hanging open.

"Oh God," Mel moaned. "Oh Jesus."

Clay shoved the SUV into park, jumped out and bounded across the lot. A police officer tried to stop him, but he knocked the guy back and took the steps three at a time. He kept seeing Ellen, soaked in blood, life flowing relentlessly out of her. He kept feeling her body as he'd cradled her against him, warm and limp, as if all her bones had turned to ash.

The door to an apartment stood open, and, assuming it was Jessie's, he crossed the threshold. Time seemed to slow to a crawl as he saw a lamp in pieces, books and pictures scattered, a glass coffee table shattered, blood among the shards. A roaring started in his ears, and he had to school his breathing.

Mel stumbled in behind him. "Where is she?" She clutched his arm and hung on. "Oh hell."

A policeman approached. "Can I help you?"

Clay forced himself to steady. "We're friends of the woman who—"

Jessie, walking in from another room, saw him and stopped. "Clay."

Relief loosened the muscles in his stomach. She'd been knocked around. Already, a bruise was forming along her jaw. Spatters of blood marred the white robe, and her complexion was ashen. But she was standing. Alive. "Hey," he said, much more casually than he'd thought he was capable.

Sinking onto a nearby chair, Mel dropped her head into her hands. "I'm going to be sick now."

Jessie went to her, moving somewhat jerkily by Clay, and hugged her friend. "I tried to call you back so you wouldn't worry."

Mel wiped at her streaming eyes. "I was so sure you'd be dead when we got here."

Jessie gave her a shaky smile. "Well, I'm not."

Mel focused on Jessie's bruised jaw, and her concern turned clinical as she gently grasped Jessie's chin and angled her head so she could examine the smear of purple. "He hit you. Are you okay?"

"I'm fine," Jessie said. "Self-defense class paid off." She held up the hand encased in plaster. "This came in handy."

Clay, satisfied that Jessie was in good hands, searched out Detective Mubarek, who was taking notes on the balcony. As Clay joined him outside, he took in the mangled locking mechanism on the sliding glass door. The intruder had probably used a screwdriver to bust it.

Shoving away the images of what had followed, he introduced himself to the detective.

Mubarek eyed him with suspicion, even after recognition registered in his gaze. "Ah, the surfer who was in her office today. Your relationship with Ms. Rhoades?"

"We're friends."

"For how long?"

"We met recently," Clay said, forcing himself to be patient. "Can you tell me what happened here?"

"Ms. Rhoades said you're a reporter."

"That's true."

"So you think it'd be okay with her if I discussed her private stuff with you?"

"I said I'm a friend. A concerned friend. Maybe I can help."

After a long moment of staring each other down, Mubarek pointed at the sliding glass door with its messed-up lock. "The guy got in through here. She didn't have anything in the bottom track to secure the door."

"Do you know what he was after?"

"Could have been the usual stuff. TV, stereo, computer. It's hard to tell because she surprised him. The mess he made suggests he might have been after more than what he could sell. Overall, I'd say she's one lucky lady."

"I saw blood in the debris."

"It's his. She flipped him onto the coffee table. Pretty

sure he took some souvenir glass in his back when he took off. I've alerted the local ERs. We'll run his DNA, see if we get a hit on a prior felony. She said he was wearing gloves, so it's unlikely we'll find any prints."

"This is the second attempt," Clay said.

Pursing his lips, the detective nodded, unperturbed. "Looks like."

"What are you going to do about it?"

"I already told Ms. Rhoades to get some protection. We don't have the staff to provide it for her, but I can recommend a couple of agencies."

Clay clenched his jaw against the urge to take a swipe at the guy. "You wouldn't let any bitterness over a certain news story prevent you from protecting a civilian, would you?"

The detective returned Clay's glare. "I resent that, Mr. Christopher. But like I said, we don't have the manpower. In fact, we're especially low-staffed right now because of a certain news story. So I'll repeat my suggestion that Ms. Rhoades either hire herself a bodyguard or get the hell out of Dodge."

As Clay stalked away, anger and several other, more frightening, emotions tangled in his gut. He'd just met her, and already, he had almost lost her. He didn't like how unsteady that made him feel. And scared. For her. Because of her.

It couldn't happen again, he told himself. He wouldn't, in one lifetime, lose two women he cared for. Life just wasn't that cruel. Was it?

In the living room, Clay zeroed in on Jessie, who sat calmly on the sofa, hair still damp and shoved behind her ears, an ice pack pressed to her jaw. She looked small and vulnerable, consumed by the robe spotted with blood. He swallowed against the tension in his throat, reminding himself that the blood wasn't hers.

Mel paced back toward the couch. "This is so not cool, Jess," she said. "Totally not cool. I don't want you staying here tonight. Hell, ever."

Jessie shifted the ice to the back of her head. "Could you stop moving around so much? You're making me dizzy."

Mel didn't hear her. "Twice in three days someone has tried to kill you."

"The burglar didn't try to kill me. I surprised him." She worked her jaw, as if testing its mobility.

Stopping in front of her, Mel gestured wildly. "Look around this place. What do you see?"

"A big mess," Jessie said tiredly.

Mel planted her hands on her hips. "I see your VCR, TV, stereo, and while I was getting the ice pack, I checked your office where your laptop sits untouched. Yet, there are books scattered all over the place, your tree dumped out of its planter. Why make such a mess? Unless he wanted to scare you. Or set up a crime scene that would scream interrupted burglary." Mel knelt before her. "Maybe I'm overreacting, but this is scaring the hell out of me. Someone tampered with your brakes. For God's sake, you just got jumped in your own apartment. It looks to me like that son of a bitch has tracked you down."

Jessie glanced toward Clay, and he saw the annoyance at what Mel had said register in her eyes.

Mubarek stepped into the room. "Ms. Rhoades? I have a few more questions."

Taking Mel's arm, Clay said, "You need some air," and steered her out onto the balcony.

Mel curled her fingers around the top of the railing so

tight her knuckles went white. "Damn it! Why won't she listen?"

"Who's the son of a bitch?" Clay asked.

Mel looked askance at him and seemed to weigh her options. "She'd never forgive me."

"That intruder could have killed her, and you obviously know something the rest of us don't."

Wrapping her arms around herself, she shivered, though it was warm for a March night in Florida. "Her ex-husband. His name is David. When they were married, he was a lawyer at a good firm in Chicago. They'd been married seven years when she found out he was cheating on her. That was a couple of years ago. She left him, moved here and changed her name."

"Changed her name why?"

Mel hugged herself tighter. "David's firm got into some trouble, and the newspaper where Jessie worked was about to break a big story about it. She told me someone from the firm threatened her if she didn't get the story killed. So she took off and covered her tracks."

She shuddered before going on. "I didn't know Jess when she was married to him, but I know her well enough now to put together that she probably left out the more grisly details of their marriage. And I'll tell you, when I first met her, she looked over her shoulder a lot. She was afraid."

Clay glanced at Jessie, found her watching them as she answered Mubarek's questions. More than anything, he wanted to protect her, as he had been unable to protect Ellen.

"Check him out, Clay," Mel said. "He's got to be behind this."

"Do you know his last name?"

"I'm pretty sure it's Collins. I saw it on some papers she had out once." She paused, then added, "I wasn't snooping. I saw the name at a glance. Maybe that's not even it."

He squeezed her hand. "You did the right thing telling me, Mel. I can't do anything to help if I'm in the dark."

Her lips trembled as she smiled. "I'll keep that in mind when she rips into me."

"Who's going to rip into you?" Jessie asked from the doorway.

Mel laughed easily. "The chief of staff when I show up for work with circles under my eyes." She crossed to her friend. "How are you doing?"

Jessie leaned a shoulder against the open door. "They're done here," she said.

"Good," Clay said. "You're both coming home with me."

Jessie's smile was weary. "I'm not up to a pajama party."

"He's serious," Mel said. "You're not safe here. And you may not be safe at my place, either."

Slipping an arm around Jessie's waist, he felt her lean against him. It felt natural, right, but it also worried him. Her exhaustion had to be bone-deep for her to allow herself to lean. "Mel's right," he said.

"Don't bother to gang up on me," Jessie said. "I'm down for the count."

"Does that mean you're not going to argue?" Mel asked.

"Bingo."

"Wow. A monumental moment," Mel said. "I'll go throw some clothes in a bag for you."

As Mel disappeared into the bedroom, Jessie drew away from Clay.

He reluctantly let her go. "Where are you going?"

"I have to sit down."

She sank onto the sofa, and Clay recognized the concentrated movements of someone still shaky on her feet.

"Can I get you anything?" he asked.

She skewered him with eyes so dark they no longer looked gray. "She told you."

"Told me what?"

"Don't pretend to not know."

He sighed. "She's worried about you, about what's happening."

"This isn't connected to him."

"How can you know that?"

"It's not like him."

"Protecting him isn't going to—" He fell silent when she leaned forward and covered her face with one hand. The sudden show of emotion shook him. As a crime reporter in his early days, he'd been around plenty of emotional people, men and women alike, who had tragically lost children, spouses or friends. He'd never felt as awkward, or as helpless, as he did now. "Jess, don't."

"I'm fine," she said from behind her hand, her voice hoarse. "Just give me a minute."

Mel returned with a purple nylon sports bag that was stuffed. "I didn't know how much to pack, so I just grabbed—" She stopped when she saw Jessie, and her gaze went to Clay. "Uh, I'll wait in the car."

"No," Jessie said, lowering her hand. Her eyes were dry. "I'm fine. I need to get dressed."

Clay helped her up, then was reluctant to release her. She pulled her arm free, as if she sensed his desire to cling and it irritated her. "Just give me some space, please."

He held up his hands in a defensive gesture. "Sorry."

She didn't acknowledge the apology as she went into the

bedroom and pushed the door partially closed.

Mel gave Clay a small smile. "She likes you."

He dragged a hand through his hair, conscious of the tremor in his fingers. "Could have fooled me."

"You're getting to her."

"Is that a good thing?"

"With Jess, sometimes getting to her is the only way to get anywhere with her. She prefers the comfort of non-confrontational situations."

"Don't we all?"

"I suppose. But where's the passion in non-confrontation?"

Jessie, dressed in jeans and a navy T-shirt, returned, her pallor replaced by a flush that made her eyes flash as she cast an accusing glance at Mel. "I don't think Mr. Christopher needs coaching on how to get anywhere with me."

Mel shrugged, unperturbed. "If you had any sense, I wouldn't have to run interference for you."

Jessie looked like she could take a swing at her friend, and Clay would have laid odds that Jessie, backed by left-over adrenaline, could drop Mel with one punch. Stepping between them, he gently took Jessie's arm. He didn't know what else to say to her, so he asked her one of the questions that had been nagging at him. "Who else could be after you?"

She jerked away. "Don't *handle* me," she snapped. "You don't have to handle me. In fact, you don't have to handle anything. I can take care of myself just fine."

Stepping back, he raised his hands. Suddenly, he wasn't worried about Mel being the one getting socked. "I'm just trying to help here."

"What's this about?" Mel asked Jessie. "Why are you being so sensitive?"

"I just met you," Jessie said to Clay. "And now you're in my home, talking to the police about stuff that has nothing to do with you, digging up all the dirty details of my failed marriage, getting advice on how to court me from my best friend. What do you want from me anyway? Besides the scoop, I mean."

"Jess, come on," Mel said. "Clay is the good guy. It's my fault he's here tonight. I asked for his help, and he came through. So if you have to be angry at someone, be angry at me."

Mel's soothing voice seemed to suck the tension out of Jessie, and she lowered her head to rub at a spot above the bridge of her nose where stress had imprinted three vertical lines. Clay would have bet his Pulitzer nomination that she had a monster headache.

"I'm sorry," she said. "What's my problem?"

"Exhaustion," Mel said, keeping her tone light. "Stress. Fear."

Jessie released a short, uncomfortable laugh as she looked at Clay. "Leave it to Mel to answer a rhetorical question. Please accept my apologies."

He nodded, smiling gently, but his stomach remained clenched. When pushed to the wall, she came out swinging. She had proved it just now with Mel and earlier when she'd defended herself against the intruder. Which didn't wash with the passivity she showed concerning her ex-husband. Just the fact that they were divorced made him a suspect. Yet, she didn't want anyone anywhere near the guy. He could think of only one reason: David Collins, if Mel was right about his name, frightened Jessie beyond reason.

"So," Mel said. "I think Clay had a question."

Jessie's expression remained neutral, so he couldn't tell if she felt as reasonable as she appeared. He didn't imagine she could shut down her temper so easily, no matter how logical her friend had sounded.

"I don't know who could be trying to kill me," she said. "That was the question, wasn't it?"

Whatever was going on in her head, Clay decided he much preferred the fiery woman with the flashing gray eyes to the polite one. Mel was right. Passion was so important. "No threats on the cops story?"

"Like I told the detective, no. I'm not stupid. I would have reported a death threat, especially after my brake line was cut. Besides, there are plenty of *Star-News* people involved in that story who have much higher profiles."

"And have any of them driven their cars into trees or confronted intruders ransacking their homes?" Clay asked.

Jessie's eyes narrowed, but before she could respond, Mel gave a shudder. "As much as I'd love to stand here all night and discuss death threats, I'd much rather get the hell out of here."

Chapter 9

Alone in Clay Christopher's bed, wearing one of his pajama tops because Mel had forgotten to pack a nightshirt for her, Jessie slept fitfully, her various aches waking her each time she shifted. After several hours of frustrated tossing, she sat up, drawing her knees up to her chest.

She didn't know what was disturbing her more: the events of the evening or Clay's scent on the pillow. He'd put fresh sheets on the bed for her, but they still smelled like him, like his clean, crisp cologne. She told herself that was why he kept showing up in her dreams, why his image came so easily to mind the moment she closed her eyes. It was a damned sexy image, too. With those blue, blue eyes and that dimple in a chin shadowed by a day's growth of beard.

She rubbed her hands over her face, knocking her cheekbone with the edge of her cast before remembering it. She was more fatigued than she'd thought, she decided. Her life was under siege, and the foremost thing in her mind seemed to be the way Clay had moistened his lips with the tip of his tongue when he'd said goodnight to her several hours before. Lust, pure and simple, had surged through her, and she'd caught herself taking shallow breaths to calm the turbulent response of her heart.

It was so unlike her. She prided herself on her ability to control her emotions, her reactions. But Clay made her feel out of control, and that was unacceptable. Wasn't it?

Sighing, she pushed aside the covers. Staying in his bed wasn't going to help. Besides, she needed to use the bathroom.

She slipped into the hall, trying to remember the way so she wouldn't have to turn on a light. But the darkness was thick, and she bumped a hip into a narrow table along the wall. As she guided it back into position, she heard a noise and froze. Had she awakened Clay? Mel was in the guest room down the hall with the door closed, so it was unlikely she'd awakened. But Clay was sacked out on the sofa within earshot.

A murmur, as if someone were speaking in a low tone, came from the direction of the living room.

Jessie edged down the hall, fingertips trailing along the wall to keep her oriented in the dark. As she drew nearer the living room, her eyes adjusted to the faint moonlight that came through the windows, and she saw him on the couch. His blanket had bunched on the floor in front of the sofa, and she noticed he was naked from the waist up.

He was also caught in the grip of a bad dream.

Thrashing, he knocked a pillow aside, and his murmuring turned to a tortured groan.

She couldn't tell whether the origin of the sound was physical or emotional pain, but either way, it sent a shudder of dread through her. "Clay?"

The normal level of her voice sounded like thunder in the otherwise silent room, but it didn't rouse him as his agonized moan turned to a chant: "No no no *no*."

Crossing to him, her heart knocking against her ribs, Jessie reached out to shake his shoulder at the same moment that his eyes snapped open, and he seized her wrist and twisted. He had her trapped under him in an instant, his forearm pressed against her windpipe.

They blinked at each other in shock, and Clay obviously didn't know her at first, because he looked ready to kill, his blue eyes fierce with grief and fury, his teeth gritted in rage. As soon as he recognized her, he scrambled to push himself off of her.

"Jesus, I'm sorry," he said, his voice hoarse. "Are you okay?"

Sitting up, she rubbed her wrist where his fingers had vised around it. "I'm fine."

He turned on a lamp and paced away from her, jamming both hands back through his hair. He was agitated, keeping his back to her. "I was dreaming."

"I got that," she said, her pulse still racing. "I was trying to wake you."

He took a few steps toward her, his pale face damp. "Did I hurt you?"

She shook her head, her mouth going dry as she noticed the bare expanse of his chest above the pajama bottoms that went with the top she wore. He worked his body hard. Six-pack abs looked more like a twelve-pack to her. Chest hair was either sparse or nonexistent—she couldn't tell in the dim light from the one lamp—making his skin look smooth and flawless. Her breath went shallow as her gaze dropped to the thin line of blond hair that disappeared below his waistband.

Don't go there.

"What was it about?" she asked. She wouldn't normally have asked—it was none of her business—but she needed distraction and needed it fast. Plus, the nature of the dream, his evident suffering, had unsettled her.

"I need a drink," he said.

Jessie followed him to the kitchen, noting that his back was just as ripply with taut muscles as his front.

"Want to talk about it?" she asked.

He snorted a little as he opened a cupboard and grabbed a rocks glass. "I've had to drag every bit of personal information out of you, yet you expect me to spill my guts?"

She shrugged, feeling a bit defensive while he uncapped a bottle of gin and splashed about a shot's worth in the glass. "Maybe I was just being polite," she said.

He gulped down the alcohol, then lowered the glass to the counter with a sound thunk. His eyes flashed with something—anger? impatience? "You do that well, don't you? Be polite."

She clamped down on the urge to walk away and leave him to his drink. "I suppose I've had a lot of practice, yes."

"See? That's what I'm talking about. Your eyes just told me to go to hell, but your words were cool, unemotional."

"Actually, they were faintly sarcastic."

"Same difference."

"Okay then," she said through clenched teeth, "I'm going back to bed. Have a good night, Mr. Christopher."

She pivoted and had gone two steps when he spoke again, his voice low with emotion. "I was dreaming about the day my wife died in my arms."

Stopping in mid-step, Jessie closed her eyes. She didn't turn, sensing he had more to say and that it would be easier for him if she stayed where she was and said nothing.

"We were in Sarajevo. Sniper shot her." He swallowed audibly. "I tripped over my own damn feet, and Ellen stopped to help me up. Two seconds, maybe less. That's all it took."

She heard the spin of metal on glass as he replaced the cap on the bottle of gin. "I'm sorry," she said, facing him. Her stomach somersaulted at the misery narrowing his eyes. "It was horrible for you."

He stared into his empty glass. "I haven't dreamt about that day in at least a year. Haven't felt much of anything in three. And then you slammed your car into a tree in my front yard."

He said it as if she'd done it to annoy him or selfishly steal him away from his grieving process. She didn't know what to say to that, but before she was able to form a response, he glanced up, his expression unreadable. "I hadn't looked at another woman since she died," he said. "I hadn't *thought* about another woman since she died. And now here you are."

He sounded so sad that a lump formed in her throat, but she understood now where he was coming from. And she realized with a nudge of regret that it had more to do with their circumstances than her specifically. "You saved my life, Clay. You did for me what you couldn't do for her. I imagine a psychologist would have all kinds of theories about what you're feeling right now."

He studied her, nodding almost imperceptibly, as if in agreement with her assessment. Then he gave her a small, tired smile. "You called me Clay."

She returned his smile, relieved that the storm clouds in his eyes seemed to be breaking up. "You say that like you think it means something."

"Maybe it does."

"Maybe it doesn't," she said.

"You're a tough one, aren't you? You don't need anybody."

"I haven't for a long time."

"It's safer that way," he said.

"Yes."

"Lonely."

"It can be," she conceded.

"It doesn't have to be."

"Maybe some people were meant to be alone."

"Maybe some people are too scared to not be alone," he said.

"Maybe some people over think things."

His grin chased away the remaining storm clouds. "You'd counter me all night if I let you."

"Probably."

"I like you, Jess."

She avoided his gaze, terrified of what she'd see there. Her own contradictory emotions annoyed her. A moment ago, she'd been disappointed that his conflicted feelings weren't centered on her. Now, she feared what could happen between them. Unsure of herself, and him, she sought refuge in evasion. "You don't get drunk on one shot, do you?"

His lips curved, as if he was pleased that he'd unbalanced her. "That wasn't a drunken confession," he said. "I haven't been attracted to anyone in a long time. It's not likely I'm going to walk away without a fight."

"Great," she said, hoping her casual nod masked the wild beating of her heart. "Now that we've got that ironed out, I'm going back to bed."

"Sleep well," he said.

She felt his gaze on her back as she detoured to the bathroom, and it took all her willpower not to look back. He liked her. He wasn't going to walk away without a fight.

Sleep well? Fat chance.

It was just past seven the next morning, and Clay was emptying the dishwasher, trying to be quiet about it. The last time he had checked on Jessie, she had been sleeping soundly. It amused him that she seemed to be so peaceful after he had spent the rest of the night with the image of her in his pajama top taunting him every time he closed his eyes.

"Good morning."

When he looked up, something in his stomach shifted. Jessie, barefoot in jeans and a white tank top, stood in the kitchen's doorway. Her blond hair looked as if she'd combed her fingers through it to try to tame the bed-head look. She'd succeeded for the most part, but the remaining untidiness, along with the soft, sleepy look in her gray eyes, sent a shaft of need through him that stole his breath.

But then he focused on the dark purple bruise along her jaw, and his desire iced over. He hoped he'd get a shot at the son of a bitch who hit her.

As she rested her hip on a stool at the island, he noted the shadows under her eyes. "You need more sleep," he said.

"Could you just wrap it up and I'll take it to go?"

He smiled. "Coffee?"

"That'd be fantastic."

He poured her a cup and scooted it across the counter.

She blew on the steam, sipped gingerly. "You make good coffee."

"Thanks."

"Is Mel up?" she asked.

So this is how it's going to be, he thought. They were going to dance around their conversation the night before, pretend he never said he was attracted to her and wouldn't walk away without a fight. That was fine with him. In the bright light of day, he felt like an idiot for being so candid anyway. If she hadn't caught him right after the nightmare had revived the horror of Ellen's death, he never would have said those things. "She went to work about ten minutes ago," he said, then indicated a bottle of pills on the counter. "She left you some drugs for pain."

Jessie lowered her cup. "She left without me?"

"I think maybe she thought you weren't going anywhere today."

"What else would I do besides go to work?"

"Relax? Take a nap? Recover from being attacked in your own home?"

She waved a dismissive hand. "I don't need to relax. And I haven't taken a nap since kindergarten. Even then, I faked it."

He chuckled. "I'm not surprised."

Sliding off the stool, she reached for the cordless phone next to his hand. "Do you have a phone book? I'll call a cab."

He laid his hand over the phone before she could grab it. "What if I told you Mel wants you to take the day off and rest?"

"I'd say that she should have a kid so she has someone to mother who's actually helpless."

"Well, for now, all she has is you, and I'm thinking she'd be adamant."

"She's not here right now, so that means she's not the boss of me. And neither are you." Tossing a self-satisfied smile over her shoulder, she headed for his bedroom.

For a moment, he was distracted by the sight of her retreating but very attractive backside, which filled out her jeans in all the right places. Then he snapped out of it. "Where are you going?" he asked.

"To use the phone in your bedroom. Hope you don't mind if I call Directory Assistance. I hear the charge is, like, three dollars nowadays."

He followed her. "Mel's going to be pissed at me if I let you go to work."

"Glad I'm not you."

In the bedroom, she had dialed and requested the number of an island cab company before Clay reached around her and took the phone.

She whirled on him, her good humor gone. "Hey."

He knew by the flare of temper in her eyes that he'd crossed a line, but he didn't back down. He imagined that's what other people did when faced with her displeasure. The only way to handle her was to forge ahead. "Think rationally for just a minute, Jess."

She glared up at him. "I resent the implication that I don't normally think rationally."

"All I'm saying is that you had a rough night, and giving yourself a day to heal won't bring a screaming end to the world."

"I have a job to do, Mr. Christopher. People are depending on me."

Mr. Christopher. So they were back to that. "Won't those same people be a bit put out if you drop dead on them because of your overwhelming sense of responsibility?"

"Okay, now you're exaggerating. The odds of me dropping dead are much lower now that I've survived the night. It was touch and go around two o'clock, what with the coma and all, but I have an awesome will to live. Now give me the damn phone."

Instead, he smiled. He really wanted to kiss her. The combination of the flush in her cheeks and the fire in her eyes sent his pulse skidding. He imagined her in his bed, naked and gleaming in the moonlight, imagined what it would be like to slide his body over hers—

She snatched the phone from his lax fingers. "Thank you."

He saw the glint of panic in her gaze before she turned her back and punched in the number for information. So she'd known where his brain—and other body parts—had just gone. Maybe hers had gone there, too, though he doubted it. That would have required a lack of control, and when it came to control, she had hers on the tightest, shortest leash possible.

A moment later, she handed him the phone. "Cab's on its way."

No hint remained of the panic he'd glimpsed. Which was fine, because he had a more serious concern now that he'd lost the battle to keep her close to him. "What will you do for protection? In case you've forgotten, someone has tried to kill you twice."

She began shoving the few belongings she'd left scattered on the bed—a travel-size bottle of lotion, the case that held her glasses, a hair scrunchie—into her sports bag. "I can take care of myself."

"Having a plan would be more appropriate than depending on that cliché."

She sighed, and her exhaustion showed briefly as her shoulders sagged. "It's not your problem, all right?"

"I'm making it my problem."

"Let's get something straight, all right? I don't need you to be my hero."

"What do you need?"

She whirled on him. "To be left the hell alone." She snapped it out, and her voice echoed through the quiet house. As soon as she said it, regret tightened her features. She raised a hand before he could say anything. "I'm sorry. That was uncalled for. I know you're trying to help, but I'm under a lot of pressure right now."

That was an understatement, he thought, but kept silent.

"I'm not usually like this," she said. "So . . . ungrateful . . . or whatever it is I'm being."

"Why do you dismiss your show of emotion as abnormal?"

"Because, for me, it is. I'm usually the picture of control."

He stepped up to her, ignoring the way she stiffened when he brushed a stray lock of hair from her forehead. As he skimmed a hand down her arm, he felt the tension in her and the silken texture of her skin. Both fascinated him, though not as much as the emotions that warred in her eyes as he touched her. Shock at first contact, then bewilderment, followed by a spark of desire. She quickly fought all three into submission.

Clay sighed, rasping his thumb up the side of her neck just under her ear. Her pulse thudded under his hand. "You don't see the problem in that, do you?"

She wet her lips, swallowing as the tip of his thumb grazed her earlobe. "The problem in what?"

"The *picture* of control. It's just an image. Not the real thing."

She looked past his shoulder, her eyes closing for just an instant before she moved away from him. Crossing her arms over her chest, she rubbed her arms as if chilled, or as if a shudder had gone through her. "Why do you do that?"

"Do what?"

"Keep touching me. You know it makes me uncomfortable."

He cocked his head. "Why?"

"I don't like to be touched."

"By me or in general?"

"It doesn't matter. I don't trust you."

"Because of the story?"

"Partly. And partly because I don't trust people I don't know."

"We can change that," he said.

"Maybe I don't want to."

"Because you're afraid."

"Aren't you?"

"Hell, yes," he said. "But I'm not going to pitch away a good thing because I'm a coward."

"How do you know it's a good thing?"

"I don't. But I'm willing to give it a shot."

"I'll save you the hassle and let you know up front that I'm not that great a catch."

"Why would you think that?"

"If I were, my husband wouldn't have cheated on me."

He kept his wince to himself, unable to imagine what kind of blow that had been for her. Obviously, she still reeled from it. He added David Collins to his list of people he'd like to pummel for hurting her. "That man was an idiot."

She raised her chin. "That man knew me, and you don't."

"I'll take my chances."

A horn sounded outside, and they both started. Jessie, grateful for the interruption, grabbed her bag and purse. "That's my cab. May I borrow a suit jacket? Mel forgot to pack me one."

Clay caught her arm before she could brush by him. "We're not done with this conversation," he said.

Gently, she drew away from him. "Maybe you're not. But I am."

In the cab, one of Clay's black suit jackets seeming to engulf her, Jessie focused on taking deep breaths, trying to calm the thrashing of her heart. Lord, he unnerved her.

"I'll take my chances."

He'd lost the love of his life, yet he was willing to take a chance on her, to open himself up to the possibility of being hurt.

That kind of courage amazed her. Especially because all she wanted to do was run and hide. It was easier to be alone, to push him away. Safer.

She reminded herself that he'd latched onto her because she was the one who'd made his wake-up call. Her car had crashed in his yard, and he'd saved her life. In essence, her accident had jerked him back into the land of the living, and when he'd arrived, she was the first one he saw.

He'd get over it.

Chapter 10

Clay waited until the taxi was out of sight before he hopped into his Jeep. There was no way in hell he was letting her go without some kind of protection. He'd follow her around all day like a damn stalker if it meant getting between her and a potential killer.

When he had the cab within view again, he used his cell phone to call a friend.

"Marshall, how's it hanging?"

"Clay Christopher. Haven't heard from you in a while. What's up?"

"Sorry. My last project wasn't very sinister. Endangered species."

"No need for a private eye in that, huh?"

"Why, Marshall, you're sounding a bit put out."

"Just because we're supposed to be buds, and you only call me when you need something."

"Please, you're choking me up."

Marshall chuckled. "What can I do for you?"

Clay tapped his fingers on the steering wheel, allowing himself only a heartbeat of hesitation. Jessie would freak if she found out what he was doing. At the same time, her best friend was worried enough about Jessie's ex-husband to tell Clay to check him out. "There's a lawyer in Chicago. Name's David Collins. I want to know everything you can find on him."

"A detailed profile."

"Yeah, and when you're poking around, keep it discreet. I don't want him tipped off that someone's interested."

"That's my specialty."

"Thanks."

Clay cut off the call and made another to try to set up interviews about the police scandal with the mayor and the police chief. Both offices said they would get back to him.

In the parking lot of Jessie's apartment complex, he watched her transfer from the cab to the red Mustang rental. After following her to *The Star-News*, he parked where he had a clear view of the entrance, then began jotting notes about the scandal on a legal pad.

Jessie stopped in the bathroom to put on makeup that she kept in her desk for emergencies. She was disheartened to see that she looked as wiped out as she felt. Makeup disguised some, but not much. She was applying cover-up to the bruise on her jaw, annoyed at the way her hands trembled, when Gillian Westin walked in.

"Good morning, Jessie," Gillian said cheerily. Instantly, her greeting smile faded. "What happened to you?"

Great, just what she needed, Jessie thought. "I had a rough night."

"Apparently. Why don't you meet me in the Greenhouse? We'll talk."

God, not the Greenhouse, Jessie thought. That was what reporters and editors called the conference room in the center of the newsroom because its glass walls put everything that happened in there on display. When top editor Gillian reamed a staffer in the Greenhouse, everyone could watch, and they did. People took the heat so often in there that the newsroom had a phrase for it: the Greenhouse Effect.

Most of the time, though, the Greenhouse was the gathering place for the endless stream of meetings—meetings to plan future enterprise, meetings to determine the day's news stories, meetings to peruse the latest disappointing circulation report.

Masking her dread, Jessie nodded. "All right. I'll meet you there."

A few minutes later, sitting across from her boss in one of the comfortable chairs that surrounded a long boardroom table, the door closed, Jessie forced herself to appear relaxed.

Lighting a cigarette, Gillian blew out smoke with a small, conspiratorial smile. "It's my newsroom. I can do whatever I want in it. Want one?"

Jessie shook her head.

Gillian crossed her firm legs. "So what's going on?"

"Greg is onto something with the cops story."

Gillian watched her, the tip of her cigarette glowing red. "I meant personally," she said, sending smoke swirling into the air between them.

"Oh." Jessie hunted for how to reply.

"I've known you for a long time, Jessie. I don't think I've ever seen you at a loss for words." She tapped ashes into a crystal ashtray that she kept in her office, adjacent to the Greenhouse. "If you don't want to talk, that's fine." She paused, waited a beat for Jessie to respond. When she didn't, Gillian said, "So Greg's onto something."

Jessie breathed an inward sigh of relief. "Maybe. Maybe not."

"There's a ringing endorsement."

"I told you he met with one of the women from the strip club, and she changed her story."

"Yes. He was reconnecting with other people from the club. How'd that go?"

117

"Each source failed to show."

"Hmm."

"The first woman—her name was Sandi White—died last night from an apparent self-inflicted gunshot. You probably saw the story this morning."

"I did. Stuart wrote it."

Jessie struggled to counteract her instinct to stiffen. Stuart Davis had been a bone of contention between them as long as Jessie had been city editor. "He was available."

"You know my feelings about Stuart, Jessie."

"He has excellent sources, and he's a good—"

"Yes, I already know what you think. My point is that Stuart needs to focus on his special events beat, and his ability to do that is hampered every time you pull him off to cover breaking news."

"I prefer to put my best people on—"

"We're not going to have this debate again, Jessie. Let's talk about the stripper, Sandi White. Wasn't she the one we considered the least credible because of her problems with bad checks, and what was the other thing? Unemployment insurance fraud, wasn't it?"

Jessie nodded. "That's right."

"And the women we talked to initially are avoiding us now."

"Greg suspects someone has frightened them into keeping quiet."

"What do you think?" Gillian asked.

"I'm not sure. Naturally, it sounds suspicious."

"I suppose it does."

"You don't think so?" Jessie asked, surprised.

"We're talking about what you think right now. What else?"

Jessie shifted, struck by the feeling that Gillian knew

118

something she didn't. "There's a freelancer working on the possibility that our story is bogus."

Gillian pursed her lips. The information didn't seem to bother her. "Who?"

"Clay Christopher."

"Ah, yes."

"You know him?"

"I know of him," Gillian said. "He has a good reputation. How do you know him?"

"We have a mutual friend."

"I see. He's pumping you for information."

Jessie wouldn't describe her dinner conversation with Clay the night before as him pumping her for information, but she wasn't up to arguing semantics. "We discussed the story, yes."

"What did you tell him?"

"What we know. He's not competition."

"No, but he can make us look very bad."

"He has no reason to."

Gillian gave her a hard look. "Jessie, think about it. He's a big, bad investigative reporter who sells his stories for big bucks. He can do that because he has a reputation. We don't even have a big, bad corporation to back us up. We're just a family-owned newspaper that broke a huge story. Irresponsible journalism is not popular these days. So what's the bigger story here? The possibility that someone duped us or the possibility that we let ourselves be duped? If some big newspaper like *The Washington Post*, *New York Times* or *USA Today* reports that *The Star-News* is an irresponsible newspaper, what will that do to us? We could be ruined. As its current editor, I *will* be ruined. And I won't allow that."

"Clay isn't interested in ruining us. He wants to know the truth, just like we do."

"Are you sleeping with him?"

Jessie caught herself before she could gape. "Excuse me?"

"If you are, I need to know. It's a conflict of interest."

"It's only a conflict of interest if we work for competing publications. And we don't."

"That's not an answer."

Jessie clenched her jaw so hard it began to ache. "The answer is no."

"Are you going to?"

"That isn't any of your—"

"What affects this newspaper is my business, Jessie. If this reporter is fucking you for a story, it's my business, as the editor of this newspaper." She paused to tap out her cigarette and immediately lit another one, taking her time and studying Jessie with shrewd eyes.

Jessie met her scrutiny without wavering. Her cheeks burned at the suggestion that she was too naive to recognize when she was being used. At the same time, she wondered whether she had lost sight of the fact that Clay was pursuing a story. Who knew what lengths he would go to to get it?

Gillian gave her a small smile, as if she had seen the doubt in Jessie's eyes, and it pleased her. "Let's just leave it at this: you don't trust Clay Christopher. That's an order. If you don't think you can do that, we'll be forced to have another conversation. Is that understood?"

Jessie steadily returned Gillian's stare as fury generated a roar in her ears. How dare this woman issue orders that involved her personal life? On the surface, she maintained her cool. "I understand," she said.

Gillian cleared her throat. "Good. So what is Greg doing now?"

"I have him in a holding pattern. I wanted to talk to you about our next step."

"So you're hesitating to go after this."

"If Greg is stepping on someone's toes, he could be at risk."

"Want to know what I think?"

"Of course," Jessie said.

"A chronic liar killed herself. End of story."

That surprised Jessie, considering how much mileage a dead body could add to an already titillating news story. A Gillian-style headline along the lines of "Dancer slain after tattling on cops" would have done wonders for newspaper sales.

Gillian smiled. "Not what you were expecting me to say?"

"Well, no."

"How long have you been city editor, Jessie?"

"About a year."

"How long has Greg been a reporter?"

Jessie already knew where this was going. "He's been here about six months."

"I grew up in this business. In this very newsroom. The talk at the dinner table when I was growing up centered around this business. There are rumors of a hoax? Well, there's a shock. Every time there's a big story like this, someone somewhere wonders aloud if it's a hoax. That's the nature of the business."

"I'd hate to not pursue this and find out later we were wrong."

"We make decisions like this every day, Jessie. Sometimes we're wrong."

"This story has had a huge impact on so many people. Publicly and privately."

"Are you doubting the validity of the story?"

Jessie hesitated.

Uncrossing her legs, Gillian leaned her elbows on the table, dark eyes flashing. "I'm not liking the look on your face."

"Look, Gillian—"

"No, you look. It's very unprofessional to sit there and tell me with this expression on your face that you had serious doubts about the story and didn't raise them. Especially now that a freelancer is looking into it."

"I did raise them."

"And it was my understanding that they were put to rest when Officer Drake contacted you. Is that incorrect?"

She was starting to sweat. "Not entirely."

"But you're telling me now that you're ready to take the word of a lying, suicidal stripper over that of a respected police officer who is also your friend?"

"All I want is to have Greg check further into the accuracy of the stories we were told by people connected with the club. And I'd like to talk to Taylor Drake again. I have a meeting with him in a few hours, in fact."

"Certainly you understand that the pictures we have are worth more than a couple thousand words," Gillian said.

"The rumors say the photos are fake. Checking into the rumors isn't a lot to ask."

"But it is a lot. You covered breaking news the other night because your department is so understaffed you don't have enough people to cover the daily news. You can't afford to send a reporter on a wild goose chase. And you certainly don't have time as a department head to be leaving the office to chase a story we've already thoroughly reported."

"Even if I don't think it's a wild goose chase?"

Gillian tamped out her second cigarette with concentrated taps. "Okay, look. You obviously feel strongly about this. So go after it. Confirm what we already know. We'll run a story tomorrow that says there are rumors flying. If we're lucky, we'll get the mayor and police chief to ignore our calls some more. We'll address the issue publicly—a 'he said, she said' story that shows our readers that we stand by our initial report and that our city officials are being close-mouthed jerks."

"That's going to be cutting it close for having the photos checked."

A muscle in Gillian's jaw flexed. "We have to get the story out there immediately, before your freelancer does it."

"The key to the hoax theory is the photos."

"Then get them looked at today."

"I don't know what has to be done to the disk or the photos to authenticate them. It may not be that quick and easy."

"Am I giving you what you want, Jessie? Yes, I am. Don't give me the opportunity to take it away." She paused, her eyes going to black slits. "Comments? Observations?"

Before Jessie could respond, Gillian leaned forward. "You might not have realized this yet, being so young and inexperienced, but I'm not big on being second-guessed." She smiled so genuinely that Jessie wasn't sure whether she had just issued a threat or not. "I suggest you keep that in mind if we're to continue to have the working relationship we have."

Jessie decided that, yes, her job had just been threatened. It was shaping up to be another stellar day. "I understand."

"Good." Gillian sat back, crossed her legs and continued smiling. "I like you, Jess. You're one hell of a city editor.

Probably the gutsiest I've known in all the years I've lived in this newsroom."

Jessie rose, wondering why she was feeling particularly gutless at the moment, even though she had won. "I need to get to work."

Gillian laughed softly. "Your minions are chattering away right this minute about how I just ripped you a new one. They were all watching, you know. Pretending they weren't, of course. They'll expect you to be unnerved, a little shaken, maybe even weepy."

Jessie lifted her chin a notch, offended that Gillian had called the reporters minions.

Gillian's grin widened. "Good girl. Keep that look on your face, and no one will mess with you."

Jessie walked out of the Greenhouse without a word. In her office, she slammed a couple of desk drawers to work off the anger, then hunted around for aspirin.

A light knock on the glass door brought her head up.

Greg, his complexion wan, was watching her. "Was that about me?"

Dropping onto her desk chair, she pulled her purse out, sifting through it for the bottle of pills Mel had left for her at Clay's earlier that morning. Finding it, she dumped a tablet into her hand and reached for the water bottle she kept on her desk. Naturally, it was empty. She dry-swallowed the pill.

Greg took the chair across from her. "What happened to your face?" he asked.

So much for cover-up, she thought, and aimed for a light tone. "That Gillian has a lethal right hook."

He didn't smile, and she had to laugh. "I'm kidding, Greg. It's no big deal. I surprised a burglar last night."

Amazement followed his relief. "A burglar? That's really weird."

She shrugged. "Apartment complexes aren't crime-free, you know."

"No, I mean the coincidence," he said. "Shawn's office in graphics was ransacked last night. It's bizarre to have two people in the same newsroom the victims of the same crime on the same night."

"His office here was ransacked?" she asked.

"Yes. Building services was going to check the security tapes to see who did it, but I heard the ones from last night are gone."

"How would a burglar know how to find our security tapes? I don't even know where they are."

"Hell if I know."

She thought of the fancy Mac and other expensive computer equipment in Shawn's office. "What did he lose?"

"Last time I talked to him, he was still wading through the mess checking."

"So his Mac wasn't taken?"

"That's the other really strange thing. It wasn't. Aren't those big ones worth a couple of thousand dollars or more?"

A sick feeling of dread spread through Jessie, and she rose. "I'm going to talk to him."

"Uh, can we talk about the story first?"

She eased back down. "Oh, sure. Sorry." She rubbed absently at the center of her forehead, hoping Mel's drugs kicked in soon. "Gillian wants a story for tomorrow that confirms there are rumors that the story's bogus but that we stand by what we initially reported."

Greg's mouth fell open. "For tomorrow? Are you serious?"

"We're going to do our best to do it, okay? You try to

track down the missing dancers. I'm meeting Taylor Drake at noon, so he's covered. I'll have Stuart go after the mayor and police chief."

"What about the photos?"

Before she could respond, she saw Shawn Witherspoon, his unruly mop of black hair flopping, rushing toward her office. He came in without knocking. "Jess, I need to talk to you."

He was a rail-thin man, only as tall as Jessie. His eyes were electric blue, his features angular. One of Jessie's favorite people in the newsroom, he had a savage sense of humor. He'd moved her to tears of laughter more than once with his "comments? observations?" shtick. With a pencil serving as a cigarette gripped between two fingers in Bette Davis fashion, he'd perfected Gillian's "I'm not being nearly as bitchy as I could be" expression. Jessie sometimes found herself envying his ability to loathe their boss so wholeheartedly.

Now, however, his nervousness struck her. He usually was so calm and genial under the most enormous pressure that Gillian had no idea that he often thought she was full of crap.

Shawn looked at Greg. "Can we have a minute?"

Greg stood. "I'll catch you after you're done with this," he said to Jessie.

When they were alone, Shawn said, "Gillian just told me we're having the photos checked."

"That's right." Tension began to gnaw at a spot just below her breast bone, but she said nothing, waiting for him to tell her what had upset him so.

"The photo disk is gone from my office." He dropped into her visitor's chair. "She's going to freaking kill me."

"Is that all that's gone?"

"Isn't that enough?"

"Shawn, please. Is the disk all that's missing from your office after last night?"

"I'm still sorting through stuff, but that's all I've noticed so far. In fact, I didn't even realize it was gone until Gillian told me to get it to you." Leaning forward, he buried his face in his hands. "Jesus, why didn't I think to dupe it? I'm so fired."

"You can put your nervous breakdown on hold, Shawn. I made a copy."

He raised his head, his laser eyes brimming with hope. "You did?"

"I did."

He jumped up, looking like he would come over the desk and hug her. "Thank God. Where the hell is it?"

"Don't worry. I'll pick it up later."

Then, as quickly as relief had made his shoulders droop, it evaporated. "Someone tore apart my office just to get that disk."

"Maybe."

"It had to be someone in the newsroom," he said. "There's no way in without a security card to open the door."

"I'm sure if someone is clever enough, they could find a way in. Customers walk in the front door during business hours without security cards," she said. "It wouldn't take all that much ingenuity to get into the newsroom from there."

"Building services told me the tapes from the security cameras are missing," he said. "Whoever took that disk knew what they were doing. And if they went to that much trouble to steal it . . ."

"I know."

127

He started to say something else when he stopped to study her face, concern tempering his anxiety. "What happened to you?"

She pushed hair behind her ear. "I had a little excitement myself last night. Nothing to worry about." Rising, she said, "So I'll get my copy of the disk to a couple of experts—"

"Want me to do that?" he asked as he stood.

"I should probably do it."

"You don't trust me now, do you? If you think the photos are suspect enough to get them checked further, then you must think I was wrong when I said they looked legit."

"You were under a lot of pressure that day."

"I did my job the best I could," he said.

"No one is saying you didn't."

He chewed at his bottom lip. "Jess, if those pictures are fake, I'm screwed."

"Unfortunately, a lot of us are."

After Shawn, miserable and jittery, left her office, Jessie signaled to Greg.

As he walked in and shut the door, he said, "I don't think I've ever seen Shawn that uptight. Or uptight, period. Something big's going down, isn't it?"

"Maybe. Until we know for sure, we have to play it cool." Getting her glasses out of her purse, she slid them on, at the same time retrieving a legal pad from under several papers on her desk. "We need to figure out a way to track down the guy who gave you the photo disk. You said he gave it to you at an ATM." She scrawled a name and a phone number. "I've used this private investigator before on other stories. He has connections with security people in the area, so I'm hoping he can get you to the right people.

With any luck, the ATM's security camera caught the exchange." Ripping the sheet off the pad, she handed it to him. "Be careful."

"I will. Oh, and by the way, love the jacket. The six-sizes-too-big look suits you."

Glancing down at Clay's jacket, she smiled.

Alone, her adrenaline flowing, Jessie checked her watch, used to it being on the opposite wrist now. She had plenty of time before meeting Taylor.

Grabbing her purse, she headed for the door.

Chapter 11

At her apartment, Jessie went to the bookcase where a few books sat undisturbed on the shelves, retrieved one about art and fanned through the pages until the computer disk slid into her hand. Apparently, she had surprised the intruder last night before he was done with his search.

"Hey."

She whirled with a gasp. The door she'd left open framed Clay, and she pressed a hand to her racing heart. "Jesus, you scared me."

He stepped inside, hands in the rear pockets of his jeans. The sun at his back cast his face in shadow. "Sorry. What are you doing?"

Suspicion replaced her shock at seeing him, and Gillian's warning about his motives rang in her ears. "What are *you* doing?"

"Following you."

"Why?"

"The answer to that is beyond a no-brainer, Jess. If you want to be ticked at me for trying to protect you, go ahead. It won't change the fact that someone might try to hurt you again, and I was worried."

She wanted to be indignant and self-righteous. He had no right to take it upon himself to be her guardian angel when she had repeatedly pushed him away. But instead of being angry, she was touched. Her ex-husband had never shown such concern for her safety, even after she had been threatened.

"If you're going to stalk me in the future, I'd appreciate it if you wouldn't be sneaky about it."

He stepped out of the shadows, a small smile playing at the corners of his mouth. "You mean you're not going to yell?"

She glanced down at the disk. "I've got more important things to do at the moment."

"Was the intruder looking for that last night?" he asked.

"I don't know how he could have been. I'm the only one who knows it was here."

"What's on it?"

"It's a copy of the disk that had the pictures of the misbehaving cops."

"No one knows you copied it?"

"I don't think so."

"Someone may have assumed or even seen you do it."

She rubbed at the knot of tension at the nape of her neck. "The original has been swiped from the newsroom."

Clay's brow furrowed, as if a terrible thought had occurred to him. "Jess, what happened on Monday?"

"That was the day of my accident."

"I know. Before that, what was your day like? At work, I mean."

Her knees suddenly weak, she moved to the sofa and sat. "I don't like where this is going."

"I think we have to go there."

"But it wouldn't make sense for someone to come after me. Greg would be a more logical target—he's the one doing all the digging, the one whose name is on all the stories. Or even Gillian Westin, the executive editor. She's the big boss."

"Humor me."

She took a breath, held it. "The story ran Monday, so it was a crazy day. I got several phone calls from subscribers and other people. Some of them—like family members of the cops—were irate. Others were congratulatory."

"Did anyone make any threats?"

"Other than canceled subscriptions, no."

"Greg was working on a follow-up, right?"

"Yes. And others."

"What were the angles?" he asked.

"The police closed down the strip club Monday, after the story ran, and the cops in the photos were being placed on unpaid leave. We were also getting public reaction. Outrage kind of stuff."

"Did you do anything that involved the disk?"

"No. I hid it Sunday night and hadn't thought about it until the original went missing."

"I'm curious about why you made a copy."

"It's the only hard evidence we have that the cops were up to no good," she said. "Unless, of course, the photos on it are fake."

"There's only one way to find that out."

"I'd prefer to tap someone out of town to look at them."

"For objectivity's sake," he said, nodding.

"Right. I really don't want to risk using someone who might have even an obscure connection to anyone involved in the story, but it looks like I'm not going to have enough time to be that thorough."

"You're in luck," he said, holding out his hand for the disk. "I've got just the guy for you, and he's local. I'll take it to him right now."

Gazing at his waiting hand, she hesitated, Gillian's warning blaring in her head. Handing the disk over would make it so easy for him. If he determined the pictures were fake, he could run with the story and scoop *The Star-News*. She, and so many others, would be ruined, not to mention how foolish she would look for trusting him.

"What?" Clay asked, his gaze inquisitive. "What are you thinking?"

"That I'd be an idiot to give this to you."

"I suppose some people might think so. But you've built a career on listening to your gut. What's it telling you right now?"

"To not let this disk out of my sight."

He hid it well, but she saw the hurt that shot through his eyes. It made her feel like a jerk. But she wasn't a stupid jerk.

"Okay," he said, and without missing a beat, pulled his wallet out of his back pocket. "Have you got a pen?" he asked as he withdrew a business card. "I'll give you Marshall's number, and you can call him yourself. Tell him you got his name from me."

The gesture, without a hint of recrimination, floored her. She knew her lack of trust had hurt, and probably insulted, him, but he didn't appear angry. In fact, he was going to share his source with her without a second thought. Gillian, she decided, was a terrible judge of character.

Jessie straightened from the sofa. "Clay—"

"If you don't want to use him, that's fine," he cut in, all business. "But he'll probably be able to get you what you want when you want it and objectively."

"There's just one thing."

He looked at her, guarded. "What?"

"I'm pressed for time. Would you mind taking it to him?"

A slow smile stole across his lips as he accepted the disk. "That wasn't so painful, was it?"

She returned his smile, thinking he had no idea. She also was praying she was right and Gillian was wrong. "It was excruciating."

He chuckled. "Well, you seem to have a pretty high threshold for pain because you're not even wincing."

"Like I said, I'm pressed for time. I have to go meet Taylor Drake now."

"A practical woman. Where are you two meeting?"

"Centennial Park downtown, under the bridge."

"Need a ride?"

"I've got a rental car, remember?"

"Maybe I should follow you," he said.

"I'm meeting a cop, Clay. I'll be okay." When he didn't budge, she sighed. "Did anyone besides you follow me here?" she asked. "I'm assuming you checked."

He gave her a sheepish look. "Not that I could tell."

"Then there's no one to follow me to the park, is there? And no one else knows where Taylor and I are meeting."

She could tell he still didn't like it and touched his arm, surprised at how natural the gesture was. So soon. She was also surprised to note that his arm was nothing but hard muscle. Quickly, she pulled her hand back and tried to ignore the heat that coursed through her blood. "If it makes you feel better, come there after you meet with your friend," she said, all too aware that her voice had dropped an octave.

He nodded, his expression telling her that he had noticed the color in her cheeks. "Deal."

As they left, Jessie pulled the door closed and concentrated on locking it, though she missed the key hole twice because her hands were suddenly shaking. This is stupid, she told herself. He's just a man. Get over it.

Behind her, standing too close, Clay asked, "Are you free for dinner tonight?"

She turned, but he didn't step back to let her by. Her stomach fluttered with nerves as she took him in. He was breathtaking. Tan, muscular, intense. The dimple in his chin, the blue eyes, the angular jaw—the stuff of fantasies. As she stared at him, she saw a grin forming. Nerves turned to irritation at his cockiness. "What's so funny?"

"Your first instinct was to say 'no.' But you didn't."

She angled her chin. "Then I'll say it now."

"Too late. I saw the 'yes' in your eyes. Face it, Jess. You like me. Why not just go with it and see where it takes you?"

"You have an incredible ego."

"You have incredible eyes."

She gave a short laugh, even more annoyed at the breathless sound that came out of her own mouth. "Please."

He eased closer, backing her against the door, and with his index finger, angled stray hair away from her face. His hand lingered at her jaw, his knuckles leaving trails of heat where they grazed her skin. "I'm putting the moves on you."

She dropped her gaze to his lips, distracted when the tip of his tongue wet them. Her pulse quickened, and she swallowed. "I hadn't noticed."

"I might be a little rusty," he said.

"If you ask for an oil can, you're out of luck."

His chuckle was low and seemed to vibrate from his body into hers. "You're quick with the comebacks, Ms. Rhoades."

"You're quick with the moves."

"Too quick?" he murmured, his mouth a scant inch from hers. His cool breath caressed her lips.

She closed her eyes. For an instant, she wanted him to kiss her, to touch her. But the practical side of her rejected that desire. They hardly knew each other. She wasn't foolish enough to deny that there were sexual sparks galore. But she also wasn't the kind of woman who acted on physical wants without regard to the emotional aftermath.

Placing her palms against his chest, she applied slight pressure. "Please don't," she said.

He backed off, dropping his arms to his sides. If he was disappointed, he didn't show it. "Is there someone else?" he asked.

More than anything, she wanted him back where he'd been, trapping her against the door with his bigger, stronger body, sharing his heat. Why oh why did she have to be so damned practical all the time? "There's no one," she said.

"You find me that repulsive?"

She managed a teasing smile. "Yes, I'd have to go with repulsive."

His eyebrow arched. "You wound me."

"I'm sure you'll recover."

"Would six be too early for you for dinner?"

She had to admire his persistence. "Definitely. Even more so if this story busts open."

"You'll have to take a dinner break, won't you?"

"You haven't worked in a newsroom in a while, have you? When there's big news breaking, there's no time for dinner."

"Then we'll make it a midnight snack. That's about the time you have to stop working on the story so everyone else can do their jobs to get it into the newspaper, right?"

She was glad he wouldn't be put off so easily. "All right. A midnight snack. Hold the caffeine."

Chapter 12

Shaking rainwater out of his hair, Clay handed Jessie's computer disk to Marshall Greene. "How fast can you get to it?"

Marshall, in his mid-thirties, had prematurely salt-and-pepper hair buzzed short. He and Clay had shared an apartment with two other friends during their college days. Their working relationship had begun in school when Clay had asked Marshall to help research political donations to the aldermen in their college town. Together, they had cracked open a kickback scandal that had had repercussions in the small town for many years.

Since then, Marshall's computer savvy had proved invaluable to Clay's investigative reporting. Clay had often lectured himself about how he needed to learn what Marshall, as a private detective, knew about getting around on the Internet and such, but it had seemed pointless when Marshall already knew so much and was so willing to help out. Plus, it gave Clay more time to investigate other angles while Marshall worked the Net.

"What's on it?" Marshall asked, inspecting the disk. He had crow's feet at the corners of his eyes, but they added character to an otherwise baby face punctuated by light brown eyes that were irresistible to most women.

"Naughty pictures," Clay said.

Marshall started to grin. "No kidding? I can get to naughty pictures right now." Sitting in front of one of the computers on his desk, he fed the disk into the drive. "So why are you sharing? I've never known you to share."

"Just take a look," Clay said.

As they waited for the computer to do its thing, Clay glanced around the office that Marshall maintained in the back of his Fort Myers home. Like the rest of the house, it was neat to the extreme. Computer magazines were organized on a wrought-iron rack. Plants thrived in colorful pots. Pictures on the walls—Ansel Adams prints framed in black—were perfectly straight. Clay knew Marshall did most of his detective work in this room, using two computers to sort through anyone's messy past that proved to be of interest to a client who paid handsomely for the information. Legwork for Marshall usually consisted of walking to the kitchen for a fresh cup of coffee.

As Marshall opened a photo file on the computer, he whistled low. "You're not kidding. These are naughty."

Bracing a hand on the back of Marshall's chair, Clay leaned forward to see the screen better. The image was one that the newspaper had not used because of its more explicit content.

"Aren't these our very own copulating cops?" Marshall asked.

"They are. Is the photo for real?"

Marshall glanced at him over his shoulder. "Are you kidding me?"

"Nope."

"Well, let's see."

Marshall worked fast, directing the mouse through a series of quick clicks, explaining what he was doing as he went along. "I'm importing the photo into a software program that lets me manipulate photos. Graphics people and photographers usually use the program to enhance color,

138

improve lighting, or erase flaws in photos. They also can add images, move things around—create their own special effects, in other words."

"Can you tell whether this photo has been altered by such a program?"

"Well, I can tell that someone's been playing with this guy's head," Marshall said, directing the computer to zoom in on the featured police officer's face and upper body.

"Already? How?"

"See how the lighting is coming from the front on the face?" He indicated the torso. "But down here, we're in shadows. The lighting isn't natural. Let's zoom in some more."

After highlighting an area of the officer's neck, Marshall waited for the computer to blow the image up. When it was done, he said, "Ah."

"Ah?"

"This officer's head appears detachable, Mr. Christopher. If you know what you're looking for, and I do, you can see that the artist in this case was a novice. See how the neck of the officer doesn't quite mesh with the body? The skin tones are different, and there's a lot of airbrushing going on to try to disguise the area where the body and neck are connected. It's pretty easy to make such an effort virtually undetectable. But you have to know what you're doing."

"Damn," Clay said, and looked at his watch. It had taken Marshall less than half an hour to determine one photo was bogus. "How sophisticated is the process you just went through?"

"Not even close to what the program is capable of. You'd just need to know what you're looking for."

"Would a graphics editor at a newspaper know what he's doing?"

Marshall snorted. "This is a very popular program. Newspapers all over the world use it. Even if the editor didn't know what he was doing, he should be able to figure it out."

Clay scratched his chin. So Shawn Witherspoon, *The Star-News'* graphics editor, was either a big idiot or he had lied about the authenticity of the photos. "Let's look at some of the photos the newspaper used."

"Okay." As he worked, Marshall asked, "So, any ideas on who might want to sabotage the police department? I mean, that's what's going on here, isn't it?"

"I don't know what the hell is going on here."

Marshall squinted at his computer screen. "Looks like our novice put in a little more effort on this baby," he said about the photo on display. "Probably knew the more graphic photos wouldn't be published, so he didn't work as hard on them. This one has the same lighting problems, though. Definitely fake."

Several minutes later, Marshall had examined more than half the photos on the disk and had determined that each was bogus. Ejecting the computer disk, he handed it to Clay. "Come in the other room. We'll have a beer and talk about David Collins." On the way out the door, he picked up a manila folder.

In the kitchen, which was as impeccable as the rest of the house, they leaned on opposite sides of a breakfast bar and sipped cold beers, the folder between them.

"I'm curious about the connection between Collins and the copulating cops."

"I don't know that there is one."

"What's your interest in the guy then?"

"We have . . . a mutual acquaintance."

"A woman?" Marshall asked.

Clay chuckled. "You don't have to act so shocked."

"I can't help it. I didn't think I'd ever see you show any interest in anyone again. Of course, if I were you, I wouldn't be messing with Collins or anyone close to him. He has some shady connections."

Clay swallowed some beer. "Give me the highlights."

"Couple years ago, the guy worked for a now-defunct law firm in Chicago." Flipping open the file folder, Marshall consulted one of several computer printouts. "Hale, Kravitz and Hale. Specialty was insurance fraud. And I don't mean fighting it. One of the suburban dailies busted open the scam, and the partners took a big fall. Collins escaped unscathed. Want to hear the coincidence?"

"I love coincidence."

"Collins' wife worked for the newspaper that broke the story."

"She tipped it off?"

"Maybe. Maybe not. She took off as the story was breaking. Hasn't been heard from since. For a while, investigators thought her disappearance might have been foul play, but they never turned up anything. I was becoming convinced that Collins, or someone connected with his troubles, had orchestrated something unfortunate for her. Then I came across their divorce decree, filed by her through a lawyer six months ago. I tried tracking her down but came up empty. Want to hear some theories? I have some."

Clay nodded, hoping Marshall's ideas were less horrifying than his own.

"She knew something about Collins' involvement in his firm's fraud, was involved in some way, and when the paper broke it, she ran to save her own butt. Or, she knew something, tipped off the paper, then took off because her life had been threatened. Or, Collins and his buds made her disappear and went through the motions of the divorce from her angle to make it look like she's still around. Either way, she knew something."

"You said Collins was cleared in the fraud?" Clay asked.

"I don't know if cleared is the proper term. He didn't do any time, and here's some irony: he's with the state's attorney's office now, focusing on prosecuting insurance fraud. He knows all the tricks, you see."

"Did he cut a deal to avoid doing time?"

"If he did, he should have cut himself a better one," Marshall said. "He's way over his head in debt."

"Do you know why?"

"He's invested quite heavily in private investigators."

"For what?" But Clay already had an idea.

"I'm just guessing here, but if Mrs. Collins is still out there, knowing whatever it is she knows about Mr. Collins' involvement with the fraud, it would make good business sense for him to find her and make sure she maintains her silence."

Apprehension tightened Clay's muscles.

"So she's the one you know," Marshall said.

Nodding, Clay rubbed his hands over his face. The half-bottle of beer he'd drained churned in his gut.

"She lives in the area?" Marshall asked.

"Yeah."

"You're involved with her."

"I wouldn't say that."

"It wasn't a question." Marshall finished his beer and set the bottle on the counter. "If Collins' detectives track her down, she's either dead or gone again without a trace. We're talking about a woman who will never be safe, never be settled."

"You're so optimistic," Clay said.

"I'm realistic."

"You're also doing a lot of assuming."

Marshall nodded. "Acknowledged. But she's not being up front with you or you wouldn't be here getting this info from me."

"We just met. She's not comfortable spilling her guts to me just yet."

"All I'm saying is, she's walked out on her entire life before. What's stopping her from doing it again if her ex tracks her down?"

"I plan to make it difficult for her."

Marshall smiled slowly. "You've got it bad."

"I'm not being an idiot, Marshall."

"I wasn't suggesting you are."

"The look on your face suggests it."

"This look is envy, my man." Picking up the folder, he handed it to Clay. "Here are the details on Collins, if you want a more thorough look."

Clay accepted it. "Thanks. I appreciate your work, as always."

"No problem. I appreciate the business."

Clay sat in his SUV, his fingers curled around the steering wheel, and watched rain stream down the windshield.

Shaking his head, he used his cell phone to call his editor in New York. "Yeah, Steve, it's Clay. Your rumor's right. The story's bogus."

"Hot damn."

"Yeah. I'm seeing this as an investigative piece on how something like this could happen to respectable journalists."

"You mean lazy, stupid journalists."

"No. That's not what happened. The newspaper was set up. Just like the cops."

"So who was the hoax supposed to ruin? The newspaper or the cops?"

"Don't know yet. But I'm working on it, and I'll get back to you." He was about to disconnect the call when he heard Steve say his name. "Yeah?"

"I was just saying it's good to have you back," Steve said.

Clay chuckled. "It's good to be back." The cell phone beeped, signaling that a caller had just left him voice mail. "Gotta go."

The message was from a flack at the police chief's office, agreeing to an interview.

Jessie huddled under the towering bridge that spanned the Caloosahatchee River. The area known as Centennial Park was deserted. The downtown park usually bustled with vacationing picnickers or business people seeking solace from a busy workday. Today, though, the sun didn't shoot sparks off the river, and no sailboats drifted by.

Jessie tried not to shiver against the rain. It was unusually cold, even for March, and she made a mental note to have one of the reporters track down an explanation for the next day's paper. There was nothing like a weather story to stir up Floridians. Chances were by the time she got back to the newspaper, the sun would be shining and not one cloud would mar the brilliant blue sky.

Taylor was late, but she wasn't worried yet. It gave her time to think.

If the story was a hoax, she and many of her co-workers were doomed professionally, and *The Star-News* would suffer horrible embarrassment and ridicule. She couldn't imagine how disappointed Richard Westin would be if his life's work ended up being a joke on late-night TV.

Suddenly, she missed him so much her chest ached. Not only did she like him on a personal level, with his fatherly demeanor and sense of fairness, she much preferred the way he had run the newsroom. He'd never bullied his editors into making decisions based on what he wanted. He'd let everyone have their own opinion, and he'd respected those opinions, even if he didn't agree. And he'd *never* referred to reporters as "minions."

She supposed she was biased. He'd given her an opportunity that no other newspaper editor had. After she left David, she'd had no résumé, no references. Such job-searching tools would have left a paper trail that she felt she couldn't afford. Without them, most editors wouldn't agree to meet with her, and the few who did were still too suspicious or wary to take a chance on her. She couldn't blame them. She wouldn't have hired her either. But all she wanted was a tryout. She even volunteered to work for free at first, to prove she could do the job. None would take her up on the offer, and she had been considering a new career when she met Richard Westin.

He'd seemed taken with her right away, amused that she'd be so presumptuous as to refuse to list her credentials other than to say she had a journalism degree from a reputable university and eight years of reporting experience. He'd also expressed concern for her safety. It was obvious she was running from something, and he'd asked if he could help in any way. "Yes," she'd said. "You can give me a job."

Instead, he'd given her a week. "Bring me one good story worthy of Sunday's Page One," he'd said.

Three days later, she'd walked into his office with a story about greyhounds being mistreated at a Florida dog track. Insiders were willing to talk exclusively to her about rampant abuse in the industry throughout the state. His response: "You're hired."

He'd retired a year later, and Gillian had taken over. Jessie had been tempted to quit many times since but knew it was unlikely she would find another Richard Westin out there. Plus, she felt she owed him. He'd given her what she'd so desperately needed: the chance to start over doing the job she loved. He'd also asked her to try to keep *The Star-News* on the right track, though he probably hadn't anticipated that his daughter's autocratic style of management would make that impossible.

Now, Jessie imagined that Richard was beside himself with pride and relief since *The Star-News* broke the cops story. Circulation was no doubt through the roof, which meant he wouldn't have to worry about selling to the highest bidder after all. If the story turned out to be bogus—

"Jess!"

Turning, she saw Taylor Drake jogging toward her. He was an imposing man with short black hair and football player shoulders. She'd met him during her first days on the cops beat and had liked him immediately. He was all cop and "don't mess with me, boy" attitude, but his kind brown eyes belied his gentle nature, as had his eagerness to share pictures of his two boys with her.

As he drew near now, she saw how tired he looked. Dark circles underscored his eyes, his usually ruddy complexion pale and drawn. Fingers of sympathy squeezed her heart. "It's good to see you, Taylor," she said, and meant it.

He shrugged out of his rain jacket. "You're shivering. Take this."

Before she could respond, he draped it over her shoulders on top of Clay's suit jacket. The warmth was instantaneous, and she huddled gratefully into it. "Thank you."

"I was hoping we'd be dry under the bridge," he said, squinting at the rain-drenched sky.

"It's falling sideways," she said. "The wind."

"What happened?" He had focused on her bruised jaw.

Under normal circumstances, she might have smiled at his brotherly concern. As it was, she shuddered in memory. "I interrupted a burglar last night."

His gaze zeroed in on her cast. "Your hand, too?"

She glanced down at the cast. She was so used to it she barely noticed it anymore. "That happened earlier this week. My brake line was cut, and I hit a tree."

He gaped at her. "Jesus, Jess. What the hell's going on?"

She shivered, and before she could answer, he said, "You're still cold. Let's talk in the Explorer."

She fell in step beside him, shoulders hunched as a gust of wind blew rain full into her face. She didn't bother to try to swipe away the water that dribbled into her eyes and dripped off her chin. "How are things?" she asked.

"Oh, they're fantastic," he said. "My wife is filing for divorce and custody of the boys."

Her heart sank. Of everyone involved, the scandal had cost him the most. His family, his friends, his self-respect, and probably, eventually, his job. "I'm so sorry," she said. "Is there anything I can do to help?"

He gave her a sad smile. "You still look me in the eye, Jess. You're among the few."

She paused beside his Ford Explorer as he started to open the passenger's side door. "Taylor, before she died, Sandi White backtracked on what she told us about you and the others."

147

Stopping with his hand on the door handle, he stared at her, his soft brown eyes startled. "Backtracked how?"

"She said she lied. She said someone paid her to lie."

The color drained from his face. "Oh my God." Shaking his head, he closed his eyes, leaning his head back as if asking the heavens for guidance. He didn't seem to notice the rain splashing his cheeks. "Oh my God."

Jessie stepped forward, alarmed. "Taylor," she said. "What is it? Talk to me."

Lowering his head, he met her gaze, blinking the water from his eyes. "I did, too."

Her pulse started to jackhammer. "You did what, too? Tell me what you did."

"I lied. I lied about all of it."

He looked so miserable that she put aside her shock and touched his forearm, to offer comfort, to try to be what he so desperately seemed to need, a friend. "Taylor—"

He recoiled as if she had struck him. She flinched back, thinking that somehow she had hurt him. Then his body jerked again, and she saw red bloom across the front of his shirt.

Chapter 13

Before killing the engine, and therefore the windshield wipers, Clay took a moment to watch Jessie and Taylor Drake as they stood next to a green Ford Explorer, talking intently. She was wearing Taylor's jacket, her hair soaked, her expression strained with concern. Taylor looked upset, standing with his head back, oblivious to the drenching rain.

Clay decided to wait until they were done talking. The police officer didn't know him, and he might clam up if a stranger approached.

He watched Jessie reach out to Taylor, saw the cop flinch as if her touch had zapped him. Puzzled, Clay squinted to see better through the rain splattering his windshield. That was when Taylor crumpled forward. Jessie seemed to try to catch him, but his weight was too much, and she stumbled back against the Explorer and went down under him.

Seeing Jessie fall—had something besides Taylor's weight knocked her against the Explorer?—snapped Clay out of his shock. Ramming open the door of the Jeep, he lurched out into the torrential rain. His mind was a blur of white as he tore toward Jessie and the cop.

He saw the blood first, vivid and red, on both of them. The sight of it, even as the rain diluted it, made his breath jam in his chest. Then he heard Jessie shout Taylor's name, saw her trying to move his dead weight off of her.

Dropping to his knees, Clay helped shift Taylor's body aside, relief turning his insides to water as she scrambled to her knees. If she'd been hit, she couldn't have moved like that, couldn't have ripped open Taylor's shirt with such force.

"Shit, shit, shit," she said, planting a hand over the gushing wound in Taylor's lower abdomen. More blood oozed from a second wound in Taylor's upper arm, but she ignored that one as she shrugged off his jacket. "Get help," she yelled at Clay. "Hurry!"

Clay ran back to the Jeep, scanning the area, hoping to catch a glimpse of who had shot the cop. But he knew it was too late, that he should have been looking already. Snatching his cell phone out of the SUV, he called 911 while he raced back to where Jessie gripped Taylor's hand, her cast smeared with blood, water dripping off of her hair and onto the fallen officer's ghost-white face. She had dragged his jacket over his upper torso, and blood oozed through the fingers of the hand she had clamped to his wound. "Hang on, Taylor, hang on."

"Ambulance is on its way," Clay said.

Jessie didn't acknowledge that she'd heard him as Taylor opened his eyes and tried to speak. "Don't talk," she said, her voice breaking. "Save your strength."

But Taylor persisted, curling his fingers into the front of her shirt and trying to draw her toward him. Leaning down, she pressed her cheek to his, as if she could transfer her strength, her warmth, through the contact. "Taylor, please," she said. "Just concentrate on hanging on."

Clay saw Taylor's lips move near her ear but couldn't hear what he said. A heartbeat later, his eyes closed, and his head rolled to one side, his hand going limp in hers.

Jessie jerked back to stare at his still face. "Taylor?" She jostled his lifeless hand, got no response. "Taylor!" Her frantic gaze sought Clay's. "Do you know CPR?"

Clay, kneeling beside her on the wet pavement, shook his head. "It won't help. He's breathing." Whatever damage the bullet had done, it hadn't arrested Taylor's respiratory function. It was most likely the cop was bleeding to death, in spite of the hand Jessie clamped over his abdominal injury. CPR would be useless against that.

Weeping now, Jessie bent over the police officer. "Come on, Taylor. Don't do this. *Don't do this.*"

Two police cars, sirens blaring, roared up, followed by an ambulance. Clay quickly told one of the officers what he knew while paramedics poured out of the ambulance, laden with medical equipment. As officers scattered to secure the area, Clay grasped Jessie's arm, drawing her away from Taylor. He firmly took both her arms when she started to fight him. "Let the paramedics do what they can," he said.

When her knees buckled and she staggered, he wrapped an arm around her waist to pull her close, alarmed by the tremors that shook her. He steered her toward the ambulance, where a female paramedic met them with blankets that she draped around both of them.

"Are you hurt?" she asked, taking in the blood that had spattered Jessie's clothing.

Jessie shook her head, unable to speak through suddenly chattering teeth. She couldn't seem to tear her attention away from the activity around Taylor.

"I think she's just cold," Clay said.

The woman eased Jessie down on the tailgate of the ambulance and directed the beam of a penlight into her eyes. "What's your name, ma'am?"

"J-J-Jessie."

"Jessie, I'm Mary. I'm going to take your blood pressure, okay?"

"Shouldn't you b-b-be helping th-th-them?" Jessie asked.

"They're doing fine," Mary said. "I'm helping you now." She wrapped a blood-pressure cuff around Jessie's upper arm. "Looks like you're going to have to have this cast replaced," she said, her voice soothing, her movements calm and unhurried.

Clay saw Jessie's lips were starting to turn blue, so he sat down next to her, hoping his body heat would help warm her. When he felt her stiffen, he glanced toward the Explorer in time to see a paramedic draw a blanket over Taylor's face.

The cop was dead.

Beside Clay, Jessie's breath began to hitch. "He was blackmailed," she said.

His disbelief at what she'd said was overpowered by the sight of the needle in Mary's hand. "What's that for?" he demanded.

"Sedative. She's in shock."

Jessie shook her head. "No sedatives."

Before either of them could stop her, Mary slipped the needle into Jessie's arm. "Just relax and let it do its job," she said. "You'll feel better in a few moments."

"Damn it," Jessie said, making a belated grab for the woman's hand. "I won't be able to do *my* job." She turned accusing eyes on Clay, her shudders already subsiding. "Why'd you let her do that?"

Easing her back, Mary covered her patient with another blanket, then sprinted over to where her colleagues were loading Taylor's body onto a gurney.

Jessie curled on her side, a bloody fist clenched against

her chest as she choked back fresh emotion. Clay wanted to touch her, to soothe her, but knew she'd push him away if he tried. Turning away, furious at his impotence, he felt as if something had torn inside his chest.

His gaze landed on Taylor's corpse.

"He was blackmailed."

And now he was dead.

Jessie opened her eyes as a cool, dry hand stroked the hair from her forehead. Clay sat on the bed beside her, his thigh, warm and firm, resting snugly against her hip.

"Hey," he said.

Taylor Drake was dead.

The memory struck fast and deep, slashing through the clinging residue of drugged sleep. Someone had shot him. His wife was a widow, his kids . . .

Swallowing against the wave of grief, she fought the accompanying helpless rage until every muscle in her body felt rigid with the effort.

"Relax," Clay said, his voice gentle. "You're okay."

He didn't seem to be okay, though. He was wincing. Realizing she had a death grip on his hand, she released him and pushed herself up, relieved when he didn't try to make her stay down. Her body felt like lead, the sedative still working on her system. She was rubbing her hands over her face when she noticed that a splint had replaced her cast.

"It got wet," Clay said. "You're getting a new one."

She glanced around, startled that they were in an actual hospital room and not an ER cubicle. "Where are my clothes?"

"Jess—"

"I'm not staying here. I'm fine."

"No one's going to keep you here."

She couldn't meet his eyes. Seeing his concern would undo her. She operated much better when she didn't have to deal with other people's sympathy. "He was blackmailed." Her voice cracked. *Damn it.* "Taylor." It wasn't necessary to say his name, but she'd needed to prove to herself that she could say it without caving in.

Clay touched her arm, but she lifted her shoulder against his tender caress, a surge of emotion almost toppling her.

He backed off, his expression carefully controlled, but she saw in his sad eyes that her rejection stung.

"I'm sorry," she said, her shoulders sagging. She couldn't seem to do anything right anymore. And now someone was dead because of it.

He didn't acknowledge the whispered apology, as if he knew that doing so would make it more difficult for her. "Did Taylor say anything else?"

She shook her head. "Nothing."

"He gave no indication who might have blackmailed him?"

"No. Whatever he was blackmailed with, it had to be worse than what he lied about." She became stronger as she talked. "Or maybe there was a threat against his family, and he did it to protect them."

"The pictures are fake."

That didn't surprise her, but the confirmation still sent a grinding pain through her gut. Who would do such a thing? What would be the point? So many lives had been shattered, marriages and families ripped apart, a family's newspaper forever damaged.

"Your graphics editor should have been able to see it," Clay said. "He could be part of the setup."

That set in motion a whole new dread. She liked Shawn, considered him a friend. But she couldn't help but recall the many times he'd vented to her about how much he hated Gillian. Closing her eyes, she shoved away the niggling suspicion. That's how it would be now, she thought. Everyone would look like a suspect.

"What time is it?" she asked.

Clay checked his watch. "Four-twenty."

"Jesus, I was out that long? They couldn't replace my cast in all that time?" Now she would be stuck here even longer.

"Just relax, Jess. What's the big hurry?"

I have to get back to work. She wanted to yell it at him. How could he not see that she had an urgent situation before her? *The Star-News . . . she* had been duped, and if the newspaper were to survive the blow to its credibility, she had to gather her reporters and . . . what? For a moment, her mind went blank. What could they do? How would they do it? They were part of the story now. How could they possibly report that with any semblance of objectivity?

She veered away from that dilemma and focused on the more immediate concern. "What do the police know about who killed Taylor?" she asked.

"We're the only witnesses. They're waiting to talk to you."

"Did you see anything?"

"I saw him get hit, but other than that, no. What about you?"

"It happened too fast," she said. One minute he'd admitted he'd lied, and the next, he'd been on the ground, bloody and dying. She pressed the heel of her hand between her eyes, trying to hold off the ache that was growing there. "Has anyone called his wife?" And his kids. His poor kids.

"The police said they'd take care of it."

Smelling blood, she lowered her hand, saw it crusted

and dark in the creases of her knuckles. Taylor's blood.

Clay moved away from her, and she looked up as he went into the bathroom and ran the water. When he returned, he handed her a wet hand towel.

She didn't trust her voice to thank him as she scrubbed at the blood. Its coppery scent filled her head, and nausea squirmed through her stomach as a fine film of sweat slicked her skin. She kept seeing Taylor, his white face wet with rain, the life fading from his sweet, brown eyes.

"Mel should be here any minute with some dry clothes for you," Clay said.

"Good." She kept her head down as she cleaned her hands, fighting sickness and emotion with equal fervor. "Do you have your cell phone on you?"

He didn't respond right away, but she didn't glance up, not trusting herself. When he finally spoke, his voice was low. "Why don't you let your assistants handle the story? You're too close to it."

"I need to talk to Greg, find out if he got anything on the guy who gave him the disk. And I need to see Taylor's wife. He might have told her something—"

She looked up when he grasped her arms. Frustration contorted his features. "Would you just stop? You could have been killed, Jess. The bullet that hit Taylor could just as easily have hit you."

Her heart thudded against her ribs, a small, trapped animal. He was getting too close, caring too much. She didn't think she could handle that responsibility on top of the ones piling up on her at a frightening pace. "You're hurting me."

Letting her go, Clay thrust a hand back through his hair. "I'm sorry. I just . . . seeing blood on you . . . it freaks me out. And this is the third time. At what point do you say to hell with it and run for cover?"

Before she could respond, Mel walked in, a Gap bag tucked under one arm. "Hey, kids."

Never more relieved to see anyone, Jessie slid off the bed. The cold floor under her bare feet sent a chill up through her as she went to her friend and took the bag. "Thanks, Mel."

"Are you okay?" Mel asked.

"I'm fine." Dumping the bag's contents on the bed, Jessie began dressing. She didn't care that Clay was in the room. She just wanted to get out of there and quickly.

"Just because Mel walked in doesn't mean this conversation is over," Clay said.

"What am I supposed to do?" she asked as she pulled on jeans. "Roll over and play dead? Go into hiding?"

"That's not a bad idea," Mel said.

Jessie scowled at her friend as she fumbled with the zipper, hampered by the unfamiliar splint. "Maybe that's how you guys play the game, but it's not the way I play it." Doffing the hospital gown, she had just retrieved the clean T-shirt from the bag when Clay whirled her around. She gasped, clasping the shirt to her bare breasts. The fury in his eyes stopped her from trying to shove him back.

"Game?" he repeated. "This isn't a *game,* damn you. If it were, you would have lost a long time ago because you're too stubborn to admit your life is in danger."

"Go, Clay," Mel said softly.

Jessie glared at her, then turned her narrowed gaze on Clay. "Let me go."

His grip tightened. "Not until we have an understanding."

She raised her chin. "You can't bully me."

"I'm not trying to bully you. I'm trying to save your damn life. Don't tell me you don't have the sense to let me do that."

"It's not your job to save my life."

"Then whose is it? Apparently, it's not yours or you wouldn't be so bent on self-destruction."

She gaped at him. "I'm not bent on—"

"Like hell you're not," he cut in. "I can't imagine any other reason you're being so damn stubborn right now."

"I have a job to do."

"Jess, the bullet that hit Taylor could have been meant for you," Clay said, and his voice softened. "We don't know. Either way, it's the third time someone has come damn close to taking you out, and still you insist on putting yourself in harm's way. That's self-destructive."

Her head spinning, she took a step back so she could ease down onto the bed. Clay released her, but she didn't notice as it hit her that Taylor might have died because he'd been standing too close to her. His kids would grow up without their father because he had possibly been in the wrong place at the wrong time—with her. Guilt settled so heavily on her chest that it hurt to take a breath.

"Please," Clay said. "Let me help you."

The intensity of his blue eyes struck her. How could he care so much so soon? But that didn't matter. He was at risk now. In fact, anyone close to her was vulnerable. "It's my problem," she said. "I'll handle it."

Mel released a frustrated groan. "Jesus, Jess. Would you give the guy a break?"

Jessie directed a cool, distant look at her friend as, rising, she pulled on the T-shirt. "I don't recall asking for your opinion, Mel. In fact, I'm tired of getting it all the time. Maybe it's time you just butt the hell out of my life."

Mel stiffened. "Excuse me?"

"You heard me. I'm tired of all the hovering. I don't need a mother, and I don't need a baby-sitter."

Mel's green eyes began to glitter. "What are you saying?"

"What I should have said a long time ago, back when your mother hen act first started getting on my nerves. Maybe then I wouldn't have to be putting up with your shit now."

Mel backed toward the door, shaking her head in confusion. She started to say something, but words seemed to fail her. Then, as quick as the tears had welled into her eyes, her features hardened. "Go to hell," she said, and slammed out the door without a backward glance.

Knees unsteady, Jessie sank onto the edge of the bed, shoving back the need to wrap her arms around herself and rock. Seeing the hurt in her friend's eyes had almost snapped her resolve. If Mel had not stormed out, Jessie was certain she wouldn't have been able to hold it together.

"Do you think that was really necessary?" Clay asked.

She squeezed her eyes shut, fought to shore up her flagging strength. Her throat ached with the need to scream, to cry. "She wouldn't have stayed away from me just because I asked her to," she said. Pushing off the bed, desperate to be busy, she dumped loafers out of the Gap bag, her back to Clay. Already, she felt Mel's absence like a hole in her soul and prayed that the things she'd just said would not be irreparable.

"You're not going to push me away to protect me," Clay said behind her. "I won't let you. And, frankly, once Mel figures it out, she won't either."

"Then we need to wrap this up fast." She paused while sliding on a shoe, surprised that she'd said "we." It was as if her subconscious had already acknowledged that Clay wasn't going to go away. And, for the first time, she thought that she could accept that. Maybe she had no choice. She needed someone to be on her side.

Facing him, she asked, "Do you have any ideas?"

His clenched jaw loosened, and he almost smiled. "Can I have a minute to savor this moment?"

"No."

"All right," he said, and some more of the smile seeped through. "Until this is over, you'll stay at my home with me and an armed guard."

"I can't afford—"

"Can I finish?"

She concentrated on slipping on the other loafer. He would never know how difficult it was for her to hand over control. "Yes, please finish."

"The protection will be provided at my expense because it's for my peace of mind," he said. "Apparently, you don't need peace of mind."

She gave him a sharp look. "Don't push me."

"Don't push *me,* darling."

That stopped her. Darling? Jesus, when had they gotten to that? "Fine, an armed guard. What else?"

"From now until we get this figured out, you don't go anywhere without me or the guard."

"I can't do my job with a guard hovering—"

"If you're going to interrupt me every other word, this could take awhile."

She pressed her lips together.

"I'm enjoying this new you, Jess."

"Bite me."

His chuckle was probably the most irritating thing she'd ever heard, until he shared his next idea. "You'll take the rest of the day off and get some sleep."

"No freaking way."

"Who's calling the shots here?" he asked.

"If this were the other way around, I wouldn't expect you to drop everything at work."

"Like hell you wouldn't. And, besides, it isn't the other way around. You're the one getting shot at, and I'm the one trying to keep you in one piece. So get over it."

Biting into her bottom lip, she clenched and unclenched her good fist at her side. God, he could tick her off. She'd never known anyone who could so easily. On the other hand, she knew she could be stubborn and unreasonable, especially when she felt cornered. Which he seemed to have a special knack for doing.

"Now that we have that settled," he said, doing a fairly admirable job of suppressing his satisfaction. "I'll go check at the nurse's station to see what the time frame is on your new cast."

Alone, she sat on the bed, eyeing the telephone and wondering if she had time to call the office before he returned. The newsroom was no doubt in chaos, and she longed to be in the middle of it.

Holding herself in check, it struck her again that Clay's growing attachment to her seemed illogical. Most of the time, she was a pain in the ass. She could be a major bitch (just ask Mel). She also had a tendency to focus on work to the exclusion of everything, and everyone, else in her life. That was one of the flaws that her ex-husband had constantly harassed her about. It was why he'd said he cheated on her, because she was a pain-in-the-ass, stubborn, self-centered workaholic. Why on earth did Clay seem to find that so appealing?

Returning, he said, "Someone should be here in a few minutes." He paused when he saw her considering expression. "What?"

"Why are you doing all this for me?" she asked. "Being

anywhere near me could get you killed."

He pocketed his hands, glanced down at the floor, seemed to mull over what he was about to say. "Three years ago, I failed my wife. She was everything to me. My life. I should have done everything in my power to protect her. I didn't." Glancing up, he met her gaze, and his was dead serious. "I'm not going to make that mistake again."

Shame swept over Jessie at the scope of her disappointment. She'd suspected that guilt over his wife's death still drove him, but part of her had hoped that his feelings had shifted, that she had become their focus, rather than his dead wife. "I'm not your redemption, Clay. You can't bring her back by saving me."

"I'm not trying to bring her back. I just don't want to bury you, too."

As Jessie was processing that, a nurse cheerfully entered the room. "Is someone in here waiting for a new cast?"

"I am," Jessie said.

She had to pass Clay on her way out the door and paused before him. He was a stunning man, even after being drenched, and she found herself wanting to touch his angular jaw, wanting to run her finger over the dent in his chin. She wondered what it would be like to place her hand on his chest now, to feel his strong heart beating against her palm. Wondered what it would be like to place her lips on his and kiss him so thoroughly that he staggered.

"After this is done, I'm going to work," she said, calmly, evenly. "Either you can come with me, or you can send a guard. It's your choice. But I'm not going to go into hiding."

"I'm not suggesting you hide," he said. "I'm suggesting you rest."

"I'll rest when I have time."

"Or when your body doesn't give you a choice."

"Or then," she conceded. "But it'll still be my choice. Get it?"

He nodded, his lips twitching as if he suppressed a smile. "Got it."

Chapter 14

It was after six-thirty when Clay walked beside Jessie into *The Star-News* newsroom. He admired the way she deftly turned aside various expressions of concern without appearing unappreciative or cold. On her way to her office, she signaled for Greg Roberts to follow.

As she sat behind her desk, she moved sluggishly, but Clay didn't mention it. He considered the ground he'd won considerable and didn't plan to jeopardize it now.

As Greg joined them, he shut the door. "How are you, Jess?" he asked. "Should you be here?"

"Don't worry about me. What have you turned up on the man who provided the photo disk?"

Greg shot a questioning glance at Clay. "Gillian pulled me off that to cover the, uh, shooting. I'll need to talk to you about that. When you're ready."

Jessie gave a short nod. "I expected as much. Any progress on the mystery man before Gillian reassigned you?"

Again, Greg glanced at Clay. "Uh—"

"It's okay," Jessie said. "Clay is working the story for *The New York Times*."

"And we're sharing information?" Greg asked. "Isn't that a little unorthodox?"

"People are dying," Jessie said, then made a visible effort to soften her tone. "We need to figure out who's behind this quickly. If that means we share information, yes."

Greg gave Clay a measuring look. The young reporter's

protectiveness heartened Clay. Finally, Greg said, "The P.I. you put me in touch with checked with the security people at the bank that owns the ATM where the guy gave me the disk. The camera there didn't catch the handoff."

"I don't suppose you had the disk dusted for fingerprints before it was swiped," Clay said.

Jessie shook her head. "Never thought of it."

"What's the deal with the disk?" Greg asked.

"We had it checked, Greg, and the photos are fake," Jessie said.

Greg lowered himself to a chair. "Damn."

"The guy who gave them to you is the key. If he didn't doctor them, he at least can tell us who paid him to give them to you. Hopefully." She worried her lip for a moment. "Is there anything about him at all that stands out in your mind?"

"No. Like I said before, he looked like a street person. He handed me the disk and walked away." Greg's face reddened. "I should have gone after him. A good reporter would have gone after him, but I had no idea what was on the disk at the time."

"What was he wearing?" Jessie asked.

"I don't remember."

"You did see him, didn't you?" Clay asked.

Greg glared at Clay. "Yes, sir, I did. I was in a hurry, and I barely glanced at him. He slipped the disk into my hand, said the newspaper would be interested in what was on it and walked away. I've been all over the place trying to spot him, but all those homeless people look alike to me after a while. I know that's not PC."

"The disk was passed to you that way on purpose," Jessie said. "He didn't want to be remembered. Or whoever had him give you the disk didn't want him to be remembered." Absently dragging hair back from her face, she shifted gears. "What have the police told you about Taylor Drake's killer?"

"Last Stuart told me, they had no leads," Greg said. "I've been trying to get to Taylor's wife. She's avoiding us."

A news assistant tapped on the door before opening it. "Jess, Detective Mubarek's here to see you."

"I'll keep Greg company," Clay said, motioning for her to go.

After Jessie left, Greg gave Clay a wary glance. "Don't bother pumping me," Greg said. "I've already said everything I know."

"I wasn't going to pump you."

"That's your gig, isn't it? You're just here to get what you can from us small-town folks so you can make a big splash in *The New York Times*."

"Like Jess said, we're sharing information because it's imperative that we get to the real story before anyone else gets hurt. That includes you and Jess."

"Isn't that the cops' job?"

"It's our job as reporters to find out the truth, and if *The Star-News* can help uncover it, that will do good things for its credibility."

"So what are you to her anyway? You just showed up here a couple days ago, and suddenly you two are inseparable."

So that was it, Clay thought. The kid was jealous. "Isn't that mine and Jessie's business, Greg?"

"You'd better not hurt her. That's all I'm saying."

"I wouldn't dream of it."

Greg stood. "I have to get back to work. I have a deadline."

Jessie escorted Detective Mubarek to the conference room in the center of the newsroom, hating that their conversation would be on display, but, with Clay and Greg in her office, there was nowhere else to have a private talk.

The detective didn't waste time with formalities. "You snuck out of the hospital before I had a chance to talk to you," he said. His hair was wet and slicked back, a sheen of sweat making his forehead shiny. In one hand, he clasped a manila envelope.

"I didn't sneak. I had work to do," Jessie said. "Do you have any leads on who shot Officer Drake?"

His jaw clenched as he dropped the envelope on the conference table, then took his notebook out of an inside pocket of his suit jacket. "I'm here to interview *you*, Ms. Rhoades."

She took the nearest chair. "I didn't see anything," she said, unable to keep the weariness from her voice.

Following her lead, Mubarek seated himself, resting his opened notebook on his thigh. "Unfortunately, neither did anyone else." He sounded just as weary.

"Did you know him?" Jessie asked.

"He was a good cop." He glanced past her shoulder, and sadness replaced his usual sour expression. "Until this week, anyway."

"When he lied to corroborate the photographic evidence, you mean."

His gaze flew back to hers, sharpening with anger. "How long have you known he lied?"

"He told me just before he died. No one here knows yet."

His anger dulled, and he shook his head. "Well, damn."

"Why would he lie, detective?"

"I have no idea. I didn't know him well. I knew he was crazy about his kids. That's about it."

"Do you know anyone who might have a grudge against the police department?"

"Please. Anyone who's ever been arrested or even gotten a ticket. Cops aren't heroes these days. They're just pains in the ass to some people."

"This would have to be a pretty big grudge. Whoever is behind the hoax would have to be angry enough, crazy enough and smart enough to engineer a scheme like this to devastate the department."

"We'd have to go through case files," he said. "It'd take weeks, maybe months."

"We don't have that long."

"All we got from the scene is footprints in the mud and an empty shell casing." He tipped up the manila envelope, and several eight-by-ten photos spilled out that he spread across the table before them.

Jessie wished she had her glasses, but they were in her office. Even without her glasses, she could see distinct impressions in the mud made by athletic shoes. In at least one photo, a mirror image of the shoe's brand name and trademark symbol were stamped clearly in the mud. Another photo—of a brand-new athletic shoe—looked like a printout from a Web site.

"Is this the shoe that made the track?" she asked.

"According to the manufacturer."

"Are these photos on the record, detective?"

"Not just yet. We'd prefer to keep them to ourselves until we've determined it won't matter if the perp knows we have them."

"Then why are you showing them to me?"

He slid the Web site printout so that it was in front of

her. "This is the style of shoe the man who killed Officer Drake was wearing. Do you recognize it?"

"I never saw the man."

"Look at the picture. Does this style of shoe look familiar to you at all?"

It hit her what he was getting at. "You think I was the target. How else might I recognize the shoe of the killer unless I've seen him before or maybe even know him?"

"It's my job to consider every angle."

Forcing back the renewed horror that Taylor might be dead because of her, she studied the printout. There was nothing extraordinary about the style of sneaker, nothing that would have made her look twice, or even once. The colors were usual—blue and yellow stripes of varying widths and lengths overlaying white canvas. It was so ordinary that it was possible that she had a pair in that style in her own closet.

"I'm sorry. I don't pay much attention to other people's shoes," she said. "I suppose these are a pretty common style of this brand."

He nodded. "Mass produced, mass marketed. But you never know what you might turn up when you start asking around at local retailers. Some clerk somewhere might remember something that turns it all around." He shuffled the photos back into the envelope. "I suppose I don't have to tell you that if you were the target, whoever's after you is getting bolder and sloppy."

She swallowed against the tension tightening her throat. "Precautions are being taken."

Assuming a more casual demeanor, he tapped his fingertips against the folder on the table. "I did some research on you, Ms. Rhoades."

She'd figured as much but waited for him to go on.

Maybe his digging hadn't gone very deep.

"Your Social Security number belongs to a woman who's been dead for many years." He leaned forward. "In fact, I couldn't turn up anything about you beyond two years ago. Jessie Rhoades didn't exist before you showed up here."

So much for not digging very deep, she thought.

"Using a false identity is fraud," he went on. "But you already know that, don't you?"

She took a breath, held it. "All I did was borrow a number that was no longer in use."

"You still stole someone else's identity."

"Someone who didn't need it anymore," she countered.

He stared her down for several seconds, and she returned his scrutiny without wavering, aware that if she glanced away, he might assume she was lying. Then, taking a pen out of an inside jacket pocket, he uncapped it and scrawled a short line across the top page of his notebook, as if checking to make sure the pen worked. "I've been a cop a long time, Ms. Rhoades. I've had some experience with battered women."

That surprised her. "I wasn't battered."

"Let me finish."

She stilled. "All right."

"I'm not interested in hauling you in for using a false identity because you don't strike me as the kind of woman who's hiding from the law. When I approach you, you don't flinch or try to avoid me. You look me in the eye. People hiding from the law don't do that."

"Good thing I'm not shy."

He gave her a faint smile. "So if you're not hiding from the law, I have to ask myself who you are hiding from."

"You're wasting your time, detective."

"I don't consider it a waste of time if the son of a bitch who shot Officer Drake is your ex-husband."

"It isn't him," she said firmly, at the same time wondering whether David's crooked partners had managed to track her down. She wanted to believe they hadn't. They were locked up. But she wasn't naive enough to believe that hit men couldn't be hired from prison. And if the partners thought she had found out about their illegal dealings and tipped off the newspaper, leading to their subsequent imprisonment, then she imagined their quest for vengeance could be all-consuming. So if they'd found her, she would have no choice but to leave Fort Myers, change her identity and start over again. And it had become clear in just the past four days that she wanted very much to stay here. Everything she wanted was here. The realization astonished her.

Then she saw Taylor, bleeding, dying. Possibly because of her. Wasn't it her responsibility as his friend to help the authorities do everything they could to find his killer, even if it meant making herself vulnerable? If David's partners were behind Taylor's death and her severed brake line, they already knew where she was anyway. Maybe if she'd been straight with the detective the first time . . .

Suppressing that very unpleasant thought, she drew in a breath and held it. "My ex-husband is David Collins. He's a lawyer in Chicago."

Mubarek scribbled in his notebook. "Address?"

"I don't know."

"Where does he work?"

"I don't know. He used to work for a firm called Hale, Kravitz and Hale, which no longer exists. The partners are in prison for insurance fraud." She paused. "They're probably the more logical suspects."

Mubarek raised his head. "Why?"

"One of the partners threatened me because he thought I had something to do with a newspaper story that exposed the firm's fraudulent activities. I didn't run from my husband, detective. I ran from the people he worked for."

"And you think they're capable of setting up the hoax and trying to kill you?"

"The hoax seems like a stretch, but I suppose it's possible. They were ruined by a newspaper story. Maybe they'd think it would be poetic justice to ruin me the same way."

"But then why turn around and try to kill you?"

"I'd certainly go down in a blaze of non-glory," she said. "It sounds weak, but who knows? It's anyone's guess at this point who's behind everything that's going on. We don't even know who the intended target is. It could be the newspaper, the police or someone more specific. A particular officer. Someone connected to the newspaper. The list could go on."

"And you're adamant your ex couldn't be behind it?"

She shook her head. "David wasn't like that."

"Like what?"

"Vengeful."

"You'd be surprised what seemingly balanced people will do when they feel betrayed."

"How reassuring."

The detective rose. As he slid his notebook into his jacket, he awkwardly patted her shoulder. "You did the right thing telling me."

"It'd be best if no one knows you're checking up on David or his partners. If they're not behind what's happening, I don't want them knowing where I am."

"I'll be discreet." He hesitated, then cleared his throat. "We should assume at this time that the shooter hit the person he intended to kill. Probably to keep Officer Drake from telling you what he told you."

"You don't believe that absolutely or you wouldn't be hounding me about my ex."

"Considering your severed brake line, I'd be a bad cop if I didn't investigate the possibility that you were the target. However, I also have gut feelings."

"What does your gut tell you about this?"

"Officer Drake was the target."

"How can you be so sure?"

"Had you been the target, the shooter would have kept firing until he hit you."

That made sense, Jessie thought, but it didn't make her feel any better. Regardless of intent, a good man had been murdered.

Seeing Gillian Westin enter the newsroom, obviously on the hunt, Jessie stood. "I have to get to work, Detective Mubarek."

"I'll keep you posted, Ms. Rhoades."

As he left, Gillian entered the Greenhouse and closed the door. Today, she wore royal blue silk and a harried expression. "I need an update now."

"The cops story is a hoax," she said, not bothering to ease into it. "The photos are fake."

Gillian's eyebrows shot up, and instant rage flared in her steely eyes. "Are you sure? I thought the disk was missing. How did you get them checked?"

"I made a duplicate. Before he died, Officer Drake told me he was blackmailed into lying about his own and his coworkers' behavior. The entire story was a setup."

Gillian's face flushed under her carefully applied makeup. "Well, this certainly makes us look damn stupid."

As Gillian went to the telephone on the wall and

punched in an extension, Jessie stared at her, shocked that the woman didn't express at least some horror that *The Star-News*—even as just a pawn—might have played a role in the events that led to the loss of a life. Perhaps two lives, she thought, remembering the dancer who'd presumably killed herself after changing her story.

"Find Shawn and tell him I want him in the Greenhouse immediately," Gillian said into the phone. Hanging up, she looked at Jessie, and everything about her stiff carriage screamed barely restrained rage. "You've known this all afternoon. Officer Drake was killed hours ago, and you're just now getting around to telling me what he told you."

"I was uncon—"

"I don't care what you were. My point is that you failed to keep me adequately informed. I'm very angry, Jessie. This newspaper may not mean squat to you, but it's my life. I'll protect it in any way necessary, and if that means I have to weed out the untrustworthy people on my staff, I won't hesitate. Are you following me here?"

"I didn't deliberately keep you out of the loop, Gillian."

"Did I ask for an excuse?"

"I wasn't offering one."

"I don't like your tone."

Jessie started to respond but thought better of it. When Gillian was determined to be mad at someone, there was nothing that could be said or done to soothe her.

Apparently satisfied that she had made her point, Gillian checked her watch. "How long do we have before our first-edition deadline?"

"About four hours."

"That'll have to be enough time to fashion an appropriately contrite story for tomorrow's paper." Gillian whirled as the conference room door opened behind her, but instead of the person she'd expected, her father entered.

Jessie was never more glad to see anyone than she was to see Richard Westin walk through that door. Gillian, on the other hand, had the self-righteous bluster drained right out of her. "Daddy," she said, and it was as if the sharp edges of her voice had been sanded down to a satiny finish.

Richard shut the door. "Hello, Gillian." He nodded at Jessie. "Jess." He looked better than he had a year ago. His complexion, which when he'd retired had been drawn and sallow, was tan and healthy from hours on the golf course. His pure white hair was probably as thick now as it'd been when he was twenty. He looked thinner, too, in khaki slacks and a green-and-soft-yellow plaid golf shirt. Retirement was definitely agreeing with him.

"What are you doing here, Daddy?" Gillian asked.

"I called him," Jessie said. "On my way in from the hospital. I figured we would need his expertise today."

Gillian forced a smile that under normal circumstances would have sported fangs. "That was good thinking, Jessie. You saved me the trouble." To her father, she said, "We were discussing what to do about the new developments in the corrupt cops scandal."

"Let's start with not calling them corrupt cops anymore, shall we?" Richard said.

"Well, of course," Gillian said, laughing nervously.

Brushing by his daughter, Richard took Jessie's un-injured hand in his and searched her face. His eyes, the color of faded denim, were filled with concern. "How are you doing, Jess? I'm so sorry about your friend, Officer Drake. I understand he was a good man."

Her throat constricted with emotion that she had to fight to contain. He was so different from his daughter that she had a tough time believing Gillian was his flesh and blood.

175

"Thank you, I'm fine," she said, relieved that her voice didn't crack.

"You're not fine," he said with a fatherly smile. "But you're doing a stand-up job of faking it." Glancing at her cast, he asked, "How long are you stuck with that?"

Before she could respond, Gillian cleared her throat. "Our deadline is four hours off," she said. "Perhaps we should get this discussion under way."

Pulling out a chair, Richard gestured for Jessie to have a seat, then took one himself, leaving Gillian to fend for herself. Fury on a controlled burn, Gillian impatiently peered through the glass out into the newsroom. "Where is Shawn? He should have been here already."

"I asked everyone to give the three of us a few minutes," Richard said. "If that's okay with you."

"That's fine, Daddy," she said, coming to the table. "In fact, perhaps you'd prefer it be just the two of us. I'm sure Jessie needs to get her staff organized."

"No, I want Jess to stay right where she is," Richard said. "Her judgment is impeccable, and we need all the help we can get right now." He flashed a winning smile at his daughter. "Don't you agree?"

Jessie was wincing inwardly. He seemed to delight in taunting Gillian, but Jessie figured she'd end up paying for it later. Still, if not for the grim circumstances, she would have been enjoying watching her boss squirm.

"Of course, I agree," Gillian said. "I tap Jessie's solid news judgment several times a day. In fact, before you came in, Jessie and I were strategizing how to handle the stories for tomorrow's paper."

"Then let's pick up that thread," Richard said. "Jess, why don't you start?"

Chapter 15

Clay flipped on the lights. As he dropped his keys on the table by the door, he glanced back. Jessie stood just inside the door, one hand in a pocket, the one with the cast hanging at her side. Fatigue had drawn her features taut, etching lines of strain on either side of her nose. The past several hours had been hard on her. Emotions at *The Star-News* had been running high—grief over the death of a man many on the staff had known and liked, shock about the revelation of the hoax, concern about the future of careers and the newspaper.

In the midst of it all, Jessie had been a rock, and Clay had admired the way she'd kept it together. She had not once raised her voice or let impatience lace her tone. She'd been entirely professional. Now, though, her calm detachment was beginning to concern him. When she should have been starting to let down her guard, she seemed to be even more on edge.

"Can I get you anything?" he asked. "Coffee? Water?"

"I'd like to take a shower, if you don't mind."

"I'll get you some towels."

After he'd set her up with what she needed, Clay went to the kitchen. It was just before two a.m., and he was starving. He figured Jessie had to be as hungry.

He was cutting up apples and cheese for a light snack when he noticed he had yet to hear the shower. Wiping his hands on a towel, he went into the hall and was about to knock on the bathroom door to check on her when he heard it. A muted sob, as if she had buried her face in a towel to muffle it.

His arm dropped to his side, and his throat constricted as he wondered what he should do, if anything. He wanted to fling open the door and gather her into his arms, but he knew that if he intruded on her most private moment, he more than likely would damage whatever headway he'd made with her. Plus, she hadn't had one moment to herself since she had awakened from the sedative, no opportunity to begin to process the horror of Taylor's death. Perhaps what she needed most right now was to be alone.

This time, he decided, he would let her avoid him. Besides, seeing her cry would tear him up, and he'd need all the resolve he could muster to deal with her stubbornness in the next couple of days. A cop-out of mega proportions, he admitted, but also reality. He stayed where he was, feeling like an impotent and cowardly jerk, until the shower came on.

Back in the kitchen, his hands not quite steady, he finished slicing fruit and cheese, arranged the food on plates, then opened a bottle of chilled chardonnay. He was pouring wine into two glasses when Jessie wandered into the kitchen.

Except for some puffiness around the eyes, all signs of the crying jag were gone, and seeing that she had a firm grip on her composure eased his jitters. She'd slipped into a pair of slim gray shorts and a white tank top, her damp hair combed back. He thought she'd never looked sexier.

"You've been busy," she said, taking in the plates of food. "It looks yummy."

He handed her a glass over the island. "We had a date tonight."

"How could I forget?" She sipped wine, her gaze meeting his over the rim, then flitting away.

Flustered anew by the nerves in her glance, he gestured toward the living room. "Make yourself comfortable, and I'll bring this stuff out there."

As she settled onto the sofa, she watched him balance two plates, a box of crackers and a wine glass. "Want some help?" she asked.

"Think I got it. Thanks."

"You're so stubborn. Sometimes I don't know what I'm going to do with you."

He saw the teasing light in her eyes, and his relief grew. "You're one to talk."

The corners of her mouth curved before she rubbed the back of her neck with her good hand.

"Neck ache?" Clay asked.

"A little."

After depositing the plates and wine on the coffee table, he crossed behind the sofa.

She straightened, realizing his intentions. "Oh, you don't have to—"

"Just be quiet and let me." Sliding his hands up under her hair, he settled them on her shoulders and began to lightly massage. He expected her to continue to protest, but instead she dropped her head forward to allow him better access. As his fingers kneaded, he admired the curve of her neck, the smooth line of her jaw. Her skin felt silken under the pads of his fingers, her damp hair curling against the backs of his hands.

She smelled like his soap, his shampoo, which, he realized, was incredibly arousing. Then she moaned, and the soft, guttural sound was more provocative than if she had been the one putting her hands on him.

He needed conversation, he decided. Now.

"Gillian was hard on you," he said.

She stiffened under his fingers, and he regretted breaking the comfortable silence, especially with work talk, but he sensed that she needed to unload. A good cry did wonders, but venting would help more. Plus, there were some issues they needed to talk about.

"I can't blame her," Jessie said, a trace of drowsiness creeping into her tone despite her tense muscles. "Of everyone at the paper, she looks the worst because she's in charge."

"What about the graphics guy? Does he still have a job?"

"She'll probably decide overnight to fire him. Even though she put incredible pressure on him to work fast, which was why he examined only the photos we used. Whoever worked them over probably anticipated that. In fact, they probably counted on us screwing up under the gun, and that's why they gave us the disk so late in the day on a Sunday. That made it harder to find outside people to authenticate the pictures." Keeping her eyes closed, she sipped her wine. "You're so good at that," she murmured with a sigh.

Clay searched for something to say to chase away the images in his head that were getting more explicit the longer he touched her. "Gillian is certainly an intimidating woman."

"Tell me about it. She makes me sweat."

"You're kidding."

"Nope. She scares the hell out of me."

He couldn't help but chuckle. "So let me get this straight. You kicked an intruder's ass by flipping him through your coffee table, but your boss frightens you so much you perspire."

"You got it."

"Why?"

Her shoulders lifted slightly under his hands. "She's unpredictable. And I suppose I resent the fact that I feel I can't walk out and never look back."

"Which wouldn't be like you."

"Actually, it's very much like me." She sounded sad.

"You don't strike me as the walking-out type."

"You don't know me very well."

A thud outside the glass doors leading to the deck startled them both. "What was that?" Jessie asked.

"It's probably just the guard," Clay said, reluctant to leave her to go to the door.

"Oh. I forgot there's a guard."

Sliding open the door, he greeted the tall, lanky, sheepish-looking man. "You okay, Tom?"

"Sorry about that, Mr. Christopher," Tom said. Despite the warm evening, he wore a dark suit. His short dark hair was precisely combed. "I'm not used to the terrain yet. Knocked my knee into the side of the deck."

"Are you hurt?"

"No, sir."

"Okay. Is your backup going to be here soon?"

"Yes, sir. He'll be here until morning, and then I'll be back."

"Excellent. Good night." Closing the door, Clay turned to see that Jessie was on her feet, looking awkward. His hope of picking up where they'd left off evaporated. "False alarm," he said.

"He must be costing you a fortune."

He crossed to her, wishing he could rewind to the point where she'd been relaxing under his palms. "Don't worry. I have some money in the bank that I didn't know what to do

181

with. This seemed like the most worthy thing to spend it on." He didn't tell her that it was the insurance money he'd received after Ellen's death, that he'd been unable to touch it until now. It would be too weird for her, and he already hated that whenever he mentioned his dead wife, Jessie's eyes grew distant and guarded, as if the specter of Ellen quashed whatever was growing between them.

Jessie tilted her head back to meet his gaze. "I don't know how to thank you."

"Thank me by staying alive," he said.

Then, because the opportunity presented itself, and because he'd wanted to for so long, he cupped the back of her head and brought her mouth to his.

The caress of his lips was gentle but firm, with a hint of hunger. A knot formed in Jessie's stomach, loosened as his lips worked hers, grew warm and liquid. Her fingers curved around his wrist, and she felt the soft hairs on his arm, felt the leather of his watchband, felt her own knuckles brush her cheek. Every sensation seemed to make her ears ring, as if she had just bitten into a pear that was at once incredibly sweet and achingly tangy.

Just as suddenly as he'd reached for her, Clay let her go.

A tiny moan of distress escaped her, and she caught herself leaning toward him.

She thought he'd stepped back, but then she realized that only his lips and his hand had been touching her. Yet, she had felt him everywhere, as if his hard, muscled body had been pressed intimately against hers.

She fought for balance, fought for calm. He was watching her, waiting, and she couldn't form a thought. His kiss, she realized slowly, had stunned her.

How silly, she thought. It was just a kiss.

Brushing her fingertips over her lips, she felt a smile grow. But *what* a kiss.

He also began to smile. "Well," he said.

She moistened her lips, and the breath lodged in her chest when his eyes darkened with hunger. "Well, indeed."

He did step back then, shoving his hands into the back pockets of his jeans. "You know, I'm thinking this snack isn't going to be enough. Should I order a pizza?"

She wasn't the least bit hungry. Not for pizza, anyway.

"Pizza sounds great," she said.

Thirty minutes later, the pizza was due at any moment. Curled on the sofa, Jessie concentrated on the sound of the shower down the hall. She imagined Clay in there, water streaming down his ridged and ripply body. As the water went silent, she wondered whether he had tan lines.

When he walked into the room, using a hand towel to dry his hair, she sat up, stifling a sharp gasp. A towel was wrapped haphazardly around his hips. Fine rivulets of water trickled down his smooth, hairless chest and muscled stomach. She saw no tan lines. Yet.

"I was wondering," he said, apparently unaware of the surplus of color in her cheeks. "How long have you known Greg?"

She forced herself to focus on his face, though that had its own distractions, between the dimple shadowed by light beard and the way wet tendrils of dark blond hair clung to his forehead.

"Uh, he started at the paper about six months ago."

"Where was he before then?"

"Grad school."

"How much do you know about his background?"

It registered where his line of questioning was leading,

and rising defensiveness made her restless. Pushing off the sofa, she paced behind it. Greg couldn't be behind the hoax. He was a sweet kid, eager for her mentoring, never moody or cranky, always up for the next challenge. "Greg's a good reporter," she said. "He doesn't have to manufacture a story to make an impression."

"He's inexperienced. I hate to say it, but he really has no business being on such a huge story. His investigative skills—"

"Are pretty good," she cut in. "He's the best reporter I've got. *The Star-News* is a family-owned, midsize newspaper. We don't have big-time reporters like you lining up to apply for jobs. I'm lucky to have someone as dedicated as Greg on my staff."

Clay looped the hand towel around the back of his neck. "Maybe we shouldn't talk about this now."

She drew in a breath, held it. "I'm sorry. I know I'm defensive. It's just that he's the one I believe in most, the one who keeps me from becoming a complete cynic about the newspaper business."

"It's understandable. But he could have come to *The Star-News* with an agenda that you know nothing about. For that matter, anyone in the newsroom could have."

"Well, I'd rather start with the more obvious people," she said.

"You see, I'd rather get the people closest to you out of the way first. Then maybe you could stop being defensive and focus."

Shocked by his impatience, she watched him walk back down the hall into his bedroom. She followed. "This isn't easy, you know. We're talking about people I care about, people I work with."

"I didn't say it's easy," he said, his back to her. Dropping the towel from around his waist, he started to pull on clean clothing.

Jessie didn't hear what he said after that. She was too busy trying to swallow and not succeeding because the inside of her mouth was suddenly as dry as uncooked pasta. Tan lines.

Buttoning his jeans, he faced her, his expression quizzical.

She fumbled for her train of thought. It was too warm in this tiny room, she thought. In fact, it was downright sweltering. Pivoting, she stalked back into the living room. "Okay, fine. Let's dissect the people who work the closest with me," she said, nervous energy making her talk too fast now. "Stuart. Maybe he wants to destroy the place he blames for making him so miserable. Shawn. He's made no secret about how much he hates Gillian. There are any number of bitter, disgruntled people in the production department who work long hours for little pay and no recognition. Hell, maybe there's a subscriber who's ticked that his paper is thrown into the bushes every morning."

"This isn't getting us anywhere," Clay said. "You can't take it so personally."

She faced him, relieved to see that he'd donned a T-shirt. "Of course I take it personally. We're talking about my co-workers. I work with them every day. Don't you think I would have picked up on something in my day-to-day contact with—" She broke off. She'd had day-to-day contact with her husband and had never suspected he was cheating on her.

The heat inside her chilled. Needing the barrier between them, she retreated behind the sofa, where she braced her good hand on the back of it. After everything that had happened, her defenses were in shreds, so it was only natural that emotions would sneak up on her. The problem was there seemed to be too much to feel at once. Grief. Guilt. Anger. Apprehension. Desire. She couldn't process it all after two years of suppressing every little hiccup of feeling for fear of where it would lead. Plus, she was beyond tired, her body bruised and battered. It was a wonder she wasn't a quivering mass on the floor at his feet.

"I'm sorry," she said. "I'm frustrated, and I'm taking it out on you. That isn't right."

He was beside her before she'd heard him move, and when he rubbed a gentle hand up her arm, she almost let herself lean in. He gave comfort so easily. She admired him for that, wished she could be more like him.

"You're tired," he said. "Give yourself a break."

She let out a shuddery breath. "None of this makes sense if it's someone at the newspaper, Clay. It goes against everything we're about. Being the public's watchdog, seeking and reporting the truth. If the readers don't trust us, we're nothing."

"Not everyone has such a black-and-white view of what our job is," he said. "A lot of people think we're just here to sell ads and fill in the spaces around them with news, to make money. And, frankly, if the business weren't profitable, we wouldn't have jobs."

"But it's still our job to fight the good fight. Truth is our commodity."

"There are messed up people in every business." He smiled gently, catching her chin between his thumb and forefinger. "You called yourself a cynic, but you're really an idealist."

He looked like he might kiss her again, but the doorbell rang.

"Pizza's here," he said, releasing her. "I saw the disappointment in your eyes when the doorbell rang before I could kiss you."

She held his gaze a moment, then smiled. "That was relief."

He was chuckling as he went to the door.

She rounded the sofa and sat, retrieving her glass of wine and taking a long swallow. The man rattled the hell out of her. She wanted him to kiss her, to touch her. At the same time, she wanted to run as far from him as she could.

He detoured into the kitchen with the pizza. When he returned, he had plates, napkins and a six-pack of Coke piled on top of two pizza boxes.

"Good Lord, you are hungry," Jessie said with a laugh.

"Half of this is for Tom. Would you mind grabbing the door for me?"

Meeting him at the door leading to the deck, she slid it open. The air that greeted them was warm and thick with the salty scent of the beach. Clay slipped by her, and she watched him exchange pleasantries with the man charged with guarding her life. The two men were easy with each other, more buddy than boss and employee. Clearly, the guard liked Clay, this man he had just met. Clay handed over one of the pizzas and a couple of Cokes, gracefully receiving the guard's thanks before going back into the house.

"That was nice of you," she said.

Closing the door, he gestured toward the sofa. "Let's eat. I'm ready to gnaw a knuckle."

As they sat on the floor at the base of the sofa, he plopped a messy piece of pizza on a plate and handed it to her. "Dig in." When she hesitated, he frowned. "What? Don't tell me you don't like pepperoni."

"No, I was just thinking."

"Thinking what?"

She shrugged, scooping the slice up for a bite. It was hot and gooey and delicious. She wiped her mouth. "Why does pizza taste so much better after two in the morning?"

"No fair dodging. Tell me what you were thinking."

She reached for her wine glass. "You're just such a nice guy."

"That surprises you?"

"Maybe a little."

He licked a cheesy finger, amused. "Maybe you need to elaborate."

"I knew that any man who risks life and limb to pull a damsel in distress out of a burning car would be a good guy, but I suppose I also thought a one-time Pulitzer contender would be a bit of a pit bull."

"You haven't seen me in action."

"I doubt your approach bears any resemblance to a pit bull. My bet is you charm your sources until they spill any and all information you want. In fact, I'd bet you're so good at it that many of those same sources consider themselves among your closest friends."

The bemusement in his expression shifted, darkened. "Actually, I don't have many close friends. Not anymore, anyway."

That set her back. He seemed like the type of person who'd have more friends than he had time to socialize with them all. "What happened?" she asked.

"After Ellen died, I had a hard time being around people. I felt as if I was balanced on this emotional ledge, and any mention of her or expression of sympathy would send me plunging off. The idea of that plunge terrified me. It was easier to avoid contact with people who knew her, which, of course, was all of our friends."

Jessie set her plate aside, her appetite gone. She couldn't

imagine what it had been like for him then, or even now. "I'm sorry. I didn't mean to—"

"It's okay." He drank some wine. "Tell me something about you now. Where do you call home?"

"You mean besides my trashed apartment off McGregor Boulevard?"

"There you go dodging again. Why can't you ever deliver a straight answer?"

"Sorry," she said, smiling. She figured he already knew that she dodged when the question had a tough, or emotional, answer. "We moved a lot when I was a kid, so home, to me, was more of a person than a location." It was a warm voice on the telephone, a sweet note in the mail, someone who would always listen and agree with her even when she was wrong.

"Your mother?" Clay asked.

"Yes." She could almost smell her mom's oatmeal cookies, could hear her admonishments to have a cookie. "Put some meat on those skinny bones you didn't get from me," she'd say, even though she herself was as thin as a stick figure.

"She passed away?" he asked.

"Several years ago."

"I'm sorry."

"It was peaceful. In her sleep." She balanced the base of her glass on her thigh. "There must have been three hundred people at her funeral. She had so many friends. Good ones, too. Not just casual acquaintances. Everyone loved her."

He cocked his head. "It must have been hard for you to leave those people behind when you came here."

She didn't look up. "I didn't know any of them. Not well, anyway."

"But there were other people you left behind."

She swallowed, wanting to laugh, or cry, at how pathetic her life had been. She hadn't liked that life, hadn't liked herself in it. She still didn't know whether the sterility of it had been a product of who she was or whether she had become a product of that emptiness. The truth was, she had used David and his debacle as an excuse to escape a barren existence. "I left my husband and a newsroom full of colleagues I didn't really know, though I'd worked with them for years," she said, setting aside her plate and glass. "I probably couldn't recall half their names right now. I'm not nearly as nice as you. Ask Mel."

"You did the right thing with Mel," he said. "She wouldn't have walked away from you if you hadn't forced her to."

"Did you see the look on her face? I hurt her."

"Because you love her. Don't you think she'll understand that?"

She stopped a tear with an impatient swipe of a finger. "This is how tired I am. I'm getting weepy."

"It's okay."

"Of course, you'd say that."

He put an arm around her and gathered her close. "Will you tell me about him?" he asked.

She'd started to relax against him, but now she tensed and pushed away. He let her go, and as she stood, she regretted breaking the contact. At the same time, she was relieved. The conflicting feelings frustrated her. She wanted him. Physically, it was an ache that was building. But emotionally, he scared the hell out of her. He wouldn't be one of those lovers who took what he wanted and walked away. He would demand everything from her, and she feared that in the end, she would disappoint him.

Just like she'd disappointed David.

Picking up their dirty dishes, she carried them into the kitchen. "My ex-husband is not trying to kill me, Clay."

He followed with the pizza box. "How can you be so sure?"

"Because I knew him for thirteen years." She set the plates down harder than she'd intended. "I would think that if there were some homicidal tendencies in him, I would have caught a glimpse of them at some point during all those years. Our marriage failed, and I cut off all contact with him. End of story."

Clay dropped the box on the counter and paused before her. "I want to take the son of a bitch out into a parking lot and beat the living crap out of him for hurting you."

Such violent sentiment coming from such a gentle man surprised her. Moved, she touched his cheek, shivering at the scrap of razor stubble against her palm. "That's so romantic."

He chuckled, then, curving his hand around her fingers, he brought them to his lips for a light kiss. "You'll tell me about him eventually, won't you? When you're steadier?"

She nodded, catching her breath when he slipped an arm around her waist and drew her closer. His lips captured hers, tilting her head back and sending it whirling. She clutched at his shoulders for support, shocked and thrilled by the sensation of his mouth on hers.

Just as suddenly, he released her. Aching and wanting more, Jessie swayed. That was the second time he'd done only that. It frustrated her. She wanted more. So much more.

"You're so tired you're about to drop," he said, his voice husky. "Come."

Taking her hand, he led her into the bedroom. After

he'd folded back the covers, he turned to her and started to say something. But she stepped into him and covered his mouth with hers. The kiss quickly deepened, heated. And ended too soon when he placed his hands on her arms and set her back. Resting the top of her head against his chin, she tried to gather her scattered senses. A simple kiss had never felt so complex.

Clay's ragged breathing made his chest rise and fall rapidly. "As much as I want you right now, you need sleep more."

She pressed her lips to his throat, felt his body respond to her tongue against his skin. "Please don't tell me you're going to be a gentleman."

"Trust me, I'm a damn frustrated gentleman. Come on, into bed."

Crawling in, she smiled as he drew the covers over her. "You're so sweet," she said. "Sleep with me."

He laughed, but it was strained. "I'll keep you awake."

"You'll make me feel safe."

"But you might not be safe," he teased.

"I'll take my chances."

He slipped under the covers with her, and she let herself snuggle against him. Closing her eyes, she breathed in his clean, male scent. "You smell so good," she said.

"So do you." His voice had gone tight.

She smiled. "Sorry."

"Sleep."

"Okay."

And she dropped off.

Chapter 16

Clay opened his eyes reluctantly and looked at the clock. Six a.m. He lay still for a moment, wondering what had awakened him and hoping it hadn't done the same to Jessie. Then, anticipating the feel of her warm and pliant body and having a suggestion for how they might spend the morning together once she was well rested, he shifted onto his back, where he discovered he was alone in the bed.

Disappointed, he sat up and rubbed his eyes. They'd slipped between the covers less than four hours ago. So much for well rested, he thought, as he pushed aside covers and went in search of his stubborn guest.

He found her making coffee in the kitchen, still clad in the gray shorts and tank top. Pausing to lean a shoulder against the door, he took the opportunity to check her out. Her bare legs were muscled and firm but still feminine, and the tank emphasized the subtly sculpted muscles in her arms. It surprised him that she took the time to work out when her job seemed to be the focus of her life. But he supposed that she was so disciplined that when she decided to do something, she made the time to do it.

As if sensing him, she turned and flashed an apologetic smile. "Hey. Did I wake you? I was trying to be quiet."

"Don't you need more sleep?"

Shrugging, she shook her cast-free hand as if to rid herself of excess energy. "I'm too wired."

"And coffee is the obvious cure."

His comment seemed to make no impression as she retrieved a cup. "Want some?"

"Not for at least two hours."

She poured a cup, her back to him. "I'm thinking I'll head into the office early to get a jump on how we're going to follow Taylor's shooting."

"It's barely after six."

"I work better when no one else is around. No interruptions."

Walking up behind her, he snaked his arms around her waist, stilling her nervous hands by lacing their fingers. The hard edge of her cast pressed against his knuckles. "Did you wake up and start thinking too much about us?" he said softly near her ear, his chin resting on her shoulder.

He felt a shudder go through her and was pleased that he could have that effect on her.

"I'm sorry," she said on a breathless laugh. "You were saying?"

He turned her in his arms and cupped her face, intrigued by the blue rings encircling her gray irises. Her eyes were dark with anxiety, and something else that he yearned to stoke into a raging fire. "You need to relax," he said, and touched his mouth to hers.

She answered with heat, her lips parting to let him in, and he forced himself to go slow, to leisurely explore her taste, her textures, even as his body screamed at him to take, to ravage. Such need was new to him. He'd never wanted to touch a woman so badly, had never been so desperate to arouse a woman's passionate response.

"I'm pretty sure this isn't going to relax me," she said against his mouth.

He swept her up into his arms. "Sounds like a challenge to me," he said.

194

Carrying her, laughing, into the bedroom, he deposited her on the bed. Before he could straighten to begin shedding clothes, she wound her arms around his neck, arching toward him. The soft murmur of longing in her throat nearly undid him, and he caught his hands in her hair, his mouth roaming over her face, down to her throat and back up to her mouth.

Lowering himself to the bed, he let his hands glide over her smooth, warm skin. Her muscles quivered beneath the gentle caress of his fingertips, and as he kissed her, he stroked her breast through her shirt, teasing until it peaked and her lips trembled open under his.

Go slow, he told himself. Go slow.

But desire was bursting inside him, and he needed, needed.

Jessie gasped when his mouth closed over the tip of her breast through the cotton. His hands, his mouth, seemed to be everywhere all at once, stroking, tasting, possessing. Dizzying sensations flowed over her from every angle until she ached to touch him, to have him.

She fumbled at the hem of his T-shirt, seeking unimpeded skin, feverish for the feel of his flesh under her fingertips, her tongue. She swore softly when the cast made her awkward, but then, thankfully, she plunged her bare hand under the material. Before she could do much more than glide her palm over his heated skin, his fingers grazed the inside of her thigh and she tensed under him, shocked by the ragged moan that slipped out of her. He'd only just touched her.

Splaying a hand against her lower back, he held her steady against him as he caressed and stroked. She fought air, thick and hot, into her lungs, her head spinning when he drew her shorts and panties off and resumed the on-slaught. All she could do was cling to him, stunned when a powerful wave of pleasure buffeted her.

While her body quaked with aftershocks, he kissed her, his tongue toying with hers, his hand teasing and coaxing until she danced on the edge again, her muscles rigid with tension. He would have sent her flying over another peak if she hadn't gasped at him. "Stop. Wait."

His hands stilled as his brows drew together in confusion. "Stop?"

"You're still dressed," she managed, her voice strangled. "I want you naked."

"I love a woman who knows what she wants," he said, shucking his shirt, his eyes glittering with playfulness as he shimmied out of his shorts and briefs. Leaning over, he groped through the drawer of his bedside table and pulled out a condom that he quickly slipped on while his gaze held hers. "You know, you're not exactly naked yet yourself," he said.

Straddling him, she rose up to pull the tank over her head. He went still as she tossed it aside, and she looked down to see his jaw slack. His Adam's apple rose and fell as his ravenous gaze drank in her breasts.

"Wow," he murmured, reaching up to caress and mold.

Smiling, she settled more firmly astride him, dropping her head back with a groan when she felt his need press against her. "Oh God, you feel so good."

He caught at her hips with his hands, shifted her so that all he had to do was thrust to be inside her. But he hesi-tated, as if he wanted her to take the final plunge. That was fine with her, and linking her fingers with his, she sank down onto him, closing her eyes and biting into her lip as he filled and stretched her.

She immediately began to shudder, breathing his name through clenched teeth, then gasping when he rolled her under him. She dug her fingers into his lower back, drawing him as close, as deep, as possible.

When her body convulsed under him, he followed an instant later.

As they lay tangled together on the bed, breathing heavily, Jessie's mind was blank. There was something she'd been planning to do before he'd swept her into his arms and carried her to bed for the most mind-blowing sex she'd ever experienced. What was it?

Stirring, he cradled her against him and pressed a kiss to her shoulder. "Think you might be able to get some sleep now?"

"Not quite. Talk about adrenaline surge." New energy pulsed through her blood as she remembered that an hour ago she'd been on her way to work.

"I was so sure my studliness would be as potent as any sleeping pill," he said.

"Oh, your studliness is plenty potent. How about that coffee?" Bounding out of bed, she dodged his attempt to snatch her back to him.

"Where are you going?" He turned on his side, propping his head on his hand. "We haven't cuddled."

She pulled his T-shirt over her head and let it fall to her knees, delighted that it smelled like him. It sent a renewed ache through her. "I have work to do."

"Jess, come on."

"But first, a shower." She cast him a suggestive look. "Care to join me?"

He hopped up. "Don't have to ask me once."

When Jessie finally made it to the office several hours

later, her bodyguard, Tom, was at her side. He looked every bit like a Secret Service agent in his dark blue suit and mirrored sunglasses. Despite his height—his lanky frame towered above her by at least a foot and a half—his presence wasn't hulking or intrusive. She guessed he was about forty, though there appeared to be no silver in his short dark hair and no lines wrinkled his tanned face—probably because he never smiled or made any other expression.

She wondered how her co-workers would react to him, then decided it didn't matter. There was no way she would be getting rid of him anytime soon. And, surprisingly, she took some comfort in his presence as she walked into a newsroom that may or may not be the workplace of someone who was trying to kill her.

At the moment, that newsroom was abuzz with activity. Telephones rang non-stop as Jessie dropped her purse in her office and grabbed a legal pad and pen to take to the first news meeting of the day. When she entered the Greenhouse, all the other department heads—features, sports, business and graphics—were already seated in the comfy chairs that surrounded the boardroom table. Tom took up a position just inside the door, facing outward so he could scan the newsroom through the glass walls, his hands clasped before him, his feet planted slightly apart.

Gillian didn't acknowledge Jessie's entrance. "Callers seem to be evenly divided," she was saying. "Half commend *The Star-News* for its honest reporting on the hoax, and half condemn it for being so easily duped. I suppose it could be worse." Glancing up, her icy gaze landing on Tom's back, she said, "Who is that?"

"Bodyguard," Jessie said. "He'll stay out of the way."

Without missing a beat, Gillian said, "I don't want any disruptions."

"He's not here to disrupt anything," Jessie said.

"See that he doesn't." Gillian gestured around the table. "I called the meeting early today to discuss where we're going with the follow-up on Officer Drake's shooting and the revelation of the hoax. I'm sure another editor can fill you in. Mostly what I'm looking for is reaction from residents and every public official we can get to."

"What about a speculative piece?" Jessie asked as she jotted notes.

"No speculation," Gillian said flatly. "It's up to the police to find out who tried to damage them. When they do, we'll report it. Until then, assigning blame has no place in *The Star-News*. In fact, I don't want this story on the front page again until the police have a suspect."

Jessie gaped at her. "This is the biggest news of the day, hell, the decade. Just because we're part of it doesn't mean we should downplay it."

Gillian cut her a withering look. "I'm not paying you to think, Jessie. I'm paying you to do as I tell you. If you have a problem with that, there's the door."

Silence settled over the meeting. Jessie kept her face neutral, but she knew her rage showed because suddenly Gillian avoided her gaze. "Comments? Observations?"

No one dared to breathe.

"Fine. One more thing, and we're done." She passed a stack of papers to Shawn at her right. "Take one, pass it down."

As each editor glanced at the sheet, an even greater sense of doom descended on the meeting.

"This is our circulation report for the week so far," Gillian said.

Of all the reports department heads had to read, the circulation report was the most traumatic. It kept a tally of the newspaper's daily circulation and compared it with the circulation the same day the year before. If the current number on any given day was less than last year's, there was hell to pay. It meant that fewer people had been compelled to buy the paper that day, and Gillian held the firm belief that that compulsion was directly linked to the day's news content.

Jessie agreed with her up to the point where Gillian held her responsible for the day's news content when Gillian herself often dictated what that content would be. Jessie had endured many a tongue-lashing for the steadily dropping circulation, which Gillian blamed on Jessie's staff not delivering the kind of interesting reporting that sold newspapers. And if Jessie's staff wasn't delivering, that meant Jessie wasn't being a good manager.

With growing anxiety, she scanned the numbers. As she'd expected, circulation had begun an upward trajectory on Monday. Unfortunately, this time it was a bad thing.

"As you all know, we broke the cops story on Monday," Gillian said. "I wish we could have enjoyed this report before the story became the joke that it is now, because the numbers are pretty damn good."

Here it comes, Jessie thought wearily, and sat back.

"I'm sharing this with you," Gillian went on, "because I want you to see that these are the numbers we should be striving for every week. If we're going to save this newspaper, we need stories like the cops scandal—real ones, that is—every day. The news is out there, but we have to dig it up. Reporters have to beat the bushes."

Editors exchanged looks. They'd heard this speech so many times that each of them could repeat it, word for word.

"Jessie," Gillian said.

Jessie relaxed her facial muscles. "When?"

Gillian faltered, thrown. "When what?"

"You want to meet with the city reporters today to talk about enterprise and what's going on with each of their beats. Morning or afternoon?"

Gillian's eyes hardened to black ice. "Two-thirty. That gives us an hour before the afternoon news meeting. How does that work for you?"

"Fine." Jessie knew she'd crossed a line, and for a moment, she had a hard time giving a damn. The woman had become so predictable in her lectures and edicts that she had become a caricature. And she seemed to have no idea how unimpressed her managers were, or how much nearly every one of them despised her.

Shoving her chair back, Gillian stood. "We're done here. Jessie, stay where you are."

Jessie's co-workers couldn't seem to clear the room fast enough. Each gave her a sympathetic smile on the way out. A few even mouthed "good luck" at her.

Gillian cast Tom, who was staying put, an annoyed glance. "I'd prefer it if your friend would give us some space, Jessie."

Jessie carefully checked her aggravation at the way Gillian avoided addressing the man directly, as if it were beneath her. When he glanced at her, Jessie gave him an apologetic look. "Would you mind, Tom?"

He didn't budge as he searched her face as if for a secret message. "You're sure?"

"You can keep an eye on things through the glass," Jessie said.

Gillian shut the door behind him, and Jessie saw he positioned himself so he could clearly see her. Clay would have been pleased.

Gillian didn't speak until she'd seated herself. "Your attitude lately troubles me, Jessie. I don't appreciate the way you've been challenging my authority."

Jessie squared her shoulders, refusing to bristle at the woman's patronizing tone. "Isn't that what we're here for, Gillian? To challenge each other?"

"Yes, of course. This newsroom is a democracy, after all." She smiled as if she had no idea that her actions contradicted the statement. Sitting back, she began to tap her pen on the table. "I understand that the way we handled the police story bothers you. I take full responsibility for dropping the ball on that one."

Jessie kept silent. The woman sounded reasonable, but Jessie knew better than to let herself get sucked in.

Gillian crossed her legs, frowning. Still, she tapped. "We made a bad decision by going with the story without having the photos more thoroughly examined. You were right, and I was wrong. But I hope you're not the kind of professional who doesn't allow other professionals to make mistakes and learn from them."

Jessie awaited the punch line. Her boss never ended a conversation with herself in the underdog position. Coming out on top was the objective of her every move.

"What I'm getting at," Gillian went on, "is this: even though you were right and I was wrong this one time, I am still your boss. You still answer to me. My error, no matter how grave, does not make us equals. Is that clear?"

"Of course."

Gillian leaned forward. "I know you don't respect me, Jessie. That's become abundantly clear in the past two weeks. In fact, I know you've never respected me. You think I got this job because my father handed it to me. But I worked hard for it. So if you ever again put me in the posi-

tion of having to defend my decisions in front of my own father or my own staff, I'll terminate your employment here.
Do we understand each other?"

Jessie had to fight to keep from rolling her eyes. Her boss
seemed to live to pull rank. It was sickening. "May I say
something for the record?"

"Certainly."

"I would appreciate it if you wouldn't assume what I
think. You're almost always wrong." Jessie rose. "May I be
excused now?"

Fury bloomed in bright red spots on Gillian's cheeks. "I
would hope that you're not foolish enough to not have your
résumé together."

Jessie stopped at the door. "You know damn well that I
have no résumé. I'm sure your father told you the circumstances under which he hired me."

"Yes, that was unfortunate. But he's not in charge here
anymore. I am. He cut you a major break. I'd hate for you
to blow it, because I'm not a big fan of Jessie Rhoades these
days."

Jessie clenched her jaw, no longer caring if her anger
showed. "Do you need me for anything else? I have a full
day."

"No. Have a good one."

Jessie gently closed the door behind her when she would
have preferred to slam it so hard the glass shattered. Tom
fell in step a few paces behind her.

In her office, she sat and tried to talk herself down.
Gillian knew which buttons to push and seemed to take per-
verse pleasure in pushing them. The unfortunate truth was,
Gillian could do all the pushing she wanted. Jessie needed
this job. Without it, she had nothing. No income, no
résumé, nowhere to go. Gillian had her cornered, and more

than anything, Jessie hated being cornered.

Tom cleared his throat, and she looked up to see him standing in her office door, his expression as concerned as she imagined it could get. "Are you all right, Ms. Rhoades?"

Relaxing her jaw, she forced a smile. "I'm fine. What about you? Want some coffee or anything?"

The offer seemed to make him uncomfortable. "No. Thank you, Ms. Rhoades."

"There is something you could do for me, though."

"Of course."

"Call me Jessie."

He gave a short nod. "Whatever you like."

Frantic activity in the newsroom caught her attention, and she went to the door to check it out. Greg met her there. "Pileup on the interstate," he said. "Lots of fatalities." Cell phone in hand, he was already racing for the door.

"Take a photographer!" Jessie shouted after him.

Waving over his shoulder, he veered toward the photo department.

"What's going on?" Gillian asked from behind her.

Jessie turned. "Accident on the interstate."

"Jesus," Gillian muttered.

"Be happy," Jessie said. "Now we have bigger news than the hoax."

The pileup interrupted Clay's interview with the police chief, but Clay had spoken with him long enough to learn something useful. With the police chief's secretary, Clay rescheduled a time to continue the interview, then stopped by *The Star-News*. The newsroom was frenzied when he arrived. Jessie spoke to him long enough to tell him she'd see him later that night. Much later.

He checked in with Tom. "Any problems?"

"No, sir."

Hours later, Jessie buried her head in her arms on the desk. She had a headache that throbbed steadily in both temples.

It was after two a.m., and the paper had been put to bed. The news had been harrowing: a truck driver had lost control, and his semitrailer had careened off an overpass and landed on the busy interstate below, causing a chain-reaction pileup. At least twelve people died, three of them kids. Other lives would likely be lost during the early morning hours as doctors worked feverishly to put mangled bodies back together.

She raised her head when Greg paused in her office door. "You okay?" he asked.

She waved away his concern as he and Tom, at his post near the door, eyed each other. Tom's presence had unsettled her co-workers all day. Even a maintenance worker emptying the trash can in her office had looked suspiciously at the bodyguard.

Luckily, the day had been so busy, Tom eventually had been forgotten.

Glancing at the phone, Jessie longed to call Mel. No doubt, her friend had had just as lousy a day as victims of the pileup overwhelmed hospital staffs all over the city. But she knew she couldn't call. She still needed Mel to be safe, and the only way to ensure that would be to stay away from her.

Shaking off the regret, Jessie focused on Greg. His glasses were propped on top of his head as he rubbed at his red eyes. He looked as exhausted as she felt. "Good job today," she said.

He gave her a sick look. "I hate days like this."

"Me, too."

"Want to go have a beer to decompress?"

Before she could respond, she saw Clay ambling across the newsroom. Some of the heaviness in her chest lightened as she attempted to tuck stray strands of hair back into the loose ponytail at her nape. "Looks like I have other plans," she said.

Greg glanced over his shoulder. "Him again. He's like your new best buddy."

She laughed softly. He was much more than that. "See you tomorrow, Greg?"

"Bright and early."

"Not too early. You earned some sleep-in time."

"I'll come in later if you come in later."

She smiled. "See you bright and early."

As Jessie left her office, Clay noticed right away that covering the accident had taken its toll. Circles of fatigue curved under her eyes, her features drawn and pale. He wondered whether she'd taken the time to eat all day and vowed to get hot food into her first thing. Taking care of her was going to be a full-time job, he thought, as he greeted her with a quick kiss.

"Hope you don't mind me dropping in to see how you're doing," he said, catching her against him before she could step back.

"It was a long day."

Clay glanced at the guard. "How's it going, Tom?"

"No problems, sir."

Jessie wiggled free of Clay's embrace. "Why don't you sit down, Tom? You've been on your feet all day."

"Thank you, but I'm fine, Ms. . . . . Jessie."

Clay arched an eyebrow, impressed that she'd gotten the man to call her by her first name. Then he forgot Tom as she squinted, as if against too-bright lights. "Headache?" he asked.

"A little. I was just going to take something for it."

A little, my ass, he thought. "I'll wait."

She swallowed water along with one of the pain pills Mel had prescribed, then capped the water bottle and returned it to her desk.

"Can I interest you in a ride home?" he asked.

"The rental car's out in the lot."

"How about I give you a ride back tomorrow?"

"As long as you don't try to muscle me into coming in late in the morning. I missed the start of an important meeting today."

He grinned. "I didn't hear you complaining this morning. Begging maybe." He enjoyed her blush as they crossed the newsroom toward the exit.

"How'd the interview with the police chief go?" she asked.

He draped an arm over her shoulders, conscious of his need to keep her close to him, to keep touching her. He didn't wonder at his need to cling. He'd spent the day worrying about her, had even called Tom every other hour to make sure everything was okay. "The interview went great. I bet I know something you don't know."

"Yeah? What?"

"Your very own executive editor had an affair with the police chief about five years ago."

Jessie stopped in mid-step to stare at him. "You're kidding."

"Nope. The guy hated telling me, too. It was killing him to tell me, but he thinks *The Star-News* jumped on the cops scandal so fast because of his history with Gillian. It didn't end amicably, and he says he's the one who did the dumping."

"My God," Jessie said. "My God."

He had to tug on her hand to get her to follow him into the parking lot. Outside, the air was so clear the stars were sharp pinpoints of light in the midnight blue sky. A slight breeze kept the humidity down. A perfect night for a stroll on the beach, Clay thought.

At his SUV, he opened the passenger door for her and brushed his mouth briefly over hers. Her lips were soft and pliant. "I love it when you're all agog," he said.

As she got into the Jeep, Clay was peripherally aware that Tom had continued walking several paces beyond his car and was getting into a dark sedan to follow them home, where his backup would take over for the night.

"There's a whole new context now," Jessie said. "If Gillian let her personal feelings guide her decisions . . ."

"Like that never happens in a newsroom," Clay said, shutting her door.

"It shouldn't," she said as he settled in the driver's seat.

"There you go, operating as if we're living in an ideal world again."

She shook her head, as if to clear it. "You're right. So Gillian isn't nearly as ethical as I thought."

"You had your doubts before this."

"Yes, but, Jesus, their affair ended badly so she jumped on the first chance she gets to emasculate him in public? That's really sleazy." She chewed at her lip. "Except five years is a long time to carry that kind of grudge."

"Maybe she'd never had the opportunity before. The cops scandal came along, and it was perfect."

"And before that, Richard—her father—was in charge.

He never would have let her behave so irresponsibly. At least, not as a representative of the newspaper."

"You've got a point there," he said.

"Maybe the person, or people, who engineered the hoax know about her history with the police chief and used it to manipulate how the newspaper handled the story. Maybe they knew Gillian would let her personal feelings lead the way to a screamer headline."

"Or maybe it's just a coincidence."

"I don't believe in coincidences," she said, glancing at the floorboard at her feet. "What's this?"

Clay flinched as she scooped up the manila folder that held all the information that Marshall had compiled on her former husband.

"David Collins" was printed on it in neat, block letters.

Chapter 17

The initial shock of seeing her ex-husband's name on a folder in Clay's SUV froze her. Her first thought was that it was another David Collins. A fluke. But Clay looked too dismayed for it to be a fluke, and besides, didn't she just say she didn't believe in coincidences?

Her head started to spin, surprising her. Even when she'd discovered David was cheating on her, her head hadn't gotten all fuzzy and weird. Her heart hadn't raced. Nothing had whirled around her like a carnival ride on speed.

Then, suddenly, she couldn't breathe. Opening the door, she stumbled out into the night air. She heard Clay say her name, heard a car door slam.

She needed air.

He repeated her name when he reached her, and the alarm in his eyes had transferred to his voice. He grasped her by the arms, and she saw his features blur and melt. Everything began to darken.

"Jess!"

Clay called her name again, incredulous when her eyes rolled back and she sagged in his arms. He lowered her to the pavement, his heart thundering in his ears as her head lolled to the side. Her face was so white she looked dead.

He pressed his shaking fingers to her throat where her pulse fluttered against his fingertips. Jesus, he thought. She was so terrified of her former husband that just seeing his name frightened her into a faint. What the hell had the man done to her?

"Mr. Christopher?"

Clay glanced over his shoulder at Tom. "She fainted. Can you help me get her back into the building?"

Kneeling beside Jessie, Tom placed two fingers at the base of her neck. "I think the hospital might be more appropriate, sir."

Clay gaped at him. "But she just fainted." Brushing Tom's hand aside, he groped again for her pulse. This time, it was thready, irregular. He leaned over her, panic kicking into high gear. "She's not breathing." Disbelief paralyzed him for an instant, then shock turned to horror. *"She's not breathing."*

Hearing himself say it again snapped him into action. He shoved aside Tom, who was about to start CPR, straddled Jessie himself and began blowing air into her mouth.

Tom whipped out his cell phone to call 911, but Clay shook his head. "We don't have time to wait. We've got to get her to the hospital now."

Both men looked up at the sound of squealing tires. Greg shot out of a red Accord, leaving the driver's door hanging open. "What's going on?"

"She collapsed," Tom said. "Can you drive us to the hospital?"

"Hell, yeah," Greg said.

Bending, Tom grasped Jessie by the knees. "Open the back door," he told Greg.

Clay stopped CPR, conscious that Jessie's lips were turning blue, and hauled her up by the shoulders. They bundled her into the backseat where Clay straddled her again and resumed CPR. She felt absurdly tiny, and terrifyingly still, under him.

As Greg drove too fast, Clay pumped Jessie's chest, counting out loud, then forcing air into her lungs. Her lack of response began to splinter his composure, and his counting gave way to a desperate chant: "Come on. Come on. Come on."

Scenarios raced through his head. An allergic reaction? But he hadn't seen her eat anything. Heart attack from the shock of seeing her former husband's name? Jesus, could that be it? Could he have killed her himself?

She wasn't responding to the CPR, and he fought down terror. She was going to die, and he was helpless to save her. Not again, he thought. Please, God, not again. "Damn it! How close are we?"

"Two minutes."

"Make it one."

Then, miraculously, Jessie coughed and pulled in a strangled breath.

"We got her," Clay said, triumph flooding through him along with relief. "Thank Christ, we got her back." Cupping the back of her head, he angled it back to keep her airway open. "Come on, that's it, take it easy."

He expected her to open her eyes and look up at him, perhaps smile. But she didn't. She didn't move. Didn't try to sit up. Didn't even flex the fingers of the hand that dangled over the edge of the backseat.

"Open your eyes, Jess." He grasped her chin, his relief shifting back to dread. "Come on, damn it, keep breathing. Keep breathing for me."

She didn't.

He straightened, his mind white with fear, and started CPR again. "We're in serious trouble back here. How close are we?"

"We're there," Greg said, slamming on the brakes. He was out of the car in an instant, shouting for help and yanking open the back door.

Clay scrambled out of the car, then watched helplessly as Tom reached in and dragged Jessie out. He lifted her into his arms as ER workers came running with a gurney. Seeing her hanging limp in Tom's arms, her head back over his elbow, one arm swinging, turned Clay's knees weak, and he stumbled.

Forcing strength back into his legs, he raced after the ER workers. Someone shouted instructions as they entered the sterile, white ER and medical workers swarmed over the patient. A woman in a pink jacket hopped onto the gurney and began CPR as a male orderly blocked Clay and the other men from following the gurney through swinging double doors. "What happened?" he asked.

"She fainted," Clay said.

"She lost consciousness and immediately became unresponsive," Tom said, and his usual calm slipped, making him stammer. "Uh, it was, uh, about ten minutes from there to here."

"Anything else?"

Clay cursed his own inadequate knowledge of medicine. "I thought she just fainted."

"We'll take it from here," the orderly said.

The double doors swung closed, their whop-whop-whop like fists pummeling his chest as Clay clenched his hands at his sides. His pulse thrummed in his ears, and for a long moment, he concentrated on fighting down the urge to be sick.

As Greg sank onto a chair, Clay turned, searching for the bodyguard. "What the hell just happened?"

Tom's normally stony face was pale and sweaty, his forehead deeply creased. "I don't know."

The nausea returned, and Clay dropped onto a chair, gripping its arms for balance. "Jesus."

The doors through which the ER staff had taken Jessie burst open, and the orderly who'd stopped them, a test tube of blood gripped in one hand, tore down the hall, his sneakered feet slapping the floor.

Oh God, Clay thought. None of this is real. It couldn't be real.

He wanted to know what was going on beyond those doors. He needed to know.

Mel. She was a doctor. She could help.

But he'd left his cell phone in the Jeep, parked at the newspaper. He glanced at Tom. "Cell phone?"

Tom patted his jacket. "I must have dropped it."

Greg handed over his as Clay fished Mel's number out of his wallet.

His conversation with her was short and to the point. It would take her at least twenty minutes to get there.

"She was never out of my sight," Tom said. "Not for a second."

Greg straightened in his chair. "You mean someone just tried to kill Jess again?"

"It could be a drug overdose," Tom said. "I'm guessing."

Clay, unable to sit still, struggling to keep his raging emotions in check, stood. He longed to throw a fist at the wall. The agony of crushed bones in his hand would be preferable to this blinding fear. "She took a pill just before we left the office," he said, his voice guttural.

"It happened too fast for a pill," Tom said. "It had to have been in the water. But I saw her drink from that bottle on her desk earlier in the day, and she was fine."

Greg leapt to his feet. "I'll go get it."

Tom headed toward the double doors that stood between them and Jessie.

Not about to be left behind, Clay followed. He was struck by the frenzied pace behind the doors. Jessie appeared to be the only patient, surrounded by several intent medical workers. A piercing alarm beeped as a woman shouted, "Clear!"

Seeing Jessie's body convulse, realizing that she'd just been zapped with defibrillator paddles, Clay froze in the same instant that everyone else in the ER stopped.

Finally, a man's voice: "No pulse."

The doctor with the paddles shouted, "Again!"

A nurse approached Tom and Clay. "You shouldn't be—"

Tom interrupted her, but Clay didn't hear what he said. Two words buzzed in his ears: no pulse.

The nurse apparently understood, though, because she hurried to the doctor with the paddles, whose face registered astonishment when the nurse spoke urgently to her. She issued a request for a drug, followed by, "Come on, people, we've got her."

Clay grabbed Tom's arm. "What is it?"

"I'm guessing it's Rohypnol or something like it."

"The rape drug?"

"In mass quantity."

"Jesus."

"It was probably in the water."

The nurse addressed them again. "Please, you have to wait outside. I'll come get you as soon as I can."

Clay backed out, his gaze fixed on Jessie's prone body. She looked dead, even as the ER staff continued to work frantically on her. As the door swung closed, he saw someone slip an oxygen mask over her nose and mouth while the doctor plunged a syringe into her arm.

Don't leave me, he thought. Please, don't leave me.

In the waiting room, Clay sat, aware of every minute that ticked by without word. Someone had pressed a Styrofoam cup of coffee into his hands, but his throat was too tight to drink.

Inevitably, he thought of Ellen, remembered what it had been like to know the life was draining out of her body and there was nothing he could do to stop it. He felt as helpless now, only now he knew what it was like to lose someone he cared about deeply. He knew what it meant to face every day without that person, to know that he would never hear her laugh or voice ever again. He knew what it was like to replay over and over how he could have prevented what happened.

One graceless stumble, one mistake, had torn Ellen from him forever.

There had been a time when he would have gladly traded places with her. It had been in only the past week that he had begun to feel differently. Because of Jessie.

And now . . . now . . .

"Clay?"

He glanced up at Mel. She looked like hell, her red curls tangled as if she had been in bed when he'd called or had been dragging her hands through it. The tears glittering in her green eyes tightened the fist around his heart.

Kneeling before him, she clasped his hand and gave him a tremulous smile. "She's okay," she said. "She's okay."

His breath left him in a shaky sigh, his relief so intense he couldn't speak.

"They stabilized her," Mel said, glancing at Tom, who

sat with one seat between him and Clay. "She coded, but she wasn't down for very long. She's young and in excellent shape, so the damage will be minimal and should heal quickly."

The guard responded with a short nod. "What drug was it?"

"Gamma hydroxybutyric acid," Mel said. "Odorless, colorless, tasteless. The dosage was definitely meant to be fatal. She was damn lucky that you guys were there when it hit her."

Greg trotted into the waiting room from outside but paused when he saw them standing around. Trepidation washed the color from his cheeks. "Is Jess—"

"She's okay," Clay said, and a laugh of pure joy almost escaped him. "Did you find the water bottle?"

Greg, looking relieved, shook his head. "It's gone."

"It was on her desk when we left," Tom said.

"I saw it there earlier, too, where it always is," Greg said. "But it's gone now." He absently rubbed his knuckles, which Clay noticed were bruised and bloody.

"What did you do to your hand?" Mel asked.

Greg tried to shrug it off. "Nothing."

Mel snagged his fingers. "These gashes need to be cleaned. What did you do? Slam your fist into a wall?"

Greg nodded, his eyes shimmering with unshed tears. "I want to kill the bastard who's trying to hurt her."

"I think we all do," Tom said.

Mel touched Clay's arm. "You okay?"

"Not even close." Fury had settled in the center of his chest, burning like the pain from an untreated ulcer after a spicy meal.

"May I speak to you in private, Mr. Christopher?" Tom asked.

"I'm going to go back to keep an eye on Jess," Mel said.

As Clay followed him a few paces away, gratitude that this man had had the presence of mind to recognize that Jessie was in trouble overwhelmed him. But he didn't know how to thank him.

"I'd like to stay with Ms. Rhoades," Tom said. "But I understand if you want someone else to take over."

"Why would I want someone else?" Clay asked, surprised.

"If I'd done my job thoroughly—"

"You saved her life," Clay cut in. "I was standing there like an idiot thinking all that had happened was she passed out. You were the one who recognized she needed help."

"Whoever did this did it right in front of me, Mr. Christopher. She drank from that water earlier in the day and was fine, so whoever drugged her did it while I was standing right there."

"You weren't in her office all day. Anyone could have gone in and tampered with her water."

"I should have been more vigilant," Tom said.

"I'm not going to fire you, Tom. So let's move on, okay?"

The lanky man nodded, expressionless. "While I was in *The Star-News* newsroom, I noticed some things about security."

"Like it's so lousy that someone walked right in and tried to kill Jess without anyone even blinking?"

"It's actually fairly thorough. People without security cards can't get in without showing I.D. to get a visitor's pass. But I think your attention should be on the security cameras. There are at least three in the newsroom. They might be for appearances, but if not they might show you something."

Clay beckoned for Greg to join them. "Can I use your cell again?"

Greg handed it to him, and Clay called Marshall to ask the investigator to meet him at the newspaper. As he turned off the phone, he saw Detective Mubarek saunter into the ER.

"Greg," Clay said. "Can you handle the detective for me?"

Greg, still looking shell-shocked, nodded. "No problem."

As Greg intercepted the detective, Tom asked, "Are you sure about trusting him?"

"Did you see the look on his face when I told him Jess was okay?" Clay asked. "He's head over heels for her."

"People in love can do crazy stuff that makes no sense to us but makes all the sense in the world to them. For all you know, he poisoned her so he could have a hand in saving her." Tom shook his head. "I should have gone with him to get the water bottle, to prevent tampering if anything else, but I wasn't thinking."

Clay clenched his jaw against the renewed rage. He didn't think for a second that Greg was behind what was happening, but the thought of eventually standing face to face with the person who was made the need for vengeance bubble through his blood. "If that turns out to be the case, I'll take care of him."

"You'll have to get in line," Tom said.

Chapter 18

A pounding headache dragged Jessie into consciousness, and she lay without moving, assessing her situation.

She knew right away she was in the hospital. Again.

She knew she was or had recently been very sick. An IV line fed into a needle in the back of her hand, and her body felt as if it had been beaten from the inside out.

Worse than all that, she couldn't remember how she had come to be here.

Sitting up, she gripped one of the railings as the room whirled. Common sense told her to relax, that eventually someone would come to her who could explain. But it wasn't her nature to lie still and wait.

She wanted answers. She needed answers.

Clay, returning from a visit to the bathroom, was slipping quietly into Jessie's room when he saw her sitting on the edge of the bed. Relief surged through him before he realized what she was doing. "Hey," he said, moving fast.

The instant her feet hit the floor, her knees buckled.

Catching her under the arms, he felt her hand clutch at the front of his shirt for support as he lifted her back onto the bed. "What do you think you're doing?" he asked.

She sat with her head hanging forward, one arm wrapped around her ribs as if they hurt. "What happened?" she asked, raising her head to search his eyes. She was too weak to sit up without bracing a hand on the bed for support.

Her voice sounded rusty, and alarm made her eyes the darkest he'd seen. "What's wrong with me? How long have I been here?"

He rubbed her arms to soothe her, checking the need to pull her against him and hold on until his own heart calmed. He hadn't been sure she'd be okay until now, until he'd looked into her eyes and seen for himself. "It's okay," he said and smiled, however feebly. "You're okay."

"What happened to me, Clay?"

He tried to ease her back, but she stiffened with resistance. "No, tell me what happened."

"You were drugged."

She stared at him as if he'd said he'd discovered an alien in the trunk of his car. "What?"

He smiled at her shock. It was a stupid, goofy smile, but he was just so happy that she was talking to him that he didn't even care that she was being her usual stubborn self. "You've been unconscious for nearly thirty-six hours."

The shakes grabbed hold of him then, and he sat on the edge of the bed and dragged her into his arms.

Jessie stroked his hair as he held her tight, his face buried against her neck. "I thought you were gone," he murmured. "I thought I lost you."

His emotion touched her, and she took comfort in the strength of his arms around her. But what he'd said echoed in her head.

"You were drugged."

Someone had tried to kill her again. And, despite a trained bodyguard charged with the specific goal of protecting her, they had almost succeeded.

Sitting back, Clay gazed at her with damp, blue eyes. He hadn't shaved, and it appeared he hadn't slept, because dark, puffy half-circles underscored his eyes. "What day is it?" she asked.

"It's about noon Sunday."

She relaxed against the pillow, too tired to even hold her head up. "I wasted the whole weekend."

He laughed softly. "We'll have plenty more."

"You're exhausted," she said, drawing her hand down the side of his face. Touching him helped. She felt safe with him there.

Capturing her hand, he pressed a kiss into her palm. "I couldn't sleep until I knew you were okay."

She was fading already. She had so many questions, but at the moment nothing seemed more important than closing her eyes. She smiled at him. "Sleep with me now."

He stretched out beside her and drew her against him. She dropped off in an instant.

The rest of that day and halfway into Monday, Jessie drifted in and out. Along with checking on her every few hours, Clay spent every waking moment with Marshall studying two days' worth of newsroom security tapes. Unfortunately, *The Star-News'* cameras took a wide-angle view of the newsroom, which meant the goings-on in Jessie's office, on the perimeter of the newsroom, were not recorded. However, activity outside her office, including the people who walked in and out of it, had been captured. Mostly, however, it all appeared very usual.

So he and Marshall had started going through the tapes frame by frame, a painstaking process that practically made them cross-eyed. Greg volunteered to help so Clay could go home, catch some sleep and shower, then check on Jessie again.

Now, as Clay neared Jessie's room, he saw Marshall in

the waiting area. Greg was with him, shifting from one foot to the other in a nervous dance.

"You've got something?" Clay asked as he approached the two men.

Marshall, his usually wrinkle-free presence creased in more than a few places, nodded wearily. "Greg picked up on something we overlooked." He handed Clay a black-and-white still taken from one of the videotapes.

"Looks like one of the maintenance guys," Clay said.

"Name's Hank Peters."

"He's all over the tapes," Clay said, disappointed. "We've watched him do hours of cleaning and fixing and emptying trash cans and nothing suspicious."

"Check out his right arm."

Clay studied the photo, noting that the man was holding his arm against his body, as if clamping something between the limb and his torso. A white circle showed clearly at the bend of his elbow. "What is that?"

"The cap of a water bottle," Marshall said.

Clay's gaze snapped up to his friend's face. "He's trying to conceal it. He knows about the cameras."

"Yep."

Clay whistled low. "Good eye, Greg."

Greg gave a short nod. "Thanks."

"So where does he live? Let's go visit him," Clay said. The muscles in his hands twitched to clamp around the man's throat.

"He doesn't exist," Marshall said. "No address, no phone, no nothing."

"He was new at *The Star-News*," Greg added. "In just the past couple weeks."

"Who hired him?" Clay asked. "That person must have some information. A phone number, something."

"Nope. His boss, Jacob Jennings, said Peters came with a recommendation from Richard Westin himself. Jennings says he didn't even conduct an interview. Just hired him and put him to work."

"Richard Westin, the former editor?" Clay asked.

"Already talked to him," Marshall said. "Says he never heard of Hank Peters."

"Jennings admits he doesn't know Westin well," Greg said. "When he got a phone call from a man who claimed to be Westin, he didn't question it. It was a maintenance job—cleaning toilets, emptying trash."

"Murdering the city editor," Clay said. "Hasn't Jennings heard that American businesses are being more vigilant about background checks on the people they hire these days?"

"Seems to me that Jennings was so intimidated by Westin that he didn't challenge the voice on the phone," Marshall said. "Plus, he's not the sharpest knife in the drawer."

"And we're sure this Peters is our guy?"

Withdrawing a vial from his pocket, Marshall held it up for Clay's inspection. It was half-filled with clear liquid. "Found this in Peters' locker at the newspaper. It's odorless and tasteless."

"And it's not water," Greg said.

Clay glared at the vial. "That son of a bitch."

Greg's cell phone rang. "Excuse me," he said, and walked a short distance away to answer it.

"So how do we find this bastard?" Clay asked.

"You mean, besides call the police?" Marshall said.

"Well, yes, call them, but isn't there something *we* can do? I don't necessarily trust the police to be all that diligent on this one, you know?"

Marshall nodded. "Bearing that in mind, I lifted some fingerprints off Peters' locker and faxed them to a cop friend who's checking the National Crime Information Center for possible identification. Until I get that, we're pretty much dead in the water." Pausing, he rubbed his eyes. "I'm sure you've already made this leap, but there's a ninety-nine percent chance Peters is working for someone."

"Yeah, I got that. So let's track him down and find out who it is."

"It might be faster to try another tack," Marshall said.

"What's that?"

"Jessie's ex."

"She insists it's not him," Clay said.

"Clay, someone is damn determined to get at her and, apparently, only her. This looks very personal to me, and who else do we have? All I'm saying is that it can't hurt to go to Chicago and check the guy out."

Clay massaged the knot at the back of his neck. "If he catches your scent, he might be able to find Jessie through you."

"If he's the one trying to kill her, he's already tracked her down."

Clay couldn't argue with that, and every instinct told him to find out everything he could about David Collins, if only so he'd know what he was dealing with. At the same time, he feared how Jessie would react if she found out. She'd be royally ticked. But if Collins was behind the attempts on her life, and Clay and Marshall busted him, then she'd be safe, and there was no way in hell she'd be able to stay mad about that. "Okay, yeah," he said. "Go to Chicago."

Greg rejoined them. "What's in Chicago?"

"Bulls and Bears," Marshall said, then slapped Greg on

225

the back. "Good work today, kid."

The young reporter beamed. "I'm glad I could help. Look, uh, I have to go do something. You guys need me? I can come back."

"Think we're covered," Clay said. "And thanks for the help." He extended a hand.

Greg took his hand, pumped it. "I guess I was wrong about you. You're one of the good guys."

"You, too." Looking back at Marshall, Clay saw the man's fatigue. "You need to catch some sleep."

"Yeah, maybe on the flight to Chicago. How's Jess doing?"

Clay smiled, nearly giddy again with relief. "Doctor's going to release her today. She's been champing at the bit to get out of here since she woke up. In slow motion, of course."

Marshall chuckled. "From what I hear, that's about normal speed for the rest of us. You're keeping the guard on her?"

"I'm not taking any chances."

"Have you thought about getting her out of town?"

"Tom said traveling is risky. Too many variables. He seems to think my place is secure enough if she stays put there."

"He knows his stuff. That's why I recommended him."

"She's going to hate it, but I don't see an alternative."

"All right, well, I'm going to go catch a plane," Marshall said. "Say hi to her for me."

As Marshall walked away, Clay pushed open Jessie's door and found an empty room.

"So this GHA stuff is pretty scary," Jessie said, scanning one of the three printouts Mel had brought her. They flapped in a strong afternoon breeze, and Jessie flattened them over her knees.

The Florida sun was hot overhead, but she had been so desperate for fresh air, she didn't care. She'd dragged Mel and Tom to the outdoor lounge area on the roof where she had dropped onto a metal chair in her robe and stockinged feet and simply basked in the glory of being alive. Her body was unbelievably achy, and her head still throbbed with the aftereffects. But she was alive, and that made everything just fine.

Brushing windblown hair out of her eyes, Mel watched Tom. "Your bodyguard is nervous."

Jessie, perching her glasses on her head, glanced at Tom, who paced the perimeter of the roof as if he were a sentry atop a wall surrounding a maximum-security prison. "I'm probably being a jerk by insisting we come outside. I just couldn't take another minute in that stuffy room."

"He's cute, in a wiry kind of way."

"I could probably get you a date."

Instead of the laugh Jessie expected, tears flooded Mel's green eyes.

Jessie's grin faded. "Hey."

Mel swiped at her eyes. "Oops. Didn't mean for that to happen."

"If that was about—"

"It's not. I'm okay. Sorry." She smiled, still a little misty-eyed. "I'm just glad you're okay. I would have been really pissed if you'd checked out without letting me apologize for what I said to you—"

"You don't have to apologize. I provoked you, remember?"

"But I should have figured that out. I mean, you've never spoken to me like that. Ever. I guess I was too stunned to stop and think about it."

Leaning forward, Jessie snagged her friend's hand and gave it a squeeze. "I'm sorry. I was thinking on my feet, and it went badly."

"Well, you were probably right. There was no way I was going to stay away from you just because you were worried I might get caught in the crossfire."

Jessie gave her a small smile. "Are you sure? Because the danger's still there. It would kill me if you got hurt—"

"Jess, come on. You've got a bodyguard. What could possibly happen . . ." She trailed off, as if realizing that Jessie had been drugged while under guard. "Let me re-phrase that."

"It'd probably be for a few days, maybe a week," Jessie said. "Until all this blows over."

Mel's fingers clasped Jessie's harder. "Who's doing this to you?"

Jessie sat back on a soft sigh. "I don't know."

"Jess, please. Trust me."

"I do. I'd tell you if I knew."

"Is it David? Is it possible he's found you?"

Before Jessie could respond, the access door to the roof slammed open. Tom had his gun out and cocked by the time Clay, barreling through the door, froze.

"Hi," Clay said, making a visible effort to relax as he acknowledged the guard with a nod. "Sorry about that." As Tom lowered his weapon, Clay sauntered over to the two women. "There you are," he said, all too casual.

Mel flashed a knowing glance at Jessie. "He's smitten."

Jessie, her heart still tripping from the shock of seeing a gun aimed at Clay's chest, could manage only a shaky smile.

Mel stood. "I'll leave you two alone."

Clay pocketed his hands. "Actually, I ran into Jess' doctor in the hall on the way here. She said the patient's free to go, as long as she gets plenty of bed rest and takes it easy for a few days."

"Take it easy?" Jessie protested. "I haven't even seen a newspaper in three days. Who knows what's happened while I've been slacking off?"

Clay let out an incredulous laugh. "You call this slacking off? Jess, technically, you were dead for a minute or two."

"Now there's a reminder I could have done without," Mel said dryly.

"Geez, Clay, don't be so dramatic," Jessie said, pushing up off the metal chair. He grasped her arm when she swayed, and she gave him a rueful look. "Okay, so I'm a little wobbly."

"Which is why you're going home and sitting on your pretty little butt for a couple of days before diving back into work," Clay said.

"A couple of days? I'll sprout roots by then."

"You know, Jess," Mel said, "I might be mistaken, but I think you're dangerously close to whining."

Laughing, Clay curved an arm around Jessie's waist and walked with her to the roof's access door. "She's got you there."

"No fair ganging up on me."

"Yep," Clay said. "That's definitely a whine."

Chapter 19

An hour later, belted into Clay's SUV and squinting against the sun in spite of the dark sunglasses he had handed her, Jessie was angry. It began building while he had packed her things and outlined for her where they were going from there. He planned to take her to his home, where she would stay under armed guard until the person who was trying to kill her was caught, even if it took several weeks. Leaving the house to go to the office or for any other reason was not an option.

She understood the reasoning and appreciated that he took her safety so seriously. But it irked her that he had not consulted her on what precautions would be taken. It was her life. She deserved some input, even if it was to say that what he proposed was fine with her.

Worse, he was treating her as if she were made of material so delicate it would snag if it caught even a tiny rough spot. She wasn't used to being taken care of, and it annoyed her that he seemed to think she was suddenly too feeble to take care of herself.

At the same time, and perhaps even more infuriating, she recognized that she was indeed weak. Her legs felt as if they were made of rubber that would bend the wrong way at the slightest nudge. If she stood up too fast, her head whirled like a washer on the spin cycle. Every move hurt, as if each of her organs had been yanked from her body, punched like flat pillows, and tossed back in without consideration for where they belonged. Such physical limitations irritated her as much as Clay's mollycoddling.

Closing her eyes, she tamped down the rising frustration and decided that checking in with the newspaper would take her mind off of it. As Clay braked for a red light, she asked, "Can I use your cell phone a minute?"

"Why?"

"To make a call. Why else?"

"Why can't it wait until we get to my place?"

Her patience stretched taut, almost snapped. "You're really getting off on this power trip, aren't you?"

He didn't respond at first, as if taking the time to count to ten. "I assume you want to call work, and the doctor told you to give work a rest for a few days."

"The light's green."

He stepped on the gas a little too vehemently, squealing tires. In the next block, he pulled into a parking lot and killed the engine. "We should talk about this before we go any farther."

"There's nothing to talk about," she said. "You've already decided everything, remember?"

"Why are you so mad about it?"

She sighed, telling herself she was being childish. "I'm not mad."

"You're mad, Jess."

"Okay, I'm mad. Do I have to have a reason?"

"That's usually how it works."

She focused on the concern in his blue eyes, the indentation in his chin, felt the now-familiar knot in her stomach and the fluttery sensation in her chest. That made her angry, too. She was falling for him. Fast. And it was one more thing she seemed to have no control over.

"Talk to me," he said, stroking the back of his hand

down her arm. "Tell me what you're thinking."

"You're taking over," she blurted. Before she could stop it, everything poured out of her. "I appreciate your concern, but you haven't allowed me a decision in my own life all week. You decided I'd move in with you without asking me if that's what I wanted. You're dictating my work hours. You forced a bodyguard on me. Suddenly, I have no life unless you say it's okay."

"Excuse me, but forcing a bodyguard on you saved your damn life. I'm not going to apologize for that. No fucking way."

The profanity stunned her, and she stared at him. "I didn't mean—" She broke off, tried again. "I'm sorry. I didn't mean that the way it sounded. Of course, I'm grateful."

He lifted his hands off the steering wheel, looked like he might slam them down against it, but instead he gently lowered them. "I don't want you to be grateful."

"I'm not a delicate flower you have to protect. If we're going to make this work, you have to let me make my own decisions. If I decide I'm going to return to work tonight—" She broke off at his sharp glance. "Or tomorrow," she amended, "then you have to let me."

His gaze met hers, and instead of the anger she expected, he smiled.

She was disarmed. "What?"

"I like what you just said. 'If we're going to make this work.' "

Flustered now, she frowned. "Don't change the subject."

"Consider the subject changed." He reached for her, slid his hand to the back of her neck and kissed her.

Too soon, he let her go, started the car and pulled back into traffic.

Turning her head away, Jessie touched the tips of her fingers to her lips, amazed at how much his kisses made her feel. Still, she was determined to not let such feelings distract her from the point she'd been trying to make. "I suppose you think you just handled me," she said.

"I kissed you. Handling you is something I plan to do later."

She couldn't help but laugh, and anticipate.

"But you're right," he said. "I've been an overbearing son of a bitch, and I'm sorry."

"I wouldn't say you've been a son of a bitch. Overbearing, yes. But not a son of a bitch."

"All I want is for you to be safe."

"I know," she said. "I just have a hard time letting other people take control."

"I hadn't noticed."

"I feel safe with you, Clay."

He flashed her a pleased smile. "I'm glad." Then, as he steered the SUV into his driveway, he said, "You can crash on the couch for the rest of the day."

She unbuckled her seat belt. "I need to check in at work first."

"You need to rest first."

"I didn't say I was going to actually work. I just said I was going to check in. There's a difference."

"All right. Then I'll bring you the cordless, and you can do both on the sofa."

Satisfied with the compromise, she had to admit it felt good when she dropped onto his couch. It felt even better when he brought her a pillow and a soft blanket, slipped her shoes off for her, brushed a kiss over her brow and headed for the kitchen.

"I'm starving," he said. "How about some pasta?"

She groaned. "That sounds fantastic." Plucking the phone off the coffee table, she punched in the newsroom's main number. As it rang at the other end, she listened to Clay rattling pots in the next room. "You're just opening a jar of something, right?"

He appeared in the kitchen door, a tomato in each hand. "Not on your life."

"You're so domestic," she said, impressed.

"Women like that in a man, don't they?"

"Are you kidding? Women *love* that in a man."

His eyebrow arched as one of her assistant editors answered the phone. The update was disappointing considering how long she had been out of commission. There'd been no new developments in the hoax story, though Greg apparently was onto something that he hadn't shared with anyone. No one knew where to find him at the moment, which worried her a little.

After hanging up, she tried Greg's cell phone and got no answer. She had finished leaving him a voice mail when Clay called to her from the kitchen. "How do you feel about onions?"

"Tasty, but I'm not interested in sleeping with one," she replied as she tried Greg at home. No answer there either.

As she dialed her work voice mail, Clay ambled in from the kitchen, drying his hands on a towel draped over one shoulder. She met his questioning gaze, the phone cradled on her shoulder. "Voice mail."

He rolled his eyes. "You've got a problem. You know that, don't you?"

"What?" she asked, all innocence.

"It's called workaholism. There are twelve-step programs for it."

"I know, but every time a new one starts, I have to work."

His chuckle faded into the background as she retrieved a message from Detective Mubarek. A colleague in Chicago had located her ex-husband's residence, he said, but so far he was nowhere to be found. The detective said he'd update her as soon as he had something more. That had been two days ago, and no messages had followed.

Lowering the phone, she lay with it resting on her tummy and closed her eyes. She was still so tired. Perhaps she would be refreshed if she napped for a few minutes . . .

While pasta boiled, sauce bubbled and garlic bread broiled, Clay went to check on Jessie and found her sound asleep, the phone clutched to her chest.

Relieved that she had surrendered to her body's demands, he carried her to his bed and pulled the covers over her. She stirred in her sleep, murmured his name, and he sat on the edge of the mattress, emotions tangling.

He'd thought he would never love again. He'd thought he would grow old, alone and aching for his first love, the woman he had been unable to save.

But somehow he had been granted a second chance.

Bending, he lightly brushed his lips over Jessie's. Feeling the faint caress of her breath on his cheek, he closed his eyes.

He didn't deserve this second chance, he thought. But that didn't mean he wasn't going to snatch it and hang on for dear life.

Jessie woke in Clay's bed, surprised that she had no idea how she had gotten there or what time it was. Sitting up, she discovered she still had on the jeans and T-shirt she'd worn out of the hospital. After a stop in the bathroom to wash her face and comb her hair, she went in search of Clay.

She found him sitting on the deck outside, the flame of a single candle dancing in a light breeze, the waves of the gulf gently lashing the shore several feet away. The moon was almost full, the stars bright in a clear sky.

"Hey," she said.

He turned his head to look at her, his teeth a slash of white in the moonlight. "You never sleep for long, do you?"

"Give me a break. I just slept for two and a half days."

Getting up, he dragged a wooden deck chair close to the one he'd occupied. "Come, sit."

She settled onto the chair, liking the way the breeze feathered the hair across his forehead. He'd changed into khaki shorts and a white T-shirt and looked tranquil. "Where's Tom?" she asked.

"His backup is around here somewhere. He's trained to be inconspicuous."

Breathing in the gulf air, she rested her head back against the chair. It surprised her that she could relax knowing that someone wanted her dead. Being with Clay made her feel protected in a way that she hadn't since before she left David. "It's a gorgeous night."

"That it is. Are you hungry?"

"I'd rather wake up some more."

"You need to eat. There's pasta in the fridge."

"Stop mothering me, please. I have no intention of letting myself starve to death."

His chuckle was low, warm. "What a relief."

She listened to the rhythm of the waves for a while, enjoying the air that stirred through her hair. "It's because of her, isn't it?"

"What?"

"That you're so protective."

"Actually, I'm protective because someone is trying to kill you."

"But the part where you go overboard with it . . . that's because of what happened to her."

"Maybe at first," he said, reaching for her hand. "But now it's because of what's happening to you."

"What happens when this is all over and I don't need protection anymore?"

"Oh, you're definitely a passing fancy, Jess."

It was what she'd needed to hear, and she wondered how he'd gotten so good at anticipating what she needed and delivering. She wondered, too, how she'd gotten so lucky. She couldn't imagine what it would have been like to go through the past week without him. Maybe she'd have been dead by now.

Rubbing her palm over the back of his hand, reveling in the texture of his warm skin against hers, she realized that his wedding band was gone. "When did you take off your ring?"

He lightly stroked his fingertips along the inside of her forearm until she shuddered. "The first night you came here for dinner," he said.

"How could you have known where we were going that soon?"

"Leap of faith."

"I've never been good at those," she said.

"There's still time."

"How did you get so optimistic?"

"How did you get so pessimistic?" he countered.

"Born and bred, I guess."

"How so?"

"I was an Army brat."

"Your dad?"

"Military through and through," she said. "Which basically means he wasn't there for Mom or me. She put a happy face on it, but it was tough. We moved constantly, so I was never able to form the lifelong bonds that most people do. After a while, I decided it was a waste of time to let anyone get close, because I'd just end up leaving them behind the next time Dad got transferred."

"That must have been lonely."

"I didn't know any different," she said.

"But you do now. What changed?"

"I met David."

"He showed you what it was like to love someone?"

"Actually, it was when our marriage was over that I realized I'd gotten it wrong. I'd gotten a lot of stuff wrong."

"Like what?"

"I wasn't living. I was existing, going through the motions. I mean, I loved my husband. The day we got married was one of my happiest at the time. We did all the stuff that married couples do. We planned everything down to the last minute: when we were going to buy a house, when we were going to get pregnant. We were going to have two kids, move to the suburbs by our mid-thirties and retire early to Florida. I was on board with it all, because that's what normal people do."

"But you weren't normal?"

She gazed up at the stars, listened to the waves. She couldn't recall another time when she'd felt that she was exactly where she was supposed to be. "None of it was me. It all fell apart, and I was devastated. But I can't help but think it worked out for the best. I started over here, and I've formed the lifelong bonds that I'd never had. I changed."

Clay cocked his head, his gaze not leaving her face. "Can I ask what he did to make you run away?"

She didn't respond at first, taking a moment to appreciate the way the moonlight reflected in the blond strands of his hair, in his blue eyes. "You don't have it all figured out?"

"How do you mean?"

"I know you've been playing detective. I might have been drugged, but I remember seeing the folder with his name on it in the Jeep."

He nodded. "I thought you might. Are you angry?"

"I didn't give you much choice. If I'd told you the truth, you wouldn't have felt compelled to try to find out for yourself what kind of person he is."

"Is he the kind who would try to kill you?"

Tugging her hand free, she leaned back and stared out at the dark. David had hurt her terribly, but she knew in her heart that he wasn't a killer. Didn't she? "David is not a horrible man, Clay. I couldn't have loved him like I did."

"Love is blind."

"I suppose it is. But he wasn't the reason I ran."

"Then why did you?"

She drew in a breath, held it. "The newspaper where I worked was going to expose David's law firm for insurance fraud."

Mel had told him as much. "Was that a story you worked on?"

"I didn't even know about it until the editor told me. Unfortunately, David's firm seemed to think I had some kind of influence or control at the newspaper. One of the partners threatened me."

"How did he threaten you?" Clay's voice had gone low, with just a hint of anger.

"He said that if I didn't get the story killed, he'd make me disappear." Even after so much time, the memory of the threat still sent a chill through her.

"What did you do?"

"I ran. Moved here. Changed my name. Looked over my shoulder for a long time."

"You ran from David's partners. Not him."

"I'm sure David was in the wrong place at the wrong time. He was clean."

Rising, Clay strode to the edge of the deck, where he leaned on the railing, his back to her. "Did you tell your husband that you'd been threatened?"

"Of course. I was worried they might try to harm him, so I called him right after the guy left."

"What did he say?"

The phone call was vivid in her memory, as was David's disbelief. Hurt flared anew as she recalled how he had interrupted her to say that they would talk about it when he got in that night.

Clay faced her. "Was he angry?"

No, she thought. He'd been impatient, rushed. Very unlike the man she'd loved. "No," she said, unable to meet Clay's waiting gaze. "He didn't sound angry."

"If my wife called me at work and told me that my colleague had threatened her life, I would have wanted to rip his throat out." Crossing to her, he knelt before her knees. "I would have dropped everything to get to her as quickly as possible to make sure she was safe. And then I would have gone after the bastard who threatened her."

"That's you—"

"That's a man in love with a woman," he cut in, skimming his hand over her knee and tangling the tips of his fingers with hers. "That's a man who doesn't want anything or anyone to get anywhere near hurting the woman he loves. That's a man who has nothing to do with a threat that's been made against his wife."

She shook her head in denial. "He wouldn't have—"

"Have you ever contacted him from here?"

"No."

"You handled the divorce through a lawyer and never had any contact with David again, didn't you?"

"Yes."

"Why?" he asked.

She rubbed at her eyes with fingers that trembled. This was going where she'd never wanted to go. It had always been easier to deny that someone she'd loved could ever want to harm her. "I didn't want him to know where I am," she said, her voice low but strong.

"Why?"

She raised her head, met his eyes, which were warm and kind, sympathetic. "You know why."

"Why can't you say it?"

"Say what?" She pushed up, tugging her hand free of his and retreating to the place at the edge of the deck where he'd stood earlier. The moon glinting off the water was much easier to face. "That I devoted more than a decade of my life to a man who cheated on me and then might have wanted me dead?"

"That wasn't so difficult," Clay said from behind her, his tone light.

Closing her eyes, she curled her fingers around the wooden railing. "You don't understand how much I don't want it to be him."

"Maybe I do. No one wants to admit that they're wrong about someone they loved." Moving up behind her, he placed gentle hands on her shoulders. "But people change, Jess. Sometimes, they become strangers."

She might have tried to shift away from him, but his

241

hands on her, so comforting, so tender, calmed her. Instead of running away, she turned into him, wrapping her arms around him and holding tight. Here was a man who would never betray her. A man who would fight for her. A man who would never knowingly hurt her.

She shivered when he pressed his lips to the curve of her neck. Then his hands caught in her hair, and his mouth settled on hers and demanded. She answered the embrace with demands of her own, gripping his forearms when their tongues met.

Suddenly, she couldn't breathe, her senses overwhelmed by him as he angled her head back and trailed wet kisses down her throat. Slipping a hand between them, he cupped her breast, kneaded it through the cotton of her shirt. She gasped, her senses swimming, when that same hand slid under the cotton and continued its caress against bare flesh.

She tried to focus on returning the pleasure, eager to do her own damage to his sanity, but his mouth, warm and wet, replaced the hand on her breast, and she lost track of her intentions, sucking in a sharp breath at the gentle tug of teeth through her shirt. Her knees turned to water, and his arms were there to support her.

He lifted her, and she wrapped her legs around his waist as he carried her inside. She pulled his shirt over his head, laughing low in her throat when he faked a stagger. His stumble seemed genuine as, spreading kisses over his chest, she arrived at a nipple.

In the bedroom, he lowered her to the bed, his lips never leaving hers. His hands seemed to be everywhere at once, on her breasts, in her hair, gripping her hips, grazing her ribs, as if furious need were overtaking a desire to go slowly.

Jessie was caught up in an urgency of her own, wanting desperately to feel his naked flesh against her. His name rasped through her lips when he unfastened her jeans and slid them down her legs. Reciprocating, she discovered with delight that he was already hard, but he caught her hand before she could touch him.

"Not yet," he murmured, silencing her protest with a kiss. His fingers brushed down the inside of her thigh, stroked the back of her knee. He swallowed her restless moan, answered it with a more intimate caress that had her pressing against him. The caress grew bolder as he lowered his head and found her breast.

Jessie writhed on the sheets, sinking her fingers into his shoulder as a ragged sound tore from her throat. God, he knew what to do, how to touch her, how to make her crazy.

She tried to drag his head up for a kiss, but he resisted, his laugh low when she choked out a protest. "Relax," he whispered. "Just let me love you."

She thought she might burst with need as he kissed his way down her torso, his urgency in firm check when he investigated her belly button with his tongue. Everywhere his tongue touched, flames of pleasure leapt. And he was taking his damn time, one hand gently pinning her in place, the other trailing after his mouth, that caress almost a tickle.

Myriad sensations flooded over her as he tasted the back of her knee, the curve of her calf, the arch of her foot. His tongue wrapped around a toe, and the intensity of the feeling wrenched a long moan from her. She didn't think she could take anymore. Then his mouth ventured up her body and into uncharted territory. Her head arched back against the bed in shock, and control spun away as she took much, much more.

When she floated back, Clay was kissing his way back up her belly, a smug grin curving his lips. She didn't think she could move, until she realized that she may have been limp, but he was far from it.

Rolling over onto him, she scraped her nails over his nipples, enjoying the way his brow furrowed when she replaced her fingers with her teeth. His hands grasped her hips, but she pinned his wrists to the bed on either side of his head, nipped his chin and trailed her tongue down his throat. His stomach muscles tensed under her lips, and she thought he might have growled her name as she closed her mouth over him. He moved his hips restlessly, as if fighting to keep still while she savored her ability to make him squirm.

"Wait," he gasped. "Jesus, if you don't stop, I'm going to—"

Holding his shoulders to the bed, she straddled him. She knew where to find his stash of condoms now and leaned over him to retrieve one from the drawer.

When she finally took him in, and his fingers dug helplessly into her hips, she smiled. Concentrating on the pleasure that rippled over his face, she set the pace, focused on the way his jaw clenched as the tension built.

When he exploded under her, his spasms sent her flying over the peak with him.

Sliding down next to him, she fought to catch her breath. Her body quivered with aftershocks as he trailed a hand up her arm, cupped her cheek. He pressed a kiss to her temple that was so tender, so loving, that she swallowed back tears.

"I'm so lucky you happened to me," she whispered.

"We happened to each other," he said. "Sleep now."

"Are you kidding? Where's that pasta? I'm starved."

Chapter 20

Shaking Clay awake, Jessie waited patiently for him to blink her into focus. "I have to go," she said.

He looked at the clock, disoriented. "What time is it?"

"Eleven-forty. Where are the keys to the Jeep?"

He sat up. "In the morning? What's going on?"

"Evening." Finding his khaki shorts on the floor, she started going through pockets. She'd been up for several hours already, dealing with some work issues by phone and trying to convince herself that she needed to stay put. But she and Clay had spent the past two days sleeping, making love, and sleeping some more. Other than a slight, persistent headache and achy muscles, she was feeling more like herself again. Which meant she was ready to climb out of her skin with the need to jump back into work.

She'd talked to Greg the day before, but he had been coy about whatever it was he was chasing on the hoax story. She suspected he'd been told to leave her out of the loop until she was cleared to return to work. Hating it but determined to be an obedient patient for a change, she'd let him dodge her questions. She figured she'd find out soon enough what he was up to.

She'd also talked to Detective Mubarek, but he'd had nothing new to report other than that he had not yet located her ex-husband. Ditto on Hank Peters, who seemed to have vanished.

The lack of progress all around had begun to drive her a

little nutty when one of her news assistants had called with an urgent message.

"The mayor wants to meet with me," she told a bleary Clay. "I have to go now."

Swinging out of bed, he snagged his shorts out of her hands and started pulling them on. "I'm going with you."

"You can't," she said. "If he sees me with someone, he might bolt."

"What makes you think that?"

"We're not meeting at a well-lit restaurant, okay? He wants to see me in private."

"Why you? Why not Greg?"

"I don't know. I used to cover City Hall. Maybe he trusts me. Look, I don't have time for this. Keys?"

"They're on the table by the door. We go together. End of discussion."

"Fine. But you're riding in the back."

"Like hell I am."

"Let's go through the drive-thru on the way," Clay said from the backseat.

As Jessie checked her watch, she ground the SUV's gears. "No time."

"You need to eat something."

"Would you stop mothering me? I'm fine."

"It's for me then. I happen to be hungry." He grinned at her in the reflection of the rearview. "I worked up quite an appetite today."

She flushed. He'd made her scream, something she'd never done during lovemaking. The memory, and the throb of remembered passion, had her shifting in her seat. "On the way back." She ground the gears again. "Damn."

"Thought you said you could drive a stick."

"It's been awhile."

"No shit."

"Do you mind? You're distracting me."

"Where are we going?"

"Connecticut."

His head popped up in the rearview mirror. "Excuse me?"

She laughed at his expression, surprised that she could be amused when her every muscle was tense. "It's off Estero Boulevard on Fort Myers Beach."

"Oh, yeah. I know that street."

Snagging his cell phone out of its cubby near the gear shift, she tossed it back to him. "Can you call Tom and ask him to back off? He's right on our tail, and I don't want anything spooking the mayor. This meeting is very unlike him."

Clay pressed numbers, but he was smiling. "Greg said you were a slave driver."

"When did he say that?"

"We've had our chats. You need to cut the poor guy some serious slack."

"You're teasing, right?"

With the phone to his ear, he grinned. "You're wondering what else he told me."

"Am not."

"Tom, it's Clay. Hey, we need you to be not so obvious for a while. Great, thanks."

"Let's try Greg," she said and rattled off his cell number.

"And you were calling me a pit bull," he muttered. "Won't he be in bed?"

"I doubt it."

In another minute, he said, "Greg, how's it going?"

Jessie watched him in the rearview. "Don't say anything

you don't want broadcast on the airwaves."

He covered the mouthpiece with his hand. "Hello? Do I look like an idiot?"

She suppressed a smile, thinking he was cute when he was indignant. "Sorry."

Scowling, he turned his attention back to the phone. "What? No, I was just talking to your boss." He paused, chuckled. "Tell me about it."

"Hey."

Meeting her eyes in the mirror, he grinned. "Yep, she's giving me that look right now. You know the one."

"When you're done playing, may I talk to him?"

Clay waved away the hand she held out. "So what have you been up to the past couple of days?" A pause, then, "When did that happen?"

"What is it?" Jessie asked.

His jaw hardening, he ignored her. "And he's meeting you when? . . . That's good. We'll be there. Hang on. Jess wants to talk to you."

He handed Jessie the phone over the seat. "Hank Peters, or whatever his name is, contacted Greg. Says he has information about who set up the hoax. They're meeting at Greg's."

"The hoax and the maintenance guy who tried to kill me are connected?" Jessie said, shocked.

Clay nodded. "Go figure."

Cradling the phone between her shoulder and chin, she shifted gears with one hand and steered with the hand in the cast. More gears ground. "Damn."

"Jess?" Greg said. "How're you feeling?"

"Clay told me what's going on. When is Peters going to be there?"

"About an hour. It was tough to be civil to him after

what he did to you. I don't know if I'll be able to keep it to-gether when I'm face to face with him."

"You don't have to worry about that because as soon as we hang up, you're going to call the police and tell them when and where to pick him up."

"No way. I want to talk to him first. He hinted that he knows who's behind the hoax."

"Let the police deal with him," she said.

"Jess, come on."

"If you don't do as I tell you, I'll write you up for insub-ordination. I'm not kidding."

"Fine," he said. "But I think you're wrong."

"After you call the cops, get out of your apartment. Is that understood?"

"Yeah, whatever."

The phone beeped. "What's that?" Jessie asked.

"Battery's dying," Clay said. "Backup's at home. Sorry."

"Damn. Okay, so you're not going to pull any heroics, are you, Greg?"

"No."

"Good. It's really for the best."

"Sure." But he sounded distant.

"We'll talk about it more later, okay?"

"Sure," he said.

"Greg, please."

"I have to get going if I'm going to get out of here."

"All right. Thanks, okay?"

"Bye."

He cut her off before she could respond. She immedi-ately started pushing buttons.

"You calling the cops for him?" Clay asked.

"Yep, and then I'm calling Gillian to let her know what's going on." As she reported the situation to the answering desk sergeant, the phone beeped another warning. Disconnecting the call, she peered at the display. "Phone's dead. Guess Gillian will have to wait." She tossed it into the passenger seat. "God, Greg had better listen to me and get the hell out of there."

"If I were him, I wouldn't," Clay said.

"Neither would I." She pressed her lips together, checked her watch. "He said Peters wasn't due for an hour, so we'll head his way after I meet the mayor. The cops should be crawling all over his place by then."

"Can't say I'm disappointed. I'd like my own crack at Mr. Peters."

It was just shy of midnight when Jessie steered the SUV onto Connecticut, a block-long road off the main drag of Fort Myers Beach, and killed the headlights. The clouds hanging over the gulf were thick and black, blocking the moon so that no light glinted off the water a few yards from the end of the road. Jessie recognized the one parked car, a Lexus, as the mayor's.

She unbuckled her seat belt. "Try to keep your head down."

"I'm not the one who's going to be in the line of fire," he replied.

"I hate to burst your bubble, but the mayor isn't in the habit of blowing away journalists with assault weapons."

"It stuns me how you know exactly what to say to ease my mind. Just stay where Tom and I can see you. I don't think that's too much to ask."

She pecked him on the lips before she got out and walked down to the beach, her shoes scuffing in the sand.

The mayor, hands in his pockets, stared out at the water.

"Hello, Mayor Kimball," she said.

He turned to greet her, and it struck her as always that he was young for his office. Not even forty, he had no gray in his thick, light brown hair, and the only evidence of wrinkles were laugh lines around eyes as dark as expensive chocolate. As long as she'd known him, she'd liked him. He was one of the few politicians who really did seem to be in the fray to help the common man.

He took her offered hand, and his was damp. "Please, it's Paul," he said. "Thanks for meeting me. I know the circumstances are rather furtive."

"Just so we understand each other, this is on the record."

"I would prefer it to be off the record, if that's at all possible."

"I guess I'm a little confused, Paul. I don't think you requested this meeting so I could be your friend."

"No. No, I didn't. Though what I'm about to tell you few of my friends know, or would understand."

"This has to be on the record," she said. "You know that, or you wouldn't have asked me here. What would be the point?"

His shoulders sagged as he plunged his hands back into his pockets. "Will you walk with me?"

"Of course." She said a silent apology to Clay as they fell in step together.

The mayor didn't speak until they'd walked several yards up the beach. "I've made a stupid, stupid error in judgment," he said. "It's going to ruin me. Politically and personally."

She stopped near the water's edge, where the sand had been packed hard by the waves, and he faced her, his posture unusually weary. He looked beaten. "Are you sure you want to do this?" she asked.

"I have to. My conscience demands it."

"Once it's out there, you can't take it back."

"I know," he said. "I appreciate that, Jess. I know you'll be fair."

"All right. Take your time."

He drew in a long breath. "Officer Drake was blackmailed to corroborate the photos of his fellow officers."

"Yes. He told me."

"Did he tell you how he was blackmailed?" he asked.

"No."

"He was my lover."

Jessie didn't know what to say, how to react. Shock had rendered her mind blank.

He offered a sick smile. "You should have seen the look on my wife's face."

As the initial disbelief waned, she began to imagine the repercussions. "You really don't want to do this, Mayor Kimball."

"Don't tell me you'd walk away from this story," he said. "The headline would be a best seller: 'Mayor confesses to clear gay lover's name.' "

"You're right. It'll ruin you." And it was suddenly important to her that this man not be ruined. He was one of so few good guys.

"I've accepted that." Misery flooded his dark eyes. "Perhaps if I'd come forward sooner, Taylor would still be alive."

"It won't bring him back."

"I know that, but I still have to do it. I won't be able to live with myself otherwise."

"Do you know who blackmailed him?"

"I don't think *he* knew. And after we realized someone knew about us, we didn't see each other again. We were afraid there might be some legit photos out there, and if there weren't, we were determined to make sure none turned up. We didn't speak, either, for fear of wire taps and tape recordings. We ran scared, Jess. Completely, desperately scared. Taylor did exactly what the blackmailer demanded. He did it for me, to spare me. And our families."

"What did the blackmailer ask for besides backing up the fake photos?"

"That's it, as far as I know."

"So ruining you wasn't part of the plan," she said, thinking out loud.

"I don't think so, no."

"Then who did the blackmailer want to ruin? The entire police department? A particular officer? *The Star-News?*"

"I don't know."

And where did the maintenance guy fit in? she wondered. Why had he tried to kill her and no one else at the newspaper involved in the story?

"In a way, I'm using you, you know," Paul said.

She focused on him, still not quite able to wrap her brain around what he'd told her. "How are you using me?"

"When you report what I've told you, I'll have cleared Taylor's name. He was a good man, a good cop. We were together more than a year, and he was the most honorable man I've ever known. He did what he did to protect the people he cared about, no matter the cost to him." Pausing, he grasped her hand. "I know you'll be fair to him, to us."

"I'll do my best."

"I know you will. That's why I came to you."

"I hope you still feel that way tomorrow."

Chapter 21

While Clay struggled to process what she'd told him about the mayor and Taylor Drake, Jessie slowed for a red light. Her brain was racing. So many questions, so few answers. Everything that had happened to all of them in the past week was connected. But how? And why had she become a target when Greg, the primary reporter, hadn't?

Of everything, that made the least amount of sense to her. He was the one chasing the story, the one doing all the digging. True, she was guiding him, but he had developed relationships, many of them personal, with the sources. If something were to happen to him, picking up where he left off would be very difficult. To her, that made him the most logical liability to the person behind the hoax—especially now, with Hank Peters arranging to meet with him. The maintenance man could potentially answer most of their questions and expose the creator of the bogus story.

As that thought hit her, her pulse stuttered. She had told Greg to get out of his apartment to keep him from getting caught in the crossfire if Peters resisted arrest. It hadn't occurred to her that Greg's safety could be at risk *because* Peters had contacted him.

She took the turn onto Greg's street too fast. Next to her, Clay braced against the door and said something, but his words were lost in the sudden roar in her ears.

At least a dozen police cars, red lights flashing, were parked haphazardly along the curb in front of Greg's duplex. She zeroed in on the ambulance, and her heart stopped. "Oh no. Oh God, no."

Slamming the SUV into park, she leapt out and raced for the front door. She heard Clay on her heels, calling her name, but didn't slow or respond. She had to get to Greg.

On the porch, a police officer with broad shoulders, a thick neck and skin the rich shade of coffee stepped in front of her and grabbed her by the arms to hold her back. "You can't go in there."

"I'm his friend," she said. The officer was familiar, and she struggled to place his face, to make a connection that would make it easier to get him to talk to her.

"Doesn't matter," he said. "It's a crime scene. You'll have to wait over there." He gestured at a small crowd of people gathering in the yard.

She clutched at his shirtfront, placing her weight to prevent him from steering her back down the steps. "Just tell me what happened. Please."

"I'm not supposed to talk to the media," the officer said.

And it clicked who he was. "You're Officer Snyder, right? Rick Snyder? I rode with you and your partner about a year and a half ago. Remember that? You had to handle a ridiculous call about a couple at an all-you-can-eat barbecue joint who wanted to take leftovers. Remember? Jessie Rhoades."

He hesitated, his brow furrowing. "I'm sorry, Ms. Rhoades, but I can't talk to you."

"Please, the man who lives here, Greg Roberts, works with me. I'm his friend. In fact, I'm the one who called you guys."

"One of the investigating officers will want to talk to you then." He paused, looking around as if to make sure no one overheard him. "The information you gave us was a little off."

"Off how?" Her composure slipped a notch. Oh God, oh God, had she screwed up? Had she made a mistake that had gotten Greg hurt? Or killed?

Behind her, Clay put a firm hand on her shoulder. The gesture, so simple, snapped her control back, helped ease the growing pressure in her chest.

"We had an unmarked car parked on the street," Officer Snyder said, "ready for when you said the suspect was expected to show up. Turns out, he, or someone, was already inside when we got here. Next thing you know, we had shots fired."

Her vision darkened for an instant, and she clamped her hand over Clay's on her shoulder. Touching him anchored her as dread slithered through her stomach. "Greg?" she asked, her voice faint.

"Shot in the chest," Snyder said. "Medics are working on him. I'm sorry. Now, please, wait over there."

She couldn't move, couldn't breathe. Greg had been shot in the chest. Oh Jesus.

"Jess," Clay said softly. "Come with me."

He led her down the steps, and she went with him mechanically. Her legs felt stiff, as if her knees resisted bending as she walked. Everything seemed surreal. The gathering neighbors, many of them in pajamas, stood on a lawn that needed mowing, whispering and murmuring. The clouds overhead, silhouetted by the moon, moved at a furious pace, as if late for a storm on the other coast of Florida.

Standing beside Clay on the sidewalk, Jessie felt control splintering. She had to do something. She couldn't just stand there and do nothing, not when Greg was fighting for his life, or perhaps already dead. She had to find out everything she could about who did this to him so she could stop him. She wanted desperately to stop him, and then make him pay.

"Jess?"

She looked up at Clay, noticing that the porch light made his hair look golden. Seeing his face, the worry in his eyes, made her breath hitch, and she stepped back from him, raising her hands to keep him from re-establishing contact. If she let him keep touching her, she was sure she would lose it.

Tom joined them, out of breath. "What's going on?"

As Clay filled in the guard, Jessie headed for the crowd watching the scene. "Where are you going?" She heard the scrape of Clay's shoes, knew he jogged after her.

She thrust away her fear for Greg, plunging her brain into reporter mode as she approached a middle-aged man in shorts and a T-shirt and extended her hand. "Jessie Rhoades with *The Star-News*. May I ask you a few questions?"

"Sorry, I didn't see anything," he said.

She thanked him and moved on, getting the same response from two others before she reached an elderly couple huddled together in bathrobes and slippers. "Hi. Jessie Rhoades with *The Star-News*. May I—"

"Don't bother. We don't know anything."

The man, thin and balding, said it so fast that she knew he was lying. She focused on the woman, who looked like the perfect grandma: pleasantly plump, white-haired, rosy cheeked, with kind, hazel eyes.

"What about you, ma'am?" Jessie asked. "Did you see or hear anything? Anything at all?"

The woman, wearing a pink, lightweight cotton robe and pink terrycloth slippers, gave a tentative nod, then shuddered. "We retired here from Chicago to get away from the crime."

Jessie touched the woman's arm in a comforting gesture. "I moved here from Chicago, too. Have you been here long?"

Behind Jessie, Clay spoke so that only she could hear. "You're interfering with a police investigation."

"I'm just talking to this sweet woman, who's obviously upset," she replied, giving the woman what she hoped was a reassuring smile and not the wooden grimace it felt like.

"We've been here four years," the woman said, patting Jessie's hand on her arm. "I've never seen anything like this here."

"What did you see?" Jessie asked, her tone gentle, coaxing.

"Marion," the older man said, a warning in his voice.

"We heard a gunshot," Marion said. "And Dan called the police."

"Did you look outside?"

Marion's hazel eyes welled as she glanced at her husband as if for guidance.

Fearing she was about to lose her connection, Jessie said, "The young man who was hurt is a good friend of mine."

"You're lying," the man named Dan said. "You're just a reporter trying to get your story."

Jessie blocked out his hostility even as the urge to tell him to shut up threatened to overwhelm her. "His name is Greg Roberts," she told Marion. "He's twenty-three."

Marion's tears overflowed. "I know. He helps Dan with yard work. Such a sweet young man."

"Then like me, you probably want very badly to help find who hurt him. If there's anything you can tell me—"

"I saw a man running away," Marion said, casting a fleeting glance at her husband, who glowered but remained silent. "While Dan was on the phone, I peeked through the blinds."

Here we go, Jessie thought. "Did you see his face?"

"No. He, uh, had on a cap, a baseball cap. And he was kind of far away."

"What was he wearing?"

"Dark clothing. Shorts. Tennis shoes. Skinny. He had very white legs." Clasping her hands together, she worried the narrow band of gold on her left ring finger. "I'm sorry. This isn't very helpful, is it?"

"But it is," Jessie said. "Is there anything else about him? Did he limp, for example?" She was reaching, fishing for something that would set the intruder apart from half the population of southwest Florida.

Marion shook her head. "No."

"Did he get into a car?"

"No, he ran between—" She broke off, her pink face going white as she stared over Jessie's shoulder. "That's him right there."

Jessie turned to see Stuart Davis in black shorts and shirt, tennis shoes and a tattered Florida Marlins baseball cap trotting across the yard.

Clay put a restraining hand on Jessie's forearm as the older reporter, sweat streaking his red face, fell to his knees before them and sucked in air. Gray hair stuck in wet strands to his forehead and the back of his neck. "Bastard got away from me," he panted.

Shoving aside suspicion, Jessie knelt beside him, close enough to smell the acrid odor of his sweat. "What happened, Stuart?"

"I went after the guy, but he was too fast for me." He slammed a fist against the grassy ground. "Damn it!"

"Tell me what happened," Jessie said. She had locked away all emotion. "How did Greg get shot?"

"Better hurry, Jess," Clay said.

Jessie saw that a police officer had spotted Stuart and was headed their way. She clamped her fingers around Stuart's arm as he coughed and fought for breath. "Come on, Stuart, talk to me."

"Greg called me," he gasped. "Said he wanted my advice." More coughing. "Said you told him to call the cops to pick up Peters. He didn't want to. So I told him I'd come over, help him interview the guy, then we'd call the cops after. I was knocking on his door when I heard a gunshot. The front door was locked, so I ran around back, saw someone run out of the house. I went after him."

"What did he look like?"

He hung his head, his breathing steadying. "I couldn't see in the dark."

"Tall or short?"

He glanced up, and his eyes burned with fury. "I know the fucking routine. I told you I didn't get a good look."

"You saw enough to know it was the intruder," she said. "You must have seen something else."

"All I saw was the guy ran like a rabbit. I couldn't keep up."

"Large? Medium? Small?"

"I don't know. I guess medium. Maybe on the small side."

"Clothing?"

"It could have been any color. It's dark."

"Hair?"

"It was covered."

"With a ski mask? A hat? What?"

"I don't know." Staggering to his feet, he glared at her. "I don't fucking know, all right?"

"Think about it. You're not even thinking about it."

Stuart looked like he might lash out at her, and Clay

stepped between them at the same time that a police officer grasped Stuart by the shoulder. "Sir, would you come with me, please?"

Stuart jerked away from the guy. "Why?"

"Several witnesses reported seeing you running from the scene. We have some questions for you."

"I didn't do anything," Stuart said. To Jessie, he said, "Tell him who I am."

"Who you are doesn't change our need to ask you some questions," the officer said.

"Jess, Jesus, tell him."

"You have to tell the police what you know, Stuart," Jessie said.

As the officer led the protesting reporter away, Clay asked, "What do you think?"

"I think he gave Greg some bad advice," she said.

Before he could respond, paramedics appeared in the door of the apartment with Greg on a gurney. A medic held a blood-soaked towel to his chest, and an oxygen mask covered his still, white face. His eyes were closed.

Jessie started to shake, and Clay put his arm around her.

Staring out the SUV's windshield as Clay drove them to the hospital, Jessie went over everything she should have done differently. She should have been more firm with Greg, more authoritative. She should have ditched the meeting with the mayor and gone straight to Greg to make sure he did as she'd told him. She should have been more specific on the phone with the desk sergeant, telling him that Hank Peters could already have been at Greg's or that Greg's safety might be at risk. Then perhaps the police would have been more forceful rather than covertly lying in wait for Peters.

"You okay?" Clay asked, putting his hand over hers

resting on her knee. His palm felt hot against her icy fingers.

She swallowed back a wave of emotion and didn't dare glance at him. "No."

"You're blaming yourself."

She bit into her bottom lip.

"You can't go there."

"I should have known he wouldn't listen," she said.

"You're not his mother, Jess. You're his editor. The only person responsible for his actions is Greg."

"I would have done the same thing in his position," she said. "We both said we would. Why didn't I do more?"

"You called the police."

"But I didn't give them enough information. I didn't make it clear to them that Greg could be in danger."

"You didn't know that at the time," he said. "Neither of us knew."

"I didn't think it through enough. If I had—"

"You can second-guess your decisions for the rest of your life. It isn't going to change what happened."

She did look at him then. "Who shot him, Clay? Did Peters set him up?"

"Greg indicated that Peters wanted to share information about who was behind the bogus story," he said.

"Peters, or whoever it was, could have lied," she said. "He was just a voice on the phone, wasn't he?"

"Greg didn't say how Peters contacted him."

"It had to be a phone call," she said. "Greg said something about how he was worried about being civil when he met him face to face. It might not have even been the maintenance guy on the phone."

"Or it *was* Peters," he said, "and whoever's behind the hoax found out he was going to tell all."

"But taking out Greg won't stop Peters from contacting someone else at the newspaper," she said. "Maybe we'll get lucky, and Peters will figure that out."

"I hate to debunk that, but he might have shown up when he was supposed to, saw all the cops and assumed Greg ratted him out."

"Or it was all a setup to take out Greg," she said. "He'd been chasing something the past few days, but I don't know what it was. Maybe he'd gotten too close to something." She slammed the side of her fist against the SUV door. "Damn it! What the *fuck* is going on?"

They were only a few blocks from the hospital when Clay cleared his throat. "I think we need to look closely at Stuart Davis."

The suggestion didn't surprise her. She was having her own suspicions about Stuart, but it still sent a current of dread rippling through her. "You think he could be behind the hoax?"

"Stuart is a bitter man," Clay said. "He blames the newspaper for much of what's wrong with his life, even if it's unjustified. He would know the mechanics of how to set up a bogus story. He'd know what you and the other editors would consider newsworthy and what you'd call bullshit. He knows how the newsroom works, what the politics are and how to play them."

She nodded as other pieces fell into place in her head. "He could have found out about the mayor's relationship with Taylor Drake from one of his many underground sources. The man seems to know everyone in this town. That would have opened the blackmail door." She absently massaged the ache in the hand she had struck against the door. "But why would he go after me?"

"You said yourself that he doesn't care for you."

"Yeah, but I haven't gotten the impression he hates me enough to want to kill me."

"Letting on that he feels that way would be foolish, don't you think? And Stuart has had access to you like no stranger. He could have walked out into the parking lot on a smoke break, cut your brake line and been back inside the building without anyone suspecting, or noticing, anything odd," Clay said. "He also knows your habits. He knows you keep a water bottle on your desk."

"But why enlist Peters to drug my water when Stuart could walk in and out of my office without anyone giving it a second thought?"

"He wouldn't want to risk getting caught," he said.

"So you're thinking Stuart enlisted Peters' help, but then Peters got an attack of the guilts and contacted Greg. When Greg called Stuart tonight for advice on how to handle the situation, Stuart had to act fast to cover his ass."

Clay nodded. "Makes perfect sense to me."

She thought of how she had tolerated Stuart's bad attitude for months, had even defended him to Gillian Westin when he probably should have been fired for insubordination or just plain laziness. If he was behind it all, she had handed him an easy advantage by not dealing with him when she should have. And now Taylor Drake was dead, and Greg was fighting for his life.

Clenching her jaw against a rising tide of emotion, she said, "I don't understand why Stuart would shoot Greg and not go after Peters. Peters is the one he would need to keep quiet."

"Maybe he panicked. Or maybe Greg told Stuart something that indicated Greg knew what Stuart was up to."

"Damn it," she said under her breath. "I should have insisted that Greg tell me what he was chasing. There's no excuse for letting him keep it to himself for so long."

"You were letting him do his job, Jess."

"And look where it got him."

Inside the ER, Jessie went to the front desk to ask about Greg's condition, and Clay went to a pay phone to call Marshall to fill him in. With the latest developments, it seemed foolish to waste Marshall's time tracking Jessie's ex-husband when there were stronger suspects closer to home. But Marshall, who answered his cell phone at Chicago's O'Hare airport, where he was about to catch the last flight of the day to Fort Myers, had disturbing news that unraveled Clay's theories about what was happening. Before returning to Jessie's side, he took a detour to talk to Tom, who hovered, hyper alert, near the entrance to the ER.

"A public place is a bad place to be, Mr. Christopher," the guard said.

"Getting her to leave before the kid's stabilized isn't going to happen."

Tom cracked the ghost of a smile. "I figured as much."

"Look, my P.I. buddy Marshall is on his way back from Chicago. How quickly could you get reinforcements in play?"

It seemed impossible for Tom to tense further, but he did. "The ex-husband?"

"He is apparently in the area."

Whipping out his cell phone, Tom punched a speed-dial button. To Clay, he said, "We need to get Jess to a secure area right away."

"I'll work on that."

While Tom began issuing orders into his phone, Clay went to the waiting area, where Jessie sat alone, her head bowed over her clasped hands, as if praying. As he approached, she lifted her head. Fatigue had drawn dark circles under her gray eyes and sketched lines on either side of her nose. She hadn't had enough time to regain her full strength, and this new stress was taking its toll fast, physically and emotionally.

Sitting beside her, he drew her against him, and she rested her head on his chest. "I called Mel," she said.

"Does she have an office here?"

"Yes. Why?"

"You might be more comfortable there."

"I'm not going to be comfortable until we hear something about Greg." As she linked their fingers, he noticed the contrast of their hands—hers small and pale, his large and tanned. "Who did you call just now?" she asked.

"Marshall." He didn't tell her about David. She was already walking a very thin emotional line. There was no sense in frightening her before they knew what David was up to.

Mel, arriving in all her disheveled glory, looked immensely relieved when she saw Jessie. "Thank God, you're in the waiting room this time."

Jessie stood to meet her. "They haven't told us anything."

Mel dumped her purse on a chair. "I'll check on him."

Clay got up before she could run off. "Mel, can we wait in your office?"

Jessie's anxiety shifted to impatience. "Why? We're fine right here."

"The public nature of the place is unsettling Tom," Clay said.

Jessie sank back down on the chair. "Of course."

Mel dug in her purse for keys that she handed to Clay. "Jess knows where it is. I'll be right up."

The silence was tense as Jessie, Clay and Tom took the elevator to the seventh floor. In Mel's office, Tom checked it out, then left them alone with the door closed.

The space was small but classy, with navy leather furniture, smoky glass tables and bright red lamps. A large desk faced a window that looked out on darkness at the moment but by day, Jessie knew, framed a verdant wooded area of pine trees and palms. A bowl of fruit sat on one corner of the desk, and Jessie imagined the mini refrigerator under the desk held lots of yogurt and carrot sticks, testaments to Mel's commitment to healthy snacking.

Jessie felt as if she melted into one of two leather, overstuffed chairs that flanked the sofa, her eyes burning with suppressed emotion. She couldn't remember ever feeling so helpless, so powerless.

Clay went to the coffeemaker that occupied a table along one wall. "Want some coffee?"

She put a hand on her stomach and thought there was no way in hell it would welcome coffee. "Whatever you want is fine," she said.

Apparently deciding against coffee, he checked out the fruit bowl. "She's got apples. Looks like Granny Smiths. Want one?"

Jessie closed her eyes. "Please stop."

He turned from the desk. "Pardon?"

"You're taking care of me. I hate that."

A moment later, he took a seat on the sofa adjacent to her chair. "Why do you hate it so much?"

"I don't need to be taken care of."

"Maybe you don't need it," he said. "Maybe I do."

"I'm sorry I seem so ungrateful. I'm not good at being protected."

"There you go again with the grateful business. When are you going to understand that I'm not doing any of this because I want gratitude? Isn't it obvious how much in—"

The door swung open, cutting him off, and he leapt to his feet, ready to fight.

Mel entered talking. "He's in surgery," she said, shrugging off a sterile coverall. "Bullet's lodged in a lung. He's lost a lot of blood, but the surgeon is optimistic." Crossing to Jessie, she took her hands. "Greg's healthy and strong, Jess. All we can do now is wait."

Chapter 22

"Jess."

She opened her eyes, startled that someone hovered over her and even more startled when she didn't immediately recognize her surroundings. But then she saw Clay, felt his hand at her cheek, and relaxed back against the leather cushions of the sofa. "I fell asleep," she said.

"I made you some coffee," Clay said, pressing a warm cup into her hands.

Her thought processes were sluggish as she sat up, glancing around to get oriented. Where they were and why came to her in slow pieces until, groggy but cognizant, she tried the coffee. It was hot but not much else. She hoped the caffeine kicked in quick. "Any word on Greg?" she asked.

"He's still in surgery."

"What time is it?"

"Just after seven a.m. I wouldn't have awakened you, but Gillian Westin is here. She's being adamant about seeing you."

"How unlike her."

He knelt before her, his gaze searching. "Are you up to it?"

No, she thought. But what choice did she have? She'd have to face her boss eventually. "Send her in," she said, giving him what she hoped was a reassuring smile.

"I'd be happy to tell her to go away until you're ready."

"You're sweet, but I can handle it. She needs to know what happened."

Rising, he said, "I'll go get her."

He slipped out of the room without a word, and Jessie stared into her coffee. What was she going to tell her boss? The story had swerved so out of control that people were being seriously injured or killed, and the only theory they had was that an older, volatile reporter was taking revenge on a newspaper he blamed for the wretchedness of his life. At least it beat the theory that Jessie's ex-husband was engineering some kind of twisted payback. Either way, Gillian was going to glare her right through the floor.

And that would be before Jessie told her that Taylor Drake had been blackmailed to lie to protect the mayor's sexual orientation.

Gillian entered Mel's office on the whisper of blue silk, looking as poised as she would have had she just arrived for a day of work. Her brows lifted in surprise when she saw Jessie. "You look terrible," she said.

Jessie almost laughed at Gillian's accusatory tone, as if she expected everyone to look their best no matter the circumstances. But Jessie didn't laugh. She felt like she might never laugh again. "You probably already know that Greg is in surgery."

"Yes, Mr. Christopher updated me in the elevator," Gillian said as she sat in the chair across from Jessie. "I'm assuming you can tell me how one of my best reporters got shot."

Jessie took a moment to brace herself mentally. "He'd arranged a meeting with Hank Peters, who'd indicated he had information about who set up the scandal."

"I see," the executive editor said, folding her arms across her chest. "And you were fine with Greg meeting with Mr.

Peters, a man suspected of trying to kill you?"

"No, I wasn't fine with it," Jessie said, concentrating on remaining calm. "I told Greg to call the police to tell them when and where to pick up Peters. I called them, too."

"Did it occur to either of you to call me?"

"Yes, but the battery in the cell phone died."

"How convenient," Gillian said, and there was a sneer in her voice. "And there were no pay phones handy. You've spent the past several hours here, and not once did you try to call me. I had to find out about the shooting on the radio this morning."

Jessie, feeling her muscles stiffening, tried to suppress the tension. "I'm sorry. I didn't think about calling you after we got here. I was worried about Greg, and—"

"Don't lie to me."

"I have no reason to lie," Jessie said.

"Except to cover your ass."

Jessie's face flooded with warmth. "I'm not covering my ass."

Gillian's eyes narrowed to black slits. "I don't like your tone."

"Then we're even."

Gillian shot to her feet. "I don't have to sit here and let you talk to me this way. I'm your boss, and you're being terribly insubordinate."

Jessie set aside her coffee cup, fearing she might hurl it at Gillian as her tenuous grip on control threatened to slip. "A man who works for us is fighting for his life right now. I don't think it's an appropriate time to pull rank."

"I think it's a perfect time to pull rank," Gillian said. "You've failed me on just about every level, Jessie. You haven't kept me adequately informed since this story started unraveling. You have defied—"

"That's not—"

"I'm not finished," Gillian cut in, her cheeks suffusing with color. "You have defied my authority at every turn, and now a reporter you supervise may die. You're responsible for that, Jessie. Only you."

Jessie rose, clenching her fists at her sides and fighting down the rage and despair that swelled in tandem in her chest. "I have not defied your authority," she said, her voice low and shaking. "I handled the situation in the most ethical way possible. Not in defiance of you, but in *spite* of you. You can preach about responsibility all you want, but that won't change the fact that part of the reason we got to where we are now is because you lost sight of what we do—seek the truth. If we'd focused on that from the start—"

"You dare to lecture me about the truth?" Gillian asked, her gaze flinty. "You haven't been honest about who you are since the day my father hired you."

"That's different—"

"Oh, so now there are degrees of truth? It's only the truth if Jessie Rhoades, or whatever the hell your name is, says it is?"

The fight left her, and Jessie lowered herself to the sofa. She would never win, and she no longer had the strength to try. What mattered to her more than anything was for Greg to survive and for no one else to get hurt. What Gillian believed or said or did didn't matter.

"What?" Gillian prodded. "You have nothing more to say to defend yourself?"

Jessie raised her chin. "If you're going to fire me, Gillian, why don't you just get it the hell over with?"

Gillian covered her shock with a brittle laugh. "I told my father he was a fool for hiring you. But he believed in you. He believed in you more than he ever believed in me, his own daughter. God knows why." She gave Jessie a stiff, cold smile. "You're finished. Not just at *The Star-News*, but in the journalism profession. I'll make sure of it." Whirling, she stalked out.

Jessie watched her go and felt nothing.

"There's got to be something we can do," Clay said.

He and Marshall were standing outside Mel's office while Tom diligently guarded the door a few feet away. Marshall, his baby face aged by the circles under his light brown eyes, had just told him that he had called in favors all over town to try to locate where David Collins might be staying. Until they heard from one of them, all they could do was wait.

"This is a tourist area," Marshall said, "meaning there are a lot more hotels than your average town this size. It's going to take time to track Collins down, and that's only if he checked into a hotel under his own name. If he's even checked into a hotel."

Clay knew he was doing a poor job of controlling his impatience, but he couldn't help it. "Damn it, this is frustrating."

"At least we know he's here, so we can be prepared," Marshall said. "Hell, maybe the guy's just here on vacation."

"That'd be just a tiny bit too coincidental, don't you think?"

"A tiny bit, yes," Marshall said as he raked his fingers through his short, salt-and-pepper hair.

Clay scrubbed his hands over his face. "How am I going to tell Jess? She's holding it together by a thread. I don't think she can take much more."

"She's strong, Clay. You know that."

"Hell, yes, I know it. She's stronger than anyone I know. She's so strong she blows me away. But she's also spent a couple of years convincing herself that her ex is incapable of trying to hurt her. It's going to kill her if he's involved in all this."

"She'll get through it. She has you."

Clay gave his friend a tired smile. "Right. I'm a magic cure."

"I don't know about that, but I have noticed the way she looks at you. I'm envious as hell."

Clay digested that for a moment, wondering whether he should feel like a jerk about the warm and happy feeling spreading through him despite the dire circumstances.

When Marshall spoke again, Clay had to force himself to focus. Warm and happy was something he hadn't felt in a very long time.

"There's something else I've been meaning to tell you," Marshall was saying. "On my way back from Chicago last night, I checked in with that friend of mine at NCIC. He'd been trying to reach me with the results on Peters' finger—"

The door to Mel's office swung open, cutting him off, and Gillian Westin marched out. Her face was red, her steps clipped as, ignoring them, she strode down the hall.

"Madame Editor doesn't look happy," Marshall said.

Clay didn't respond as he pushed through the door Gillian had just slammed, aware that both Tom and Marshall followed close behind. Dread twisted his insides when he saw Jessie sitting on the sofa, her back stiff, her features devoid of color and expression. "I'm guessing that didn't go very well," he said.

She gave him the ghost of a smile. "She fired me. She blames me for Greg—" Breaking off, she buried her face in her hands. "Oh God, she's right."

Clay was beside her in an instant, rubbing his hand over her back, alarmed by the tremors shuddering through her. "She's not right," he said. "Don't let her do this to you. She's looking for someone to blame, and you're an easy target."

"But she's right, Clay. He depended on me, and I failed him."

Her words pierced his heart. He remembered how often he'd thought the same thing after Ellen had been killed and knew there was nothing he, or anyone else, could say to change the way she felt. All that would make a difference would be Greg's survival.

Instead of murmuring platitudes, he held her close and hoped that was enough.

Behind them, Marshall cleared his throat. "Tom and I will wait in the hall."

"No," Jessie said, gently disengaging from Clay's embrace. "I'm okay."

Clay let her go, wishing he could do more but accepting that it was out of his hands and that hovering would do nothing but upset her more. Rising, he noted that Tom had taken up position next to the door, feet planted, hands clasped before him. Clay was impressed that the guard showed no sign of weariness.

Marshall, his light brown eyes radiating concern, cast Clay a glance that asked, What can I do? Clay responded with a helpless shake of his head. To Jessie, he said, "Marshall was getting ready to share some new information on Hank Peters. Are you up to it?"

"Of course." She seemed relieved to have something else to focus on. "What did you find out?" she asked Marshall.

While the P.I. drew a small notebook out of his back pocket and flipped through several pages, Clay poured himself some coffee and refreshed Jessie's. "Coffee, Marshall?" he asked.

"No, thanks," Marshall said, scanning his notes. "Here we go. Real name is Henry Peterson. About two years ago, Fort Myers police picked up his brother for drunk driving. Cops tossed him in a cell to sleep it off. Turns out he was diabetic, went into insulin shock, lapsed into a coma and never woke up. Henry Peterson went on a one-man crusade for a while, calling for an investigation, claiming police brutality, cover-up, obstruction of justice, you name it."

"I remember him," Jessie said. "He called *The Star-News* a couple of times a week."

"You talked to him?" Clay asked.

"Covering that story was one of my first assignments as a reporter here. We covered the story heavily at first. A prisoner dying in police custody was big news, but once cause of death and lack of fault were determined, there wasn't anything else to pursue. After I talked to Peterson the first time, I investigated further, but everything was on the level from the cops' end. The coroner said there was nothing suspicious about the brother's death. He wasn't wearing an emergency I.D. bracelet, so there was no way the police could have known he was at risk."

"Did you meet Henry Peterson?" Clay asked.

"Our only contact was by phone," she said. "There was no reason to meet with him after we decided the story was dead, and I was afraid doing so would give him false hope or encourage him."

"How did he react when you told him there appeared to be no evidence of a cover-up?" Marshall asked.

"He wasn't happy, of course. He filed a lawsuit against the police, but a judge threw it out last year over lack of evidence. After that, Peterson moved on to writing letters to the editor. When they started getting nasty, we refused to publish them. I also stopped accepting his calls."

"Did he ever make any threats?" Marshall asked.

"Not overtly," she said. "More than anything, I felt sorry for him. He obviously was having a tough time accepting the freak nature of his brother's death. I think he wanted someone to blame. Some people in the newsroom thought maybe he wanted to be able to sue for damages."

Sipping coffee, Clay grimaced at the bitter taste that had developed from the carafe spending too long on the warmer. "So, feeling snubbed by both the cops and the newspaper, he set up a scandal that neither could ignore."

"First, he made the cops look bad, then it was the news-paper's turn," Marshall said.

"Right," Clay said. "He went after Jess because she was the reporter who thwarted his crusade at the beginning."

"Greg must have started putting all this together, and that's why Peters/Peterson shot him," Jessie said. But then her brows drew together. "Except that Stuart described Greg's shooter as medium to small. I remember seeing Peterson emptying the trash in my office, and he easily tops six feet and weighs at least two hundred pounds."

Marshall tapped a finger against the open page of his notebook. "We could be looking at a partner for Peterson."

Tom spoke from his position near the door. "If I might interject?"

Clay turned. "Go ahead."

"My bet's on the reporter, Stuart Davis. He could have described someone who doesn't resemble Peterson to steer suspicion away from him."

Marshall's cell phone rang, and the detective moved into the hall to take the call as Jessie got up and began to pace. "It was well known in the newsroom that Henry Peterson was gunning for the police and, after we rejected his cover-up story, the newspaper. It would have been easy for Stuart to track him down."

"You don't think it could have been the other way around?" Clay asked, heartened to see the color returning to her cheeks. Her earlier lethargy had vanished.

"I can't imagine Peterson contacting Stuart and hatching this scheme without knowing first that Stuart would go for it."

"If Stuart was the instigator, then something must have set him off," he replied.

"Knowing Stuart, anything could have been a trigger," she said. "He's been out of favor for some time, relegated to covering fund-raisers and hot-air balloon rallies. Every time there's a beat change, he gets knocked down a notch, mainly because his attitude sucks and he's not as productive as he should be." Pausing in her pacing, she faced him, her eyes bright. "Two weeks ago, I suspended him after he blew up over the latest beat change."

"Two weeks ago," Clay said. "That was right before your brake line was cut."

Before Jessie could respond, Mel rushed in with good news. "Greg's going to be okay. He's in Recovery."

Jessie, beaming with relief, threw her arms around her friend and hugged her. "When can I see him?"

"Not for several hours, so you might as well go home and get some sleep," Mel said. "I've arranged for someone to call me if anything changes, but his surgeon doesn't expect there to be any complications. The surgery went really well, and Greg has taken good care of himself, so he was in excellent health going in."

"I have to see him before I go," Jessie said.

Clay shrugged when Mel rolled her eyes at him, but she

was smiling. "Fine. I'll take you to Recovery, but then you have to leave. I insist on it as your doctor. Deal?"

"Deal."

Mel arched a surprised brow at Clay. "That was far too easy. Is she mellowing?"

Clay laughed, his own relief at Greg's prognosis making him feel as giddy as Jessie looked. "Don't count on it."

As Jessie headed for the door, Mel on her heels, Marshall returned from his cell phone call. The look on his face stopped Clay from following the women out the door. "What is it?" he asked.

"One of my contacts got a line on Collins," Marshall said. "He's registered at the Clipper Inn downtown."

Chapter 23

Stepping out of the shower, Jessie quickly dried herself. Tom and two other guards had brought her home to Clay's less than half an hour ago after Clay and Marshall had rushed off without a word about where they were going or what they were chasing. Their urgency, and lack of information sharing, unnerved her, but there wasn't anything she could do until they returned and explained. Mel had offered to stay with her, but Jessie knew her friend had a long shift coming later in the day and needed sleep.

In the meantime, Jessie savored the joy of knowing Greg would be okay. She'd seen him in Recovery, and while the tubes and machinery attached to him had appeared ominous, Mel had assured her he'd be up and around in a week, maybe less. Full recovery would take months, but Greg was strong and, Jessie knew from experience, exceptionally determined. Her only wish was that Taylor Drake had been as lucky.

Shrugging into Clay's robe, she paused to breathe in the scent of him in the terrycloth. Missing him was an ache in her chest, and such a strong feeling surprised her. She couldn't remember experiencing such a pang when separated from David. Did that mean she was in love with Clay?

Now, that's a silly question, she thought. Of course, she was in love with him. She'd fallen hard and fast, and while that defied everything about herself that she took pride in, she discovered that she didn't really care. Control be damned. When she was with Clay, nothing mattered but the way he made her feel. Loved.

In the face of Clay's love and Greg's recovery, being fired didn't weigh on her mind as much as she'd expected it would. She wondered whether it had sunk in yet. At the same time, she acknowledged that, more than anything, she felt relief. The thought of starting over was daunting, yes. But she'd done it before, and while it was unlikely she'd encounter another Richard Westin, she had faith that she'd find a way to do the job she loved.

In the bedroom, she reluctantly shed Clay's robe to pull on clean jeans and a white tank top. For the first time in days, she experienced a twinge of hunger and headed for the kitchen. Perhaps by the time she put together something for breakfast, Clay would be there to share it with her.

Opening his refrigerator door, she perused the offerings, impressed. The man knew how to shop, she thought, as she retrieved mangoes, strawberries, peaches and blueberries. Her mouth was watering as she dumped it all on the island and hunted around for a knife.

As she washed and sliced a peach, she thought about how she should handle the mayor's confession of his affair with Taylor Drake. No doubt, Gillian would take the sensational approach to the story with no regard for the impact on the community at a time when strong leadership was needed. Technically, because Jessie no longer worked for the newspaper, she wasn't obligated to share what she knew. Yet, keeping it under wraps would deny the mayor his goal of clearing Taylor's name. It occurred to her that she could let Clay tell the mayor's story in the project he was working on for *The New York Times*. Not only would that get the information out there, but it would also be in a far more credible newspaper than *The Star-News*.

Smiling at the prospect of scooping Gillian out of the story, Jessie began to hum.

Clay hung back as Marshall worked the electronic lock on the hotel room door. "This is highly illegal," Clay said.

"You want to know what Collins is doing here or not?" Marshall asked.

"Just hurry."

Popping open the door, Marshall gestured for Clay to precede him into David Collins' hotel room. "I don't want to know how you did that," Clay said.

"Good, because I'm not going to tell you. Next thing I know, you wouldn't need me anymore."

Clay checked out the room, noting the Florida-related décor: a tropical fish comforter, matching pastel pink curtains and wicker chairs facing sliding doors that looked out over the Caloosahatchee River. A royal blue sports bag dropped on the floor inside the door was the only indication that anyone had checked in. "Looks like he just dumped his stuff and left," Clay said.

"He apparently doesn't plan to be here for long," Marshall said, hefting the bag onto the bed and zipping it open. Sifting through the contents, he said, "Toiletries, couple of shirts, socks . . . nothing weird."

"You mean like a manifesto titled *Why I Want My Ex-wife Dead?*"

Marshall didn't laugh. "Why don't you try the redial button on the phone?"

Lifting the receiver, Clay hit the appropriate key. While he waited for an answer, he watched Marshall draw a large white envelope from a side pocket of the bag and dump its contents onto the bed.

At the same time, a voice on the phone said: "Thank you

282

for calling *The Star-News*, how may I direct your call?"

Clay hung up the phone as the air began to back up in his lungs. Spread over the colorful depictions of happy fish on the bed were photos of Jessie leaving work with Clay at her side, Jessie getting out of his SUV in his driveway, Jessie walking with Tom across *The Star-News* parking lot. An accompanying newspaper was folded to the Local section, where Jessie's name in the flag was highlighted in yellow. "Oh shit," he said under his breath.

Flipping the envelope over, Marshall added his own soft expletive. "Damn." Handing it to Clay, he added, "We'd better get to her fast."

Clay's name and address, circled several times in red ink, were scrawled on the envelope.

Jessie called Tom's name as she peeled a juicy mango. She knew his cohorts had planned to order food to be delivered as soon as they returned to the house, but Tom had mentioned that greasy fast food didn't appeal to him. Maybe he would be interested in fruit.

When she heard footsteps crossing the living room toward the kitchen, she asked, "Are you hungry?"

She glanced up when there was no response, and her smile died on her lips.

Henry Peterson grinned at her. "Starving."

"Goddamn draw bridge," Clay said.

A large yacht passing through the causeway had caused a morning traffic jam leading onto Sanibel Island, the only way to access Captiva by land.

Marshall clicked off his cell phone. "Your home phone's out of service. I'll call the police."

Clay slammed his fist against the dashboard.

As Peterson skirted the island in the center of the kitchen, Jessie backed away fast. Her back hit the cool metal of the oven door, and cornered, she brandished the knife, her first thought of the guards. No one could have entered the house without being spotted. "Did you do something to Tom?"

Peterson, hulking in jeans, an untucked khaki T-shirt that showed sweat stains and mud-caked sneakers, continued smiling. "If I was you, I'd be more worried about myself." He stopped before her, his gaze flicking down to the knife, then back up to her face. His stupid grin, showing white teeth with a gap in the middle, didn't falter. "You think that little old thing is going to stop me?"

She thrust it at him, counting on the element of surprise.

The three-inch blade tore through the cotton of his T-shirt and met flesh. Grunting, he leapt back and stared down at the hole in his shirt. Only a small amount of blood seeped through, indicating the damage was minimal. Raising his head, he glared at her, his foolish grin gone. "That was stupid," he said.

She was trapped by his body in front of her, the oven at her back and the counter to her right, but she couldn't wait for him to make the next move, not when madness gleamed in his eyes. Lunging to the left, she jerked back to the right when he reacted, and squeaked by him. He grabbed her by the shirt, and she whirled, jamming down with the knife. The blade stabbed into the back of his hand. "Bitch!" he yowled, sending the knife to the floor with a flick of his hand. It skittered across the tile and under the oven.

Free, Jessie raced toward the living room without looking back. The sliding glass doors that led to the deck, where she'd glimpsed Tom less than an hour ago, were about ten feet away.

Peterson took her down in a full-body tackle about a foot shy of the doors, and together, they slid violently into the glass. Stunned and breathless, with two hundred pounds of madman bearing down on her back, Jessie strained to move, to wriggle free. But moving was impossible until Peterson eased back and flipped her over. Before she could do anything more than gulp in air, he straddled her. She writhed under him, straining to buck him off, trying to hit him in the head with her cast.

He backhanded her, and she lay still, dazed and tasting blood.

He leaned over her, his breath smelling as if he'd recently eaten a mint. The scent sent her back to the night in her apartment when an intruder had attacked. That man had had fresh breath, too, and she suddenly knew Peterson was the one she'd thrown through her coffee table.

Grinning, he said, "Suddenly, this is so easy. I always said the direct method was the best. Screw subtlety." He bracketed her throat with one hand and squeezed. "I'm almost sorry it's over. You've been such a challenge."

Jessie, her head spinning, black spots spattering her vision, wrapped her fingers around his wrist and tugged, frantic to loosen his grasp. She needed to get him to talk, to stall him. "Why are you doing this?" she choked out.

His grip eased, and she sucked in air, not caring that it set her throat on fire, just thankful to be able to breathe.

Peterson sneered. "I thought you, the big bad reporter, had all the answers."

"Just tell me why."

He bent so that his nose nearly touched hers. "I'm going to kill you."

Swallowing against the rising fear, she fought to speak calmly, coherently. "Please tell me why. I deserve to know why."

He gave her a grim smile. "That wasn't the plan originally. The plan was to scare you. But you weren't easy to scare."

His hand on her throat loosened further, but she didn't move, didn't struggle for fear of setting him off again. Plus, he had yet to restrain her hands, and she didn't want to tip him off. "Whose plan?"

"You assume I have a partner," he said.

"I assume that when you go down, you won't want to do it alone."

He barked with laughter. "You've got balls, lady. You're dead in less than ten minutes, and you're still talking tough."

She reined in the panic that lunged into her throat. "So if I've got only ten minutes, tell me who's giving the orders."

"I don't think my boss would like that at all."

"At least tell me why."

Pursing his lips, he seemed to consider it, then shook his head. "Nope. Sorry."

She smashed her cast against his temple with a sharp crack, and his weight sagged to the side, giving her the opportunity she needed to kick free and gain her feet. He scrambled up, too, and blocked her escape, swearing when he put his hand to his head and it came away bloody.

"You're so dead," he said.

She didn't wait for him to do the attacking. She tried to kick him, but he caught her leg, jerked her toward him and up, then slammed her hard on her back on the floor. Unable to breathe, Jessie stared up at him, her vision wavering as if ripples of water separated them. He smiled, and she saw the gun in his hand. Where the hell had that come from?

"Game over," he said.

"Hold it."

Peterson spun toward the voice, but he was too slow. A body bowled him over as Jessie rolled onto her side and curled into a protective ball. In the time it took for Peterson to collapse near her feet, bleeding and unconscious, she still had not been able to draw in a breath. She felt a hand on her arm.

"Jess?"

Looking up at the man who had just saved her life, she gasped out his name on her first wheezing breath.

"David."

Chapter 24

Clay drummed his fingers on the steering wheel while Marshall talked to the island police on his cell phone. The draw bridge had just lowered, and the morning's beach traffic was creeping along. Marshall dropped the phone in the cubby at the base of the gear shift.

"They're involved in a water rescue on the opposite end of Sanibel," Marshall said.

"What does that mean?"

"They don't have enough people to send someone to your place, and when they do, it's going to take them awhile to get there."

Jessie fought to pull air into her burning lungs as her ex-husband roughly hauled her up by the arms. Even with legs too weak to support her, her senses swimming, she struggled to push him away, desperate to live, to survive.

It wasn't until he clasped her tightly to him that she realized he was hugging her.

"Thank God," he said against her neck. "Thank God."

Coughing, she dragged air into her starved lungs, trying to make sense of what was happening.

David, his hands gentle on her back, soothed. "Take it easy, take it slow," he said. "The bastard knocked the wind out of you."

When she was breathing easier, he set her back from him and quickly looked her over. "My God, look at you." His fingers lightly stroked a bruise along her jaw. "Are you all right?"

She edged back from his support, wary. "What are you doing?"

He laughed, and it was short. "I thought I was saving your butt. Tell me what's going on. Who is that guy?"

Her brain was short-circuiting as she tried to make sense of what was happening, but she couldn't stop shuddering. Her jaw throbbed where Peterson had struck her, and the muscles in her back began to seize up. "I have to sit down."

David looped her arm around his neck and led her to the sofa. After he eased her down, he knelt before her. "Can I get you anything? Water? Some ice?"

"Shouldn't we tie him up?" she asked, her gaze fastened on Peterson.

David stripped off his belt, wound it around Peterson's wrists and secured it. "I don't know how well that will hold him, but it should."

"He had a gun."

"It's right here," David said, then nudged it under the sofa with the toe of his sneaker, as if he didn't want to touch it.

With Peterson secured and his gun mostly out of reach, Jessie looked at her ex-husband. He had changed in two years. Gray salted his light beard, the corners of his blue eyes crinkled, and a paunch that the David she knew never would have tolerated had grown around his middle. His clothing was shabby, too, his jeans faded and his white linen shirt absent the crisp, ironed creases he preferred. Even his sneakers, which he'd always been fastidious about, were in need of replacement. All in all, he looked as if he had aged ten years rather than two.

She didn't know what to say to him, how to react to his

appearance. And then her bewilderment vanished, and she leapt to her feet. "Oh my God. Tom."

David stayed close behind her as she slid open the deck doors. "Where are you going?" he asked as a wave of moist heat struck her along with the terrifying sight of Tom sprawled on his back on the wooden slats of the deck.

"Oh no." She ran to the guard and knelt beside him to search for his pulse.

"I'll call 911," David said, and raced into the house.

Tom's heart beat strong, but he had a nasty knot at his temple. Sitting back on her heels, Jessie scanned the immediate area for the other two guards. Gulf waves lazily sloshed just yards from the deck, but no other men were in sight.

David returned, Clay's cordless phone in his hand. "It's dead," he said. "I'll get my cell phone out of the car."

Pushing to her feet, she went in search of the other guards. She found one along the side of the house, sitting with his back against the stucco as if he'd sat down for a nap. He didn't appear to be injured, and his pulse thudded against her fingertips when she pressed them to the inside of his wrist. A few minutes later, she found the remaining guard in a similar position on the opposite side of the house.

How had Peterson managed to disable each man without alerting the others? Was that even possible to do alone?

"Hey, Jess," David called from the deck. "Where are you?"

She wasn't more than twelve feet from him, just around the corner of the house, kneeling next to the third unconscious guard. She heard the scuff of David's shoes in the sand, felt the warm morning breeze stir through her hair and rattle the palm fronds overhead. Peterson had a partner, she thought. He'd said so.

By the time her ex-husband rounded the corner, she had the guard's gun in her hand.

"There you are. Help's on its way," David said. It took him a moment to focus on the weapon braced in her hands, and then he stopped in mid-step, his face draining of color, his eyes quizzical. "What are you doing?"

Her hands shook. His distress looked genuine, but she couldn't trust him. She'd already misjudged him long ago. "What are *you* doing?"

He raised his hands, palms out. "I thought I was having really good timing by arriving when you obviously needed some help. What's with the gun?"

"How did you find me, David?"

"A detective tracked you down for me. Jess, come on. You don't need the gun." He stepped toward her, hands still up. "Put it down."

"Stop."

He obeyed. "Look, I know it's a shock to see me, but you can't imagine how relieved I am to find you. I thought for sure you were dead, that the partners at the law firm had made good on their threat." His sneakers crunched on sand and pieces of shells as he chanced another step. "Of course, whatever's going on here is freaking me out. What kind of trouble are you in?"

She cocked the gun. "I said stop."

"Jess, Jesus, you're aiming a gun at me. *Me*. David."

"You knew they were going to threaten me," she said, annoyed that her voice broke. "You didn't do anything to stop them."

His eyebrows arched sharply. "What? I didn't know anything. I was as shocked as you were."

She fought the swell of emotion in her chest, but her

feelings of anger, hurt and betrayal had gained plenty of momentum in two years. "You weren't surprised when I told you."

He took another step. "Jess—"

She snapped her arms straight, her finger flexing on the trigger. "Don't."

"Okay, okay. I'm staying right here." He scrunched up one shoulder to stop a trail of sweat tracking down the side of his face. "Look, Jess, I know how it must have sounded on the phone. I've replayed that conversation in my head over and over and wished to God I'd been able to respond differently. But your call interrupted a meeting. The firm's partners were all right there, listening. I had to play it cool."

"You're lying."

"I'm not lying. I swear. I've invested a lot of time and money trying to find you, so I could make sure you're okay and explain to you what happened." He gained another foot.

"Damn you, I told you to stop," she said, her hand shaking. "I'm warning you."

"You won't use that on me, Jess," he said, and boldly took another step. "You loved me at one time. We loved each other."

"I got over it."

"Well, I haven't. I can't tell you how happy I am to find you alive and . . . somewhat well." He smiled slightly, with a hint of his former cockiness. "Give me the gun, and we'll go inside and wait for the police. You should put ice on your jaw."

The police, she thought. He'd called them several minutes ago, yet she heard no sirens. It was a small island. It shouldn't take so long for the cops to arrive. "You didn't call the police."

His smile faded. "Of course, I did."

She strengthened her stance, convinced now that he was the partner Peterson had refused to give up. She'd been in denial long enough. "What was the plan, David? Ruin me the way you think I ruined you?"

"What are you talking about?"

"Your law partner accused me of tipping off the newspaper about the insurance fraud. Is that what you think?"

"*I* didn't know anything about it, so how could I think *you* knew something?"

"You set this whole cops scandal up to shatter my reputation. You helped Peterson take out the guards and then ambushed him to make it look like you saved me. Why? Why not just kill me and get it over with? Why the games?"

He shook his head, his expression incredulous. "I don't know what you're talking about. I just got here a couple of hours ago. My detective got a tip that someone from Fort Myers was asking about me. I couldn't imagine who that might be because I don't know anyone here. I don't even know why, but I had a hunch and suggested he look for you here, starting at the newspaper because I know newspapers are in your blood. Yesterday, he called to tell me he'd found you, and I was beside myself with happiness." He paused, and his eyes glimmered as if with tears. "I had to find you so I could tell you how sorry I am about what happened. I screwed up, Jess. I really screwed up. We had a good marriage, and I pissed it away with that law clerk. But I've had a lot of time to think, and I know now that I did it to get your attention. You were so wrapped up in that damn newspaper, and all I wanted was for you to notice me."

She gaped at him. "You're kidding me, right? You *cheated* on me to get my attention?"

"Look at me, for Christ's sake. I haven't had a decent

night's sleep since you took off. I'm over my head in debt. Detectives cost a lot of money, you know. Hell, I haven't been with a woman since you left me. Not one. Why would I do all of this if I didn't love you?"

"You don't know the first thing about love."

"I want you back—"

A roar to her left had her swinging around with the gun, but she was too late. Peterson smashed into her, knocking her hard into the side of the house. The gun went flying, and she went down. Pain was lightning in her side, but she scrambled to her knees, then to her feet.

Peterson and David were fighting for the pistol she'd dropped. She didn't know what to do. Helping either of them seemed like a bad idea. As Peterson landed a punch against David's jaw, she ran to call the police.

She made it as far as the edge of the deck when a gunshot had her diving for cover. Huddled with her back against the side of the deck that faced the gulf, she peered around the corner, expecting to see the men grappling for the gun.

Instead, David staggered to his feet. There was blood on him, but it didn't appear to be his. He lurched toward her, holding out the weapon as if to give it to her. "Jess, I—"

His head snapped back with a sharp crack. Shock swept over his features before he fell backward in the sand and lay still. Realizing the cracking sound had been a gunshot, Jessie looked up.

Mel stood on the deck above her, feet braced apart, a gun grasped in her hands.

Chapter 25

"Are you all right?" Mel asked.

Jessie didn't register the flatness of her friend's voice as, knowing her legs wouldn't support her, she crawled to David's side. Blood poured from the wound at his temple, soaking the sand beneath his head. "Oh Jesus," she said.

Mel dropped the gun and raced for the house.

Still conscious, David groped for Jessie's hand with sand-caked fingers. His lips moved, and she bent closer.

"I'm sorry," he whispered. "So very sorry."

She grasped his hand, confusion and despair ripping at her. "Just rest. Mel is calling for help."

He blinked, as if his vision kept sliding out of focus. "I already called—"

He lost consciousness as Mel knelt beside her. "Christ, what a mess," she said. "I was aiming for his shoulder." Violent tremors shook her hands as she wrapped a white towel around his head. Then, sitting back on her heels, she jerked a cell phone from her pants pocket. Before she could push any buttons, sirens sounded in the distance.

Mel raised her head. "Someone must have heard the gunshots and called." Her hands were steadier as she monitored his pulse. "He's breathing okay. That's good. Can you stay with him while I check on the guards and the other one?"

Jessie didn't move as she struggled to decipher what had just happened. Mel touched her arm. "Jess, are you okay?"

"He was handing me the gun."

The harried color in Mel's cheeks faded. "He was *pointing* it at you."

Jessie shook her head. "No. He was handing it to me."

Someone called from inside the house, and Mel pushed to her feet. "I'll get the paramedics."

Feeling sick, Jessie held David's hand, conscious of its growing clamminess and the red that soaked through the thick white material encircling his head. He'd said he was sorry. He'd said he'd searched for her so he could explain. He'd shown no familiarity with Peterson when he'd fought him. But if David wasn't Peterson's partner, who was?

"Jess! Jess!"

Before she could get to her feet, Clay was pulling her up and against him. Pain flashed through her side as he hugged her close, and she released an involuntary moan even as she wrapped her arms around him.

He eased back from her, his palm covering the hand she pressed to her ribs. "You're hurt," he said.

Seeing the concern replace the wild fear in his eyes helped clear her head. She gave him a tremulous smile. "I'm okay."

Unconvinced, he led her to the edge of the deck, where she gingerly sat, grimacing. "You're not okay," he said. "Where's Mel? She should look at you."

"I'm right here," Mel said, joining them. Strain had drawn her face tight. "Except for Tom, who was hit over the head, the guards were drugged. Looks like they'd just eaten."

Jessie stared at her friend. Drugging was easy for one person to handle, she thought. Access to the food was the only requirement. After that, all Peterson had to do was wait for the drugs to kick in, then take out Tom.

"My guess is it's the same stuff that psycho used on you, only less of it," Mel said.

"How do you know it's less?" Clay asked.

"They're already coming out of it. Tom, too, though he's got one hell of a headache."

"Jess is favoring her side," Clay said.

"It's nothing," Jessie said. She squeezed his hand to reassure him as she looked at her friend. "How'd you know I was in trouble?"

"Marshall called her," Clay said. "We were stuck in traffic."

"Let's go inside where I can check you out," Mel said.

An hour later, Jessie sat on Mel's leather sofa while her friend wrapped a wide Ace bandage around her sore ribs.

They had left the activity next door less than ten minutes ago. Two ambulances had whisked David, Tom and Peterson to the hospital. David had been unconscious but stable. Tom had been pale but insisting that he was fine. And Peterson had been sullen, with a broken nose and a non-life-threatening shoulder wound. Tom's two co-workers, woozy but functional, had been helping the police rope off Clay's house with yellow crime scene tape. Last she'd seen Clay, he was talking to two police detectives furiously taking notes.

"You really should have X-rays," Mel said. "Something might be broken."

"Nothing feels broken."

"Cracked, then."

"They're just bruises," Jessie said.

"Excuse me, but who's the doctor here?"

"Will you call to check on David?"

Mel's shoulders drooped, and she sat back on her heels.

Jessie had never seen such deep lines of stress in her forehead. "I called while I was getting this," she said, gesturing with the roll of bandage. "He's still unconscious. They're going to drill a hole in his skull to release the pressure on his brain from swelling."

"Oh God."

Mel swallowed, growing even more pale. "He pointed the gun at you. He was threatening you with it. Wasn't he?"

"I don't know." Tears of frustration burned, but Jessie held them back. "I don't know."

Mel's hand was cold as she grasped Jessie's. "He came here to hurt you. He hit you."

Jessie shook her head. "No. No. He . . . that was Peterson. David saved me from Peterson."

Before Mel could respond, Clay walked in. "How's it going here?"

Rising, Mel helped Jessie don a fresh T-shirt from Mel's drawer. "Someone's being stubborn about getting X-rays, but I don't imagine that surprises you," Mel said, her movements efficient but shaky. "Anything new at your place?"

"One of the cops told me Detective Mubarek's been questioning Peterson downtown. Apparently, the son of a bitch can't seem to tell his story fast enough."

As soon as he sat on the sofa next to her, Jessie leaned against him, needing his strength, his warmth. "Doing okay?" he asked, cradling her gently against his side.

She rested her head on his shoulder. "Did Peterson mention David?"

"Several times, in fact. He said your ex-husband contacted him about a month and a half ago. Said he offered him a ton of money to take you out."

Mel sat heavily on the floor and dropped her head into her hands. "Thank God," she whispered.

Jessie shut her eyes as pain spread through her chest. She should have been relieved. It was over. But it stunned her how much it hurt that David really had wanted her dead. Unable to continue to hold in the emotion she'd been suppressing for so long, she curled against Clay and let it go.

Chapter 26

Many hours later, Jessie sat on Mel's deck, one hand resting over ribs that throbbed, her legs bent under her. Humidity hung in a cloud over the gulf, hiding the moon and stars and making the night even darker. Gentle waves sloshed against the shore.

When she had left the bed in Mel's guest room, Clay had been snoring softly. Sleep had eluded her, though, even as fatigue seemed to flow like lead through her veins. But her brain had insisted on trying to maneuver the pieces into place, pieces that didn't quite seem to fit.

Unfortunately, answers to the questions that stalked her wouldn't be available any time soon: David was in a coma. His doctors were optimistic, but they said it would take time.

Greg, who no doubt had some answers of his own to add, had awakened from surgery, but Mel had said he was too groggy and drugged to be much help yet. It could take days to find out what he knew, if anything.

"Don't you ever sleep?"

She smiled as Clay, settling into the chair next to hers, reached out a hand. She clasped it and held on. It amazed her how much the contact helped. It also amazed her that she didn't feel the least bit embarrassed by her earlier crying jag. "I can't stop thinking."

"About your ex and Peterson?"

Mimicking Clay's relaxed position, she rested her head

300

against the back of the chair. "I thought I knew David."

"People change."

"But so drastically?"

"Sure."

"You didn't."

He turned his head without lifting it from the chair back and gazed at her. "What do you mean?"

"You lost your wife, and it didn't make you psychotic."

"Maybe not overtly."

"I'm serious," she said.

"So am I. The night you crashed your car in my front yard was the third anniversary of Ellen's death. I'd been grieving for three years. That's probably not normal."

"You loved her so much."

Sitting forward, Clay ran both hands back through his hair. "I used her death as an excuse to give up. You were my wake-up call."

Her lips curved. "I remember thinking that last week."

"Well, I'm glad I picked up the phone. You changed my life, Jess. Maybe you saved it."

She moved her shoulders restlessly, wincing at the resulting discomfort in her rib cage, then got up to roam the deck, albeit slowly. "If I was such a happy pill for you, where did I go wrong with my husband?"

"You assume that you're the one who went wrong."

"I was obsessed with my job."

"You're still obsessed," he said, laughing softly behind her. "We'll work on that."

She braced a hand on the railing. "He certainly knew where to hit me where it would hurt the most. My career."

"He didn't win, you know. You lost your job, and you're still okay."

She didn't know about that. It wasn't going to be pretty

when it finally sank in that she was unemployed. "What I don't get is how he figured that a scandal involving the police would eventually lead to my downfall at the newspaper. I mean, how could he possibly anticipate how Gillian, or any of us, would react?"

"It's useless to try to figure it all out before we have the chance to ask him how he did it."

"There are other things that don't make sense," she said, unable to let it go. "Peterson said David promised him big money. Putting aside the question of how David even knew about Peterson to begin with, Marshall's check on David turned up huge debts. He couldn't possibly have delivered on that promise."

Joining her at the railing, he touched her arm so that she faced him. "The man cheated on you," he said, "and you still expect him to be honest when he deals with other people. Surely you see the lack of logic in that scenario."

"How's this for lack of logic? If Peterson and David were partners, that puts Stuart in the clear, which means he didn't lie when he said he saw a small or medium-sized guy running from Greg's. David and Peterson both weigh at least two hundred pounds each."

"So Stuart got it wrong. He was upset and worried about Greg. He admitted he saw the guy from a distance, and size is tough to judge like that."

"But why would David try to kill me in the midst of trying to ruin me?" she asked. "That doesn't make any sense at all."

"The guy's a nut case, Jess. You're going to find contradictions in his behavior all over the place."

"Do you suppose Marshall could check on something tomorrow?"

He glanced at his watch. "You mean later today?"

"David said he called 911, but I assumed he lied because it took the police so long to get here."

"I can explain that," he said. "Marshall called while we were stuck in traffic. The police were in the middle of a water rescue and couldn't spare anyone right away. When they did arrive, it was probably from Marshall's call."

Deflated, she closed her eyes. He had an answer for everything, and she had no idea why it frustrated her. Except that the idea that David was the bad guy countered everything she thought she knew about him. Plus, he'd seemed so sincere when he'd apologized. Why had he bothered to say he was sorry when he very well could have been uttering his final words? Wouldn't he have taken that opportunity to tell her how much he hated her?

"Look, I know it's hard for you," Clay said. "You loved the guy at one time. Maybe a tiny part of you still loves him. Realizing that he wanted to hurt you, even *kill* you . . . that's going to mess with your head. And it's inevitable that there will be things that don't add up, things he said or did that don't make any sense. The unanswered questions will drive you crazy if you let them. All you can do is let the police figure it out. Then you'll have to accept what they tell you and move on." Taking her by the shoulders, he gazed deep into her eyes. "I'm going to be here for you for however long it takes."

Tears flooded her eyes. "How did I get so lucky to find you?"

He smiled, catching a tear on his knuckle as it trickled down her cheek. "I believe I was the one who found you, remember?"

"Oh, yeah. That whole burning car thing. I'd heard that no man could resist that."

"Ah, so you set me up from the start."

"Hooked you and reeled you in," she said.

"I'm glad you did. I love you."

Stunned, she gazed up at him and felt a little light-headed. "Are you serious?"

His chuckle sounded nervous. "That's not exactly the response I was hoping for."

"We've known each other only . . ." She trailed off, trying to add up the days in her head but unable to focus on anything but what he'd just said. He loved her. Clay loved her! Joy swelled in her chest.

"We've known each other twelve days," he said. "Maybe it's nuts, but I don't care. I want to marry you."

Floored, she could only stare at him, her ability to speak, or think, gone.

Grinning, he drew her into his arms. "I'll take that as a yes."

Chapter 27

When Jessie rose at dawn, she took a moment to stand beside the bed and watch Clay sleep. He was on his back, one arm angled above his head, the sheet riding low on his belly. She admired the tanned expanse of his muscled chest, the lean lines of his waist, resisting the urge to trail her fingertips over his smooth skin. She considered waking him to tell him that she loved him. Earlier, she'd been too stunned by his proposal to say it. But he looked so peaceful now that she didn't want to disturb him. There'd be plenty of time later to tell him, with words and with actions.

Smiling, she jotted a note to let him know that she was going to clean out her office at *The Star-News* before her coworkers started arriving for their workday. If she did it when they were around, there would be endless questions and quite possibly public displays of emotion, none of which she wanted or felt especially strong enough to handle right now. She left the note on her pillow and brushed a kiss over his brow.

Mel had gone to work even earlier, so Jessie silently slipped out into the moisture-laden morning air and walked the short distance to Clay's driveway, where her rental car was still parked from the day before. Getting into it took some time, as her battered ribs seemed to protest every move, but it still felt incredibly liberating to drive away without an armed guard following close behind. It was so liberating, in fact, that she put the convertible's top down and enjoyed the warmth of the early morning sun. Life might not exactly be good just now, but it was showing definite signs of improvement.

She arrived at *The Star-News* to find the newsroom dark and silent, as she'd expected. After finding an empty box on the loading dock, she flipped several light switches and looked around, waiting for sadness to dig in.

Surprisingly, it was minimal. She would miss her co-workers, but she could easily check in with them whenever she wished. The list of what she wouldn't miss was longer. The unreasonably long hours. The stress of striving to achieve Gillian's often unrealistic expectations. The difficulty of cajoling another story out of a burned-out reporter. The anxiety of pursuing a fair and balanced report that seemed counter to her boss' preoccupation with sensational headlines and ad sales.

At least she wouldn't be out of work for long, she thought. After she and Clay had returned to bed in the early morning hours, they had cuddled close. Her bruises had prevented lovemaking, but they had talked about the future. He persuaded her to help him with his *New York Times* project on the unraveling of the hoax. He said he pictured a double byline on the story, which he planned to pitch to his editor as a three-part series. Once his editor worked with her, Clay had said, he'd fall instantly in love, and then she'd have more requests for stories than she'd ever be able to handle.

Jessie hoped that proved true, because she couldn't imagine how nerve-racking it would be not having a steady job to go to every morning. "We'll find a way to fill your mornings," Clay had said, with a suggestive nip at her shoulder.

In her office, Jessie dropped the box on the floor. Her

desk was piled high with newspapers and various deadline and circulation reports that had been tossed on it in her absence. Deadline reports she happily dumped in a pile for her successor. She started to do the same with the most recent circulation report, then paused when the numbers caught her eye. Fumbling in her purse for her glasses, she slipped them on and examined the report, stunned.

There certainly would have been no tongue-lashings over these astounding numbers. She scanned up, seeking the headlines that had generated the most impressive leaps in papers sold.

"Copulating cops: Your tax dollars at work" started the roll, as she already knew, followed by several related stories. Then there was "Police thwart water park bomber," followed by "Police scandal a hoax" and "Sniper kills cop at center of scandal" on the same day. "Twelve perish in interstate pileup" also had scored big.

In short, the past weeks had been extremely good for *The Star-News*. Jessie imagined ad revenue had enjoyed similar surges. It was the nature of the beast: when bad news happens, papers sell, and when papers start selling, advertisers buy more ads.

It was ironic, Jessie thought, that the very scandal that had threatened to destroy the credibility of the newspaper, and therefore its ability to survive, had actually given it a huge boost. Whether the long-term impact turned out to be good or bad remained to be seen.

It cheered her that she didn't have to chew her nails over it. In fact, she realized, if she did pursue a freelance reporting career, she would no longer have to think twice about circulation reports. She would never again have to defend the least-productive or crankiest reporter on her staff. She would never again have to worry about how she was going to flesh out a weak story budget on a slow news day.

Whatever happened next, all she had to do was seek the truth and report it. Handling the bureaucracy of upper management would be someone else's problem.

Waking alone, Clay groaned in frustration. He guessed he was cursed to forever wake up alone in bed as long as he shared it with Jessie. He was perusing her note, smiling goofily at the scrawled endearment at the end, when the phone in the other room began to ring.

When Mel didn't answer it, he assumed she was gone for the day and sprinted to grab it before her machine kicked in. "Hello?"

"Thank God, you picked up," Mel said. "Greg's awake. He's asking to talk to Jess right away."

"She's at the paper cleaning out her desk. What's up?"

"He's pretty agitated. She needs to get here as soon as she can. The anxiety isn't good for him."

"I'll give her a call and have her meet me there."

Jessie was dropping several days' worth of newspapers on the floor to be recycled when the pile shifted, and a headline a few layers down caught her eye: "Police release evidence in water park bombing."

Curious, she drew the paper out of the stack. The date was five days before. She had been in the hospital recovering from the drug overdose and had missed it. Accompanying the story was a large photograph of footprints the police had found near the bomb before they removed it to be detonated far away. Police had hoped the picture would prompt someone with information to come forward.

Jessie was gazing at the picture, thinking that the page

designer had run it too big, when something about one of the muddy impressions struck her as familiar. The brand name of the shoe was stamped clearly in the mud.

Heart pounding, she reached for the phone and called Detective Mubarek. "Hello, detective, it's Jessie Rhoades."

"How are you, Ms. Rhoades? Recovering from your ordeal, I hope."

"Yes, thank you. I have kind of a strange question for you."

"What is it?"

"What kind of shoes was Henry Peterson wearing when he was booked? I remember he had on sneakers but nothing about them."

"They're locked up with his personal belongings, but I can check. Mind if I ask why you want to know?"

"I'd prefer not to say in case it's nothing. Can you call me back right away?"

"No problem."

After giving him her office number, she hung up.

At Mel's, Clay got a busy signal on Jessie's office phone, so he tried *The Star-News'* main number and hoped someone would pick up. He was surprised when Gillian Westin answered.

"Clay Christopher here. I have an urgent message for Jess," he said.

"She no longer works here," Gillian said, her tone prim.

"She's there cleaning out her office. Apparently, she's on her line. Could you get a message to her for me?"

"What's the message?" She sounded irritated as she shuffled papers in the background.

He didn't care. "Greg's asking to see her."

Gillian didn't respond right away.

"Ms. Westin?"

"He's awake," she said. "That's good news."

"Yes, but he's agitated and wanting to see Jess. Will you let her know right away that I'll meet her at the hospital?"

"Of course. I'm so pleased to hear he's—"

Clay hung up on her and headed for the door.

Gazing down at the picture of muddy footprints, Jessie's mind began to race.

Detective Mubarek had shown her photos that bore the same brand name and, if not the same pattern then a very similar one, on the sole. Those impressions had been made by Taylor Drake's killer. These had been made by the man who planted a live bomb at a crowded water park. Could Henry Peterson be the bomber, too?

The phone rang. "Jessie Rhoades."

"It's Detective Mubarek. When Henry Peterson was arrested, he was wearing Nikes."

She leaned back in her chair, a sense of excitement jangling through her. "I think Peterson and the water park bomber wore the same style of shoes."

"Hang on," the detective said.

She heard the roll of metal wheels on a tile floor, followed by the glide of a file cabinet drawer being opened. Some shuffling sounds, then, "I'll be damned. I'm comparing the photos, and the footprints are indeed identical." He slammed a drawer. "I'm going to pay Mr. Peterson a visit right away. Good eye, Ms. Rhoades. Very good eye."

After hanging up, she stared at the newspaper photo, trying to make sense of this new information.

If Peterson was the bomber, what could he have been trying to accomplish? He told police he'd agreed to work with David because he wanted to ruin the police and the newspaper. But someone, presumably the bomber, had called to tip off *The Star-News* about the bomb, giving the paper the jump on other media. Then, because the device had been detonated in a remote area after the TV news cycle, *The Star-News* had been able to report information that the news stations hadn't had, leading to a more thorough report in the paper the next day. All of that had made the newspaper look very good, so why would Peterson as the bomber, and David as his partner, think that would *damage* the paper?

Something else didn't make sense: the police department had won kudos for how it handled the potentially catastrophic water park situation. The cops ended up looking like heroes, which also contradicted Peterson's goal of destroying the police.

Sifting through the paperwork for the circulation reports she had set aside, Jessie looked again at the numbers. As she'd noted before, circulation the day the water park story ran skyrocketed. In fact, she realized, *all* of David's and Peterson's activities—from the cops scandal to the bomb to Taylor's murder—had resulted in very good news for *The Star-News*. Even the follow-up reports on the bogus nature of the scandal had boosted the numbers.

She imagined the report that reflected circulation for yesterday—the day the story ran about Greg's shooting—would be just as impressive. It was possible that the numbers could be sustained for many weeks as readers ate up the kind of murder-and-mayhem stories that sold newspapers.

Massaging her temples, her elbows braced on the desk, Jessie closed her eyes. None of it fit. David and Peterson had failed on a mammoth scale. The hoax might have dented the paper's credibility, but it had boosted circulation and ad revenue, and when it came to the bottom line, circulation and ad revenue beat credibility any day. Reporters and editors all over the country would vehemently refute that, but the truth was, if the industry didn't make money, corporations wouldn't own newspapers.

It was a horribly cynical view of the profession, and Jessie would have been among the first to argue that profit for many newspapers was the result of a balanced, fair report that provided readers with important information they couldn't get anywhere else. But, financially, *The Star-News* was a different animal. It didn't have corporate support, and it was no secret that making money had been a struggle the past year. In the corporate world of chain-owned newspapers, when a smaller paper struggled to make ends meet, there often was a bigger publication that could make up the shortfall. The Westin-owned *Star-News* had no such backup. If it went under, a family was ruined.

The pieces fell into place in Jessie's head at the same time that her phone rang. She snatched it up, thinking it might be the detective again. "Jessie Rhoades."

"Hey. It's Clay."

Background noise told her he was on a cell phone. "Where are you?"

"In the Jeep. Did Gillian give you my message? I tried your line earlier, and it was busy."

"Gillian is here?" Raising her head, she scanned the empty newsroom.

"I just talked to her a few minutes ago. That was nice of her to deliver my urgent message so quickly."

Hearing the tension in his voice, she sat up straighter. "What's going on?"

"Mel called. Greg's asking to see you."

"He's talking? Thank God."

"She says he's getting worked up, which isn't good. I'm on my way, but you'll probably beat me there."

"I'm leaving right now." Hanging up, she reached for her purse.

"Hello, Jessie."

Gillian Westin, in a killer red dress that accented every curve, stood in her office door.

Clay arrived at the hospital, surprised to discover that Jessie had not shown up yet.

Mel shrugged. "I figured she'd be here by now, too."

He pulled out his cell phone. "She can't still be at the office, but let me try her again."

But Mel put a hand on his arm to stop him. "Maybe Greg will talk to you. It's imperative that he calms down soon, or he's going to have some serious problems. The doctor wants him sedated, but I've asked him to hold off as long as possible so he could tell Jess whatever it is that's upsetting him." She led him down the hall and into the young reporter's room.

Clay approached the bed where Greg lay, hooked up to intimidating-looking equipment that monitored his every vital sign. "Hey, kid, how's it going?"

Greg's eyes widened, and he struggled to talk even as a coughing fit choked him.

Clay patted his shoulder. "Take your time. I'm not going anywhere."

The coughing gave way to wheezing as Greg grabbed at Clay's hand and whispered something.

Clay had to lean down to hear him better.

Jessie flinched at the sight of her former boss.

Gillian gave her a smile that didn't touch her flat eyes. "I didn't mean to startle you."

Jessie got to her feet, certain her body language would give her away in an instant. "I was cleaning out my desk."

"I can see that."

"I'll be out of here in less than an hour."

Gillian didn't respond as she casually took a seat across from Jessie's desk and crossed her legs, as composed as ever. "Sit down, Jessie. Let's talk."

"What is there to talk about? You've made your feelings about my employment here perfectly clear." Jessie cursed herself as her voice wavered.

Gillian gestured at Jessie's chair. "Come, don't be foolish. Sit."

Jessie put a steadying hand on her desk. Gillian sat between her and the door. If she made a run for it, it would take little effort on Gillian's part to stop her. It would be better to play it cool. And better to stay on her feet, poised to bolt if the opportunity arose.

Gillian cocked her head to one side. "I was watching you just now. You were very intense."

Jessie cleared her throat. "I was looking at our—the—circulation numbers for the past few weeks."

Gillian laughed softly, easily. "Ah, yes. Impressive, aren't they?"

Jessie hoped her contempt didn't show on her face. "Yes. Your father must be very proud."

"Oh, he's tickled to death. He didn't think I could do it. But I showed him, didn't I? In fact, *we* showed him. Didn't we?"

Jessie began rearranging papers on her desk. "I'm afraid I don't have time to chat. Greg's asking for me at the hospital."

Gillian's face hardened almost imperceptibly. "I'm not

going to tell you again to sit down."

Jessie froze, her heart thudding. Gillian had intimidated the hell out of her for two years, but she'd never frightened her. Until now.

Clay, bending over Greg to hear what he had to say, straightened so fast his head spun. "Oh shit."

Behind him, Mel asked, "What is it? What did he say?"

Clay fumbled with his cell phone, swearing when his fingers tripped and he had to reset the connection and try again.

"Clay, what's going on?" Mel asked.

He turned away as Jessie's office phone rang once, twice, three times. On the fourth ring, her voice mail picked up.

Clay shut his eyes, frustrated.

No answer could mean she was on her way here. Except she should have arrived by now.

Or it could mean she wasn't able to answer.

He tore out of the room.

When the phone began to ring, Gillian was studying her own impeccable manicure.

Jessie reached for the receiver. It was probably Clay.

"Don't," Gillian said.

Jessie considered defying her. All she'd have to do was lift the phone from its cradle, and Clay would know she was there. But then her gaze fastened on the gun that had been concealed in the folds of Gillian's skirt.

Her former boss gave her a shrewd smile as she rested the gun against her silk-covered thigh, oh so casual. "I'm going to tell you to sit one more time."

Jessie sat.

Once the phone stopped ringing, Gillian delicately

cleared her throat. "You know what impresses me about you, Jessie? You constantly question things. Even when the answers seem obvious, you're always looking at situations from another angle, always considering a different scenario. It can be maddening, but most of the time, it's admirable. It's what my father says makes you an exceptional journalist." Her hard smile turned derisive. "He once told me I needed to learn to be more like you. Then, in the same breath, he said that probably wasn't possible because what you have is gut instinct, and we're either born with it or we're not. It can't be learned. That's what he said."

Sighing, Gillian rose and brushed the creases out of her dress. "At the time, I didn't know who to be angry at, him or you. Luckily for you, he retired a week later and handed me *The Star-News* reins. I figured I could just browbeat you until you got annoyed and quit. Of course, I wasn't seeing the big picture then. And I certainly didn't count on you being such a tenacious little bitch." She arched a perfectly plucked brow and smiled. "Comments? Observations?"

Jessie glanced past Gillian into the still-deserted newsroom, wondering how long before her former co-workers began to arrive or Clay got worried about her continued absence at the hospital and showed up. Either way, she needed to stall. She focused on Gillian, who watched her as if expecting Jessie to actually share her comments and observations.

Jessie forced herself to relax back in her chair, as if settling in for a heart-to-heart chat. "So when did you start seeing the big picture?" she asked.

The question apparently pleased Gillian, because her smile grew, and she nodded. "When dear old Dad told me to shore up flagging circulation or he'd sell the newspaper to the highest bidder. Can you imagine how much the idea of that hurt? I grew up in this newsroom. The people who are retiring now used to baby-sit me. This place is my life."

"There are tons of newspapers out there, Gillian."

"Yes, but they're not *The Star-News*. None of them are *mine*. I'd have to start over at another newspaper. Sure, I could walk in the door as a managing editor or even executive editor, but there'd always be someone to answer to, always someone to second-guess my decisions. Here, I'm the end-all and be-all of decision-making. I hold the power."

"Power?" Jessie repeated, unable to blunt her incredulity. "This whole thing has been about *power?*"

Gillian slapped a hand on the desk between them. "You don't know what it's like to fight for respect. To *crave* the respect that someone else, who's younger and brighter, gets with little or no effort. He never listened to me the way he listened to you. He used to side with you in news meetings so often it made me sick. It made me want to—"

She broke off, as if she'd run out of air. Drawing in a deep, calming breath, she straightened her spine and squared her shoulders. "I've gotten off track. I'd hate for you to get the impression that this has been about you, Jessie. No, it was never about you. You were just the one who kept questioning a story that was fake from the start."

"Fuck!"

Clay swore explosively as he encountered locked door after locked door at *The Star-News*. He pounded on each and got no response. Back at the employees' entrance, he glared at the glass door that required a key card to open.

Next to the door sat a newspaper rack that displayed the day's front page. The main headline screamed: "Hoax leads to editor shake-up at *Star-News*."

Hauling up the rack, Clay heaved it against the glass door.

The rack bounced harmlessly back.

The glass was shatterproof.

Jessie tapped her fingers on the desk. Across from her, Gillian looked as blissful as anyone who was about to get everything she'd ever wanted. "I suppose it never occurred to you that eventually the hoax would be exposed," Jessie said.

Gillian shrugged. "No, that never occurred to me. I had everyone in this newsroom, including you, quivering at the sound of my voice. Shawn, bless his cowardly, unsuspecting heart, authenticated fake photos because he was so terrified of me. I didn't expect anyone to question how I wanted to play the story. When the stripper recanted, I had her taken out and ran the others out of town. By then, the police had no credibility, and the more the police chief denied what was clearly proved by the photos, the more people would doubt the veracity of anything he said ever again."

"Which was part of the plan, wasn't it? Kill two birds with one stone, so to speak."

Her dark eyes narrowed. "So you know about our failed relationship." She gave a nod of approval. "You're even better than I thought."

"Someone else deserves the credit for that one."

"Ah. Your friend Clay Christopher probably. He's also been a big pain. I haven't figured out how I'm going to deal with him yet."

Regretting the comment that had shifted Gillian's attention to Clay, Jessie searched for something to steer her away. "What'd the police chief do? Dump you?"

Gillian's neck reddened. "He humiliated me by making

promises he never intended to keep."

"Let me guess. He said he'd leave his wife for you. That's such an old line. I'm disappointed in you, Gillian."

"What would you know about love? You've been too busy burying yourself in work to allow yourself to love a man. The chief—I can't even say his name—taught me a lesson. Love makes people stupid. *He* made me stupid. That's something I won't ever forget."

"So the scandal was intended to ruin him as much as it was intended to save the newspaper. And you used Peterson to do your dirty work while leading him to believe he was avenging his brother's death at the hands of the police."

As the flush of remembered shame faded, Gillian began to smile again. "He was so easy to play. Hatred blinded him. He hated the cops, and he hated you for debunking his conspiracy theory. I blamed that on you, of course. Told him I knew nothing about his repeated calls begging you to look further into his story. I promised him a Page One story about how the cops killed his brother and then covered it up, but before that could happen, you had to be taken out of the picture."

"And he bought that because I have so much power over you," Jessie said, not bothering to temper her sarcasm.

Gillian made a dismissive gesture with the gun. "Most people have no idea how the newspaper business works, Jessie. They don't know who makes the decisions about what stories get covered and how they're played from day to day. As far as Peterson knew, I sat in my office without a clue about what my staff was doing."

"Little did he know."

"Oh, and he was the *perfect* tool," Gillian said, nodding with approval. "I worried at first that he might turn squeamish, but he had no qualms about putting the gun in that stripper's mouth and pulling the trigger to make it look like suicide." She paused, relishing the moment. "He told me you put up quite a fight when he jumped you in your apartment the night he was there looking for the backup disk I correctly assumed you'd made. He said you flipped him onto a glass table. I think you scared him."

"You can never have too little self-defense training," Jessie said.

"I'm impressed that you can still joke, Jessie." She waved the gun absently, as if it were as insignificant as a cigarette. "I didn't pull this on you for no reason."

But Jessie refused to let her former boss see the fear that threatened to ambush her. No doubt, Gillian would kill her and not feel a moment of remorse. Falling apart wouldn't change that, and if nothing else, she needed to maintain her composure so she could think clearly. At the moment, however, her only option seemed to be to continue to stall. If she was lucky, Clay had overreacted to her failure to show up at the hospital and was now on his way to find her.

Jessie pursed her lips. "So you know me pretty well, don't you?"

"I do, yes."

"Then you know that stories with holes drive me up the wall."

"In other words, you've got more questions," Gillian said, making a big show of checking her watch. "First one here—usually our resourceful but cranky Stuart—should be walking in in about an hour. So we've got some time. Fire away."

"What did Greg turn up that got him shot?"

"Ah, Greg. Our most intrepid but inexperienced reporter. He actually connected Peterson to the bogus story long before any of you did. It was pure luck, of course.

He'd gone through *The Star-News* archive hunting for someone who might have a beef with the cops. The Peterson name popped up, and Greg remembered hearing about all the grief Henry Peterson had given you about the cops' involvement in his brother's death. Lucky for me, you were out of commission at the time, so Greg brought his theory to me. Next thing you know, Peterson, who at the time you all knew as Hank Peters, gave Greg a call and said he had information."

"But he had no intention of sharing it."

"Nope. I just wanted to make sure Greg stayed home that night."

"So you could kill him," Jessie said. Rage, gaining momentum the more Gillian talked, began to burn behind her eyes.

"Stereotypes played in my favor that night," Gillian said. "It never occurred to anyone that Stuart saw a woman running away from the scene of the crime."

"Why didn't you just have Peterson do it?"

"This might be difficult for you to understand, seeing as how you're the kind of manager who tends to let the people who work for you get away with murder." She paused, smiling at her joke. "But Peterson didn't have the best track record for achieving the goals I set out for him. Look at how many times he tried to kill you and failed. I couldn't afford for him to mess up again, especially when Greg was on the right track."

"So you did it yourself." Jessie said it through her teeth, and it took all her strength not to lunge across the desk and grab Gillian by the throat.

"It wasn't as difficult as I'd expected," Gillian mused. "I kind of enjoyed it, to be honest. You should have seen the look on his face when I pulled the trigger. It was priceless.

You know how much I love shocking people." She sighed. "Of course, it was never my plan to kill anybody. It wasn't until that stupid stripper caught the guilts and you kept hammering at authenticating the photos I paid good money to have altered that it became necessary for people to die."

A fissure of confusion interrupted Jessie's fury. "But my brake line was cut before Sandi White recanted."

"Ah, yes, your little accident," Gillian said. "I didn't have anything to do with that, actually. Peterson wanted you dead for blowing him off, and I told him to go for it. I considered it his bonus for doing such a good job up to that point. I didn't actually want *you* dead until you suddenly got the balls to stand up to me. That was when I realized that you were going to be a problem that was not going to go away anytime soon."

"What about killing Officer Drake? Was he a problem, too?"

"Well, I couldn't very well have him spilling his guts to you, could I? That was probably the moment when Peterson screwed up the most. He was supposed to nail you both, but he told me later that Drake was all over you, blocking his shot."

Jessie, realizing that Taylor had saved her life when he'd fallen on her, thrust the memory back. "I'm curious about how you found out he was the mayor's lover."

Gillian's dark eyes widened. "How do you know about that?"

"The mayor told me."

"Well, I'll be damned. It never occurred to me that either of them would ever come clean about their sordid affair."

"You haven't told me how you found out," Jessie said. Damn it, where the hell was Clay? She was sure she wouldn't be able to keep Gillian talking much longer.

Gillian cocked her head. "Here's where you might learn a little something about being a good journalist. It pays to have good friends in high places. One of mine, who works in the mayor's office, spotted the cop and the mayor during a moment in which they thought they were alone. She's promised to be an exclusive source when we break the story."

"I'm surprised you haven't already splashed it across the front page. The boost in circulation would probably top the one that followed the cops scandal."

"Oh, it's on my budget, all right," Gillian said. "We just haven't gotten there yet."

"Don't you think readers are going to get suspicious about all this juicy news all of the sudden?"

"Readers want to be entertained, Jessie. They're not even going to think about it as long as we keep turning out stories that pique their interest." With a disappointed sigh, she glanced at her watch. "Shall we go for a drive? I need to get you out of here before your former co-workers start trickling in. I'm sure you don't want to involve any of them in something that's about to get very ugly." She used the gun to gesture for Jessie to stand. "Come."

Jessie stayed put. "I have one more question."

Gillian gave her a serene, unperturbed look. "All right."

"David Collins. Do you know who he is?"

"I wondered whether you would get around to him."

Jessie didn't respond, keeping her gaze steady on the older woman.

Gillian returned the scrutiny, her eyes narrowed. "This David Collins, he's important to you."

"I just want to know how he was involved."

Gillian shrugged. "I heard that name for the first time

when Peterson called me yesterday after being arrested for attacking you. He told me what happened, how this guy he'd never seen before thwarted him and that you acted like you thought they were partners. I told Peterson to say they were—to cover for me, of course—and then I made him all kinds of promises about how I would spring him, all I needed was time. Like I said, he was very easy to play."

Jessie felt sick. Everything that David had told her, about how he'd tried to find her, about how sorry he was, had been the truth. When Mel had shot him, he really had been trying to hand over the gun.

"Interview over," Gillian said. "Get up."

Rivulets of sweat raced down Clay's face as he pawed through the tools in the back of his SUV in search of something he could use to pry open the door to the newsroom.

Curling his fingers around a crowbar, he sprinted back to the door, jammed the flat edge of the tool between the door and the frame, and froze.

Through the glass, he saw Jessie walking toward him.

Relief surged through him, even as he noticed that she held herself stiffly, her face taut with tension.

Then he saw Gillian a pace behind her.

As Jessie walked ahead of Gillian, she considered trying a move like the one that had left Peterson flat on his back among the shards of her coffee table. But she feared she lacked the necessary strength after her tussle with him the day before. Of course, the gun pressed against her sore ribs was the biggest deterrent of all.

Then she spotted Clay through the door. He braced his palm against the glass when he saw her, but the light of relief in his eyes lasted only an instant before his gaze fixed on

Gillian and darkened with menace.

Somehow he knew that Gillian was the bad guy, Jessie realized. What he didn't know was that Gillian had a gun.

Fear of what he might do, how he might jeopardize himself to help her, Jessie took matters into her own hands.

Pivoting, she shoved at her former boss, driving her back against the wall in a flurry of red silk. Gillian's lips formed a surprised "O," and before she could react, Jessie took a swing at her.

The punch, square on the jaw, sent Gillian sliding down the wall, a thin trickle of blood at the corner of her mouth marring her perfect makeup.

With pain radiating through her hand, up her arm and down into her ribs, Jessie bent to retrieve the pistol from Gillian's limp fingers.

But Gillian's fingers were not the least bit limp.

On the other side of the door, Clay watched, helpless, as the smiling Gillian aimed a gun at Jessie's face.

Frantic, he worked the crowbar on the door.

The metal refused to give.

Gillian, that ridiculous smile on her face as she sat on the floor with her skirt pillowed around her, wiped a hand across her mouth, smearing blood and lipstick. "You think one punch is enough to bring me down?"

Stepping back, Jessie raised her hands before her. "Gillian."

Gillian, keeping the weapon leveled at Jessie, used the wall for support to get to her feet. Her laugh was breathless. "You've been wanting to do that for a long time."

Jessie didn't dare glance at Clay or the door.

"I know he's there," Gillian said. "I saw him at the same

time you did. He'll never get through that door. It's reinforced steel. Even if he does, he'll be too late."

"This is between you and me, Gillian."

"You know how foolish that is, Jessie." Gillian worked her jaw and grimaced. "I imagine that punch felt pretty good from where you're standing. A real David-slaying-Goliath kind of rush."

Jessie was peripherally aware of Clay hammering the crowbar against the glass, which splintered but didn't break. Time, Jessie thought, he just needed time.

"You want to hit me again," Gillian said. "I can see it in your eyes. Now you know how I feel, Jessie."

"We're nothing alike."

"Of course, we are. We're a lot alike, you and I."

"I'm not like you, Gillian. I never will be."

"I used to be an idealist like you. Believed in the good in people, that the good guys always win. But they don't. I learned that the hard way when that bastard dumped me. I learned it again when my father repeatedly told me I needed to be more like you. And yet again when he gave me the impossible task of increasing circulation in a town where the news never seems to get that bad. So you know what my conclusion is? The people who win, Jessie, they're not the good guys. They're the people who play the game the best. And in our little game here? I'm going to win. I beat my former lover. I beat my father. And now I'm going to beat you."

"Yeah, well, you cheated."

Gillian laughed. "I cheated. That's good. That's very good." She used her free hand to brace the one that held the gun. "This moment is poetic, you know. Your lover gets to watch you die, and there isn't a damn thing he can do about it. And when I'm done with you, he's next."

Jessie charged her former boss.

Clay stopped battering the door, horror paralyzing him as Jessie tackled Gillian and both women crashed into the glass right in front of him. They hit the floor in a tangle of limbs, less than a foot from where he stood. And he could do nothing but watch.

Jessie cracked Gillian a good one on the side of the head and was scrambling for her feet when Gillian swept them out from under her. Going down hard on her back, Jessie rolled toward the door, her body curving as if to contain the agony that ripped through it.

Clay, his lungs constricting as he recalled her already damaged ribs, dropped to his knees, both hands flattened against the glass only inches from her where she lay. Her eyes were clenched shut, her lips white.

"Oh God, oh Jesus," he said, his voice breaking with desperation, with terror for her. "Jess." He slammed a fist against the glass. "Jess, come on."

Remembering Gillian, he raised his head, saw her looking around, searching for the gun.

"God, Jess, get up," he said. Shooting back to his feet, he rammed against the door. He felt something give in his shoulder and didn't care. "Get up, Jess. Get up." He rammed again. And again.

"What the hell are you doing?"

Clay whirled.

Stuart Davis was striding up the walk.

Jessie, on her side on the floor, heard Clay's shouts through the door and opened her eyes to see him driving his body against the unyielding glass.

"Get up! Get up!"

But she couldn't move, couldn't breathe. Firecrackers of pain had exploded in her chest, stealing her breath, making her head swim. Consciousness threatened to skitter away, but she clung to it with the same desperation that Clay used on the door.

Feeling pressure against her hip, she realized it was Gillian's foot forcing her onto her back. Jessie had no choice but to roll with it, and more pain detonated. She might have had bruised ribs before, but at least one was broken now.

On her back, Jessie blinked up at Gillian, black spots peppering her vision.

Standing at Jessie's feet, Gillian cocked the gun, triumph shining in her black eyes. "Sorry about that, but I want to see your face when I pull the trigger. When I win."

Gritting her teeth, Jessie drove her foot against Gillian's ankle in one last furious effort to stop the inevitable. But she succeeded only in tilting her own world on its side when the effort sent shards of pain knifing through her.

"Now, that was truly pathetic," Gillian said.

A rush of wind jerked Gillian's head up, and Jessie was vaguely aware of a dark shape flying over the top of her, the rustle of silk, followed by a grunt, then nothing more.

Clay rolled to his feet. His knuckles smarted where he'd struck Gillian, but he didn't notice as he stumbled to get to Jessie, who lay on the floor, unmoving.

"Jesus, is she okay?" Stuart asked.

"Get help," Clay said.

As Stuart trotted away, Clay cradled her gently on his lap and stroked her cheek. It took him a second to realize that she was gazing up at him. Seeing the familiar dark blue rings around her irises, Clay couldn't speak at first. Finally, he said, "Hey."

She gave him a wan smile. "Hey."

He leaned his forehead against hers. "Jesus, Jess, you scared me."

"Sorry. Can I get up now?"

"Just stay put for once until help gets here."

"Where's Gillian?"

"I knocked her flat."

"My hero." Threading her fingers through his hair, she brought his head down so she could kiss him. When they parted, she said, "I want to get up now."

Clay was grinning. "Can you just wait?"

She moved restlessly, winced. "Ow."

"Jess—"

"It'd hurt less if you gave me a hand," she said.

Groaning with frustration, he helped her to her feet, catching her against him when she hissed in pain and swayed.

Forcing a smile for his benefit, she pressed a hand to her side. "See?" she said. "All better."

"Right," he said, unconvinced.

"How'd you get in?" she asked.

"Stuart opened the door with his key card."

"Lucky break." Staring down at Gillian, unconscious at their feet, Jessie whispered, "Comments? Observations?"

Epilogue

"You're sure you won't reconsider, Jess?"

She and Richard Westin were standing in the waiting room outside Greg's hospital room. Though Greg had weeks of rehabilitation ahead of him, he was in good spirits and recovering fast.

The past couple of days had been rough on all of them, but most of all on Richard Westin, who, in one afternoon had seen his daughter charged with everything from fraud to murder and had decided to sell *The Star-News*, a part of his family for decades. Even so, he had offered Jessie her job back.

"I appreciate the offer, but I have other plans," she said.

"Plans that involve that reporter Clay Christopher, I hope." He gave her a wink.

Relieved to see some of the sparkle reclaim her mentor's faded blue eyes, she laughed, glancing at where, across the room, Clay, Mel and Marshall chatted. Her pulse stammered a little when Clay met her gaze. Smiling at Richard, she said, "Clay Christopher is part of my plans, yes."

"Whatever you do, you'll be good at it."

"Thank you." She hesitated, then gripped his hand. "You gave me a second chance, no questions asked. I can never repay you for that."

"After what my daughter just put you through—"

"You can't blame yourself for that," she cut in.

"You're really okay? She didn't cause you any permanent physical damage?"

"One broken rib, and it'll heal. My friend Mel gave me some excellent drugs, so I don't even really feel it at the moment." Which was a slight lie, but she would have bet her physical discomfort was nothing compared with his emotional misery.

He wiped moisture from his eyes, and for a moment, didn't seem to know what to say. "You'll keep in touch with an old man, won't you?"

She gave him a hug, feeling his hand pat her gently against the back, as if he were afraid that anything with more strength would hurt her. "Of course, I will," she said. "Please take care of yourself, Richard."

Watching him walk away, she wished she could do more for him.

She'd been wishing she could do more for another man just two hours before when she had been standing at her ex-husband's bedside when he had opened his eyes. "Thank God, you're okay," David had mumbled.

Remembering that moment, Jessie almost choked up again. They had talked then, about the past. He'd been groggy but coherent. Mostly, though, he'd been earnest about telling her how sorry he was that she had felt she had to run away two years ago to be safe. With tears rolling back into his shaggy hair, he'd told her he still loved her, but he understood if she had moved on.

She'd told him that she had, and then she asked him to rest.

Nodding, he'd closed his eyes. "Maybe I can now."

"You okay?"

Drawn back into the present, Jessie turned, leaning easily into Clay as he slipped an arm around her waist, mindful of her wrapped ribs. The warmth of his body was solid, reassuring. "I'm perfect," she said. Then she glanced askance at him, caught the conspiratorial glint in his eyes. "What?"

He kissed her on the nose. "I know a secret."

Grinning up at him, she ran her finger over the dimple in his chin. "Spill it."

He rolled his eyes and played coy. "I don't know whether the parties involved would appreciate that."

She wrapped her arms around him, drawing him against her. With her lips a breath from his, she said, "I see we're going to have to sort out the logistics of our working relationship, Mr. Christopher."

He tried to kiss her, but she retreated. He chuckled. "Okay, I give. Mel and Marshall just made a date."

Jessie cocked her head to one side. "Really?"

Clay claimed his kiss, his warm hands cupping her face. When they parted, he rested his forehead against hers. "I don't think I'll ever get tired of doing that."

Snaking her arms around his neck, she pressed her lips to his again. Desire rushed through her, and she embraced it, embraced him. "I love you," she said against his lips.

His lips curved under hers. "I was hoping you'd say that."

"Yeah? Why?"

"Because I love you, too."

Jessie grinned, truly happy for the first time in two years. "Now, about the logistics of our working relationship."

"You're in charge, right?" he said.

She laughed. "A fast learner. I love that in a man."

About the Author

Joyce Lamb was born and raised in Rockford, Illinois. She followed in her father's footsteps to become a journalist, but writing fiction has long been her passion. She wrote *Relative Strangers* while working in Fort Myers, Florida. Currently an editor at *USA Today*, she lives in the Washington, D.C. area, where she loves cooking out with friends, playing tennis, reading, and working hard on her next novel.